ACCLAIM

"Augustine, in her signature wit, creates a story full of laughter, swoon, and, of course, hockey. With arching themes of grace and second chances, the reader is sure to fall in love with not only the main characters but also with the beauty of growth and change."

—DREW TAYLOR, author of The Politics of... series and the Designated series

ACCLAIM FOR BY BLOOD AND BLADE

"*By Blade and Blood* is mystifying and powerful, every page filled with emotion and authenticity, showing the kind of courage needed to truly love and be loved. Augustine delves deep into difficult topics with grace and compassion, offering hope to the hurting and ashamed, and giving readers the chance to know what love is by experiencing it with Dhamar and Inara."

—ERIN PHILLIPS, author of *A Crown of Chains*

"A breathlessly romantic tale of courage and healing. Enter the vibrant, twisted world of Taletha and you're sure to fall in love with its broken characters and their fight to stand up for what's right."

—MEGAN MCCULLOUGH, author of *We Could Be Villains*

"Almost from the first page, we are enraptured by Inara's struggle for belonging and Dhamar's desire to do what is good and right. Set against a colorful and vibrant backdrop that comes alive on every page, we find ourselves centered around the stories of two characters whose desire to love and to be loved is palpable. As the threat of war looms on the horizon, the shining heart of *By Blood and Blade* is the characters' unshakable devotion - to themselves, to each other, and to what is really and truly right."

—BRIAN MCBRIDE, award-winning author of *The Mamoth Series*

"A timeless love story fraught with struggle and the beauty that rises from fighting those struggles together."

—AJ SKELLY, bestselling author of *The Wolves of Rock Falls* series and *Magik Prep Academy* series

ACCLAIM FOR BY LIGHT AND LOVE

"The romance is complex but also complete, full of grace and selfless love."

—ERIN PHILLIPS, number one bestselling author of *A Crown of Chains*

"With vivid imagery and depth of heart, Anna Augustine weaves together a short and sweet love story. Her characters and world feel so real that they could leap off the page."

—ALISSA J. ZAVALIANOS, Author of *The Earth-Treader* and *Endlewood*

"*By Light and Love* is a heart-warming, captivating tale surrounding two souls who overcome the odds stacked against them and learn what it means to truly love. With humorous banter, vivid imagery, and an *Arabian Nights* vibe, Anna packs this novella full with important life lessons and themes that any reader can connect to and resonate with."

—DREW TAYLOR, author of *The Politics Of...* series and *The Designated* series.

By the Sun and Stars

Also By Anna Augustine

Novels

When You Found Me

A Love Like Ours

Teletha

By Light and Love

By Blood and Blade

By the Sun and Stars

Anthologies

The Depths We'll Go To

Fool's Honor

Aphotic Love

Casting Call: Havok Season Six

Animal Kingdom: Havok Season Seven

Quill & Flame
PUBLISHING HOUSE

By the Sun and Stars

To the family we're born with...
and the ones we find along the way.
And to my Missional Community:
Thank you for showing me that perfection is never necessary to be loved.
In fact, sometimes the imperfections are what bring us closer.

A Taletha Novel

BY THE Sun AND Stars

Quill & Flame
PUBLISHING HOUSE

ANNA AUGUSTINE

CHAPTER ONE

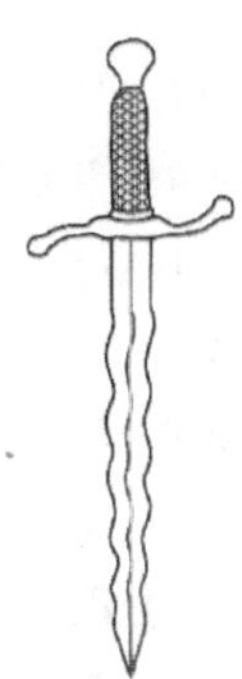

Aysa

The warm morning sun chased away the chill of the desert night as I strode among the multicolored tents of my people. The coins that hung on a string around my neck jingled, turning heads in my direction. I greeted everyone with a beaming grin and skipped forward with a little leap. Chuckles followed me, but I ignored them as I spun, enjoying the sun on my skin.

"Where are you headed?" Emre, my guard and best friend, asked as he fell into step beside me. He wore his normal blank expression, his arms swinging loosely at his side. One of his dark brows rose as he studied the bounce in my stride. "You're in a good mood."

"I am. Otac asked me to come to breakfast with him today." I grinned up at him. "It's been a while since he's called for me."

My otac was the leader—or šefe—of all Šeri. He was extremely busy, not only with running our tribe but also with organizing and overseeing the dozens of other tribes across our lands. Otac tried to be a good father, a dutiful husband, and a capable šefe. But there were times I'd go weeks with only a good morning kiss on my forehead and nothing more. To be asked to have breakfast with him and Majka was a rarity and one I was honored to accept.

"That doesn't worry you?" Emre's lips twisted with skepticism.

I pulled up short, turning to face him. "No, and for three reasons. One—" I raised my first finger. "—we're no longer at war, so it has nothing to do with Dhamar or Inara or any of the Talethians. Two—" My second finger popped up. "—I know that I'm not in trouble because I haven't done anything to upset the tribal leaders recently." Emre snorted, but I ignored him. "And three, Otac loves me, and as the next šefe of our people, he will listen and treat me with respect."

"I don't doubt that." Emre rolled his eyes but motioned me on to Otac and Majka's tent. "He's a good otac and šefe. Not like the old malek of Taletha." He made the gesture to ward off spirits—a circle with a slash from top to bottom over the chest. "Just be careful, Aysa."

I nodded at my friend. Emre was a steady, comforting presence at my side. Had been since the day I was ten and a man had tried to assault me behind some empty tents in the camp. Back then, the fifteen-year-old boy had merely been passing through our tribe—a desert wanderer. He had leapt to my aid, soundly beating the man and dragging him to my otac, who was enraged and sentenced the man to death. For Emre's part in protecting me, Otac had hired him as my guard, and Emre quickly became my ever-present shadow.

The man was infuriating, however. He always questioned my decisions, hated my impulsive spirit, and constantly worried about what scrape I'd get into next. There had been plenty of times I'd slipped his watchful eye and ended up with an injury to show for it—not because I was reckless, but because when I knew what needed to be done, I did it. No matter the cost. Though Emre never said the words *I told you so*, it was often implied with raised brows and a soft sigh of exasperation.

Yet there was no one I'd rather have at my back. Emre was my support, the one person I felt comfortable enough with to ask my wild questions and share the struggles that I kept hidden from everyone else. When there wasn't anyone else, there was always Emre. He was my very best friend.

The camp was beginning to come alive as the sun continued to rise.

Sheep bleated from their pens as children laughed and ran about the tents, rubbing the sleep dust from their eyes. Their giggles brought a smile to my face and another hop to my step. The smell of samoon and falafel filled the air from the cooking tents, making my mouth water and my stomach growl rancorously.

"You sound like a half-starved desert wolf, my princezo." Emre bumped into my shoulder, though I couldn't tell if it was an accident or intentional.

Maturely, I stuck my tongue out at him. He chuckled and I opened my mouth to reply, but Otac pulled back the tent flap, cutting off my scathing retort.

"Aysa, my love! Come in, come in. We have much to discuss."

I ducked inside, breathing in Otac and Majka's tent—vanilla and frankincense. Their space was lavish. Silk pillows were on the floor, scarves and other tapestries draped around the sides of the tent, while an incense burner hung from the support beam. While it boasted of my otac's wealth and power, it was also homey, safe, and comforting.

Majka sat like a queen in her violet kaftan. With colorful scarves of bright yellow and green belted around her waist, she looked stunning. Her dark brown hair had streaks of gray, a testament to her wisdom and knowledge and possibly the four kćerkas she'd birthed and raised.

"Thank you for inviting me to breakfast, Otac." I rose up on tiptoes and pecked his cheek.

He smiled, lines creasing his face, and pressed a good morning kiss to my brow. Otac hadn't smiled much in the recent months. With the leaders of the tribes calling for war against Taletha, the scarcity of grazing lands for our animals, and the everyday weight of being šefe, his brilliant smile was hidden most days. It made my heart soar to be able to pull it out of hiding.

Emre stood at the door, his eyes scanning the tent before he bowed—first toward Otac, then to Majka, and finally to me. "I shall stand guard."

"Thank you, Emre." Otac gave my friend a nod of his head, the highest acknowledgement he ever bestowed. At twenty-five, Emre had something few of our people ever had—Otac's respect. It was hard earned, harder kept, and something I knew Emre took great pride in and care to retain.

After he'd ducked out, Otac turned to me. His brown eyes softened. "How are you this day, kćerka?"

I loved when he called me *daughter*. It wasn't something he did often, usually choosing to refer to me by my title of *princezo* or by my name.

"I am well, Otac." I grinned at him as I took my seat beside Majka. "Though I would still like it if you'd allow to me travel as the ambassador to Mordova."

It had been nearly eight months since the confrontation at the border of Šeri and Taletha that had brought a tentative peace to both of our lands. Dhamar—my cousin and the new malek of Taletha—had written a few days earlier to acknowledge that his council had agreed with our terms of peace and wanted an official ambassador to travel to their capital of Mordova to finalize the documents. I had volunteered and, so far, had heard nothing in reply.

Otac's brows lowered, a few strands of his black hair brushing against his forehead as he shook his head. "Let's save such talk for after breakfast, hm?"

Majka sighed and rolled her eyes. "Honestly, Aydin. Do you think she'll drop her case so easily? Do you know nothing of our kćerka?"

I laughed, stifling it by shoving a piece of samoon into my mouth. Otac's narrowed gaze cut to me, and the food turned to sand in my mouth. His eyes squinted as he drummed his fingers against the low table. It was his calculating expression, the one that meant I wouldn't like whatever was about to come out of his mouth. It was the same look he'd given me when he'd ordered me to marry Dhamar—which I had promptly ignored once I'd learned the young malek was my relative.

"Otac?" I asked after swallowing.

He took a bite of lamb, chewing slowly as he studied the rest of the food on his plate and refusing to meet my gaze. It was so unlike him. My pulse hammered harder than a runaway stallion as I turned to Majka and asked, "What is going on? Am I to be the ambassador or not?"

Otac set his fork delicately beside his plate—too precise in the movement. "The short answer is yes."

I nearly leapt to my feet, but Majka's grip on my arm prevented it. Her light brown eyes narrowed a fraction as she added, "Barring a few conditions, kćerka."

My heart dropped to my toes. I glanced between her and Otac, not liking the seriousness that shrouded them like a wet blanket. I barely managed to force out, "What conditions?"

Otac pressed the pads of each finger together and rocked them forward and backward. The long sleeves of his red robe swayed with the motion. "There will be a contest of sorts. I have called for the sons of each tribal leader to come here."

"A contest?" My stomach soured, and I pushed my half-finished plate away from myself. "Why are we hosting a contest? What is the prize?"

Otac and Majka shared a look. They didn't say a thing, but an entire conversation passed between them in the span of seconds. At last, Majka turned and patted my hand as if that would lighten the horrible news that she dropped on me like a bucket of cold water. "You, kćerka."

"Me?" I squeaked, feeling a sheen of sweat coating my upper lip.

"The leaders think it's high time for you to marry, Aysa," Otac stated.

"What?" I leapt to my feet, ripping away from Majka as my pulse thrummed in my ears, causing my head to ache with the force. This wasn't our way. We had never forced marriage on women in our tribe, unlike our neighbors in Taletha. Confused and angry, I balled my hands into fists at my sides. "Why do I have to marry?"

"You are twenty summers, Aysa," Majka interrupted before Otac could say anything. "I had been married to your otac for four years by the time I was your age."

"But I don't want to marry! I'm happy the way I am." I turned to Otac. "Why are you forcing me to do this now?"

"We are glad that you are happy, Aysa." Otac's shoulders stooped in what appeared to be defeat. *Surely not.* But there was no mistaking it. His brows furrowed and he sighed. "If I could choose, I would let you marry for love, as your majka and I did. But the family heads believe you're a bit too..." He trailed off and turned to Majka.

"They think you're too wild and reckless, kćerka." Majka sighed.

The words stung. I'd been trying to do what was best for Šeri and the tribes since I was old enough to understand what my role in life was. I was their future šefe, the one who would rule and guide them once Otac handed me the position. To hear that they still found me too wild and unpredictable hurt. What was wrong with my passion? My fire? It meant I wanted to succeed. But I wasn't perfect, and a perfect princezo is what they desired.

"It's not only that." Otac ran his fingers through his beard. "They want to see you married before they allow you to go anywhere near Taletha."

"Why?" I asked, bitterness leaking into the word. "Are they afraid that I'll ruin the very alliance I helped to create?"

"No, my dear. It's because they care about our family line." Majka patted my hand, but I yanked it away.

"They don't care about the family line. They don't like *me.* They never have. Besides, if I am married, my koca shall go with me to Taletha." I crossed my arms. "Doesn't that put both of us at risk?"

"No. A koca means you would always have protection even at night," Majka stated calmly. "And a koca means the possibility of an heir, protecting the line further."

Heat filled my face at that thought. I wasn't ready to be a majka, let alone a wife. I cleared my throat before asking, "But I have sisters. If something happened to me, Dilan would be next in line, yes?"

"Yes, yes. And all these arguments have already been presented to them. But the fact remains that they want their princezo wed and safe. You may be headstrong and wild, but they can't ignore the fact that *you* were the one to bring peace to Šeri."

Headstrong and wild. Is that all they're ever going to see? I groaned, rubbing at one of the coins on my necklace. "How many men are coming?"

"Eight." Majka began to tick names off on her fingers. "Two from the southern tribes, three from the western tribes, one from the northeastern tribes, and two from the central tribes."

"None from ours?" I asked, surprised.

Besides our tribe, there were eight others that held positions on Otac's council. Each specialized in a specific skill set, and they all had herds of some sort. The tribes often traveled across Šeri to different oases to feed and water their herds and trade their goods with others in our desert home. Of all the tribes, Tribe Hamid was the most stationary along the eastern coast.

Otac shook his head. "No, the family heads decided they wanted a chance to have one of their sinovi as the šefe's spouse." He scowled, as if he knew it was going to become a political game—win the hand of the šefe's kćerka, win the position of power. I didn't like it any better.

After a prolonged and suffocating silence, I sullenly asked, "Who will pick my koca?"

"That is where we will have some control over our stubborn people." Majka smiled, and the conspiratorial spark that I'd inherited flashed in her eyes. "You will choose."

"Me?" They were leaving this choice to me? Placing it in the hands of the wild kćerka the leaders thought couldn't lead? I nearly scoffed at the irony.

"Yes." Otac chuckled and rubbed his hands together like the little boys when they were planning to snatch a sweet treat from the food tent. "You are the one who must wed the scoundrel—" He cleared his throat when Majka raised a brow at him. "—ah, the young man, and therefore, should have some say."

My eyes burned, but I hurriedly blinked it away. I wasn't prone to tears and wouldn't start now, despite being touched by Otac and Majka's love on display. Instead, I interlocked my fingers and straightened in my seat. "What should I look for in a man?"

"What do you long for in a partner?" Majka asked, clasping her hand over mine.

"Nothing. I don't want one," I stated with a small laugh. It wasn't that I hadn't thought about marriage and the man I would marry. But that was in the someday—far off and hazy. Of course, I wanted a family. A koca to lean on when leading my people became a burden. But my people had always been at the forefront of my mind—the tribes of Šeri. *Not* the mysterious man who would be my koca.

Besides, I was only twenty, after all, and wanted to live some life before settling down into the role of šefe and wife. But now the choice was out of my hands. I would have to marry one of the eight young men coming to our camp. *Nicar above, is this actually happening?*

Otac's gray eyes sparkled in the lantern light. "If I were to pick a man for you to wed, I would like someone who would fight for you. Protect you. Speak well of you as šefe and kari."

"And I would like you to wed someone who is gentle, yet firm. Someone who isn't afraid to stand up to that stubborn streak of yours." Majka tweaked my nose, a motion she'd done to all us girls when we'd been young and underfoot. "And whomever you choose, he will be a lucky man. You are a stunning woman, Aysa. A bold and fearless leader and a woman who deserves to be loved and cherished for all those things."

I smiled, but my words, for once, were failing me. That's what they saw in me? And those were the attributes they petitioned Nicar to bless me with in a spouse?

Clearing the emotion from my throat, I stood. "Is that all Otac? Majka?"

"Yes, my kćerka." Otac rose and abruptly tugged me to him. He smelled good—like fresh air and the vanilla incense that burned in the tent. "Just remember that if you want to be the ambassador, you *must* choose a koca. Whomever you choose will be a lucky man. And your majka and I will always be proud of you."

"Always?"

"Yes." Majka hugged me as well, pressing her lips against my forehead. "Now, go. I know you'll want a ride to think all this over."

I smiled, glad Majka knew me so well. Kissing them both, I hurried out of the tent. Emre fell into step as I all but ran to the corral where our horses stood. The corral's design was such that it transported easily, yet also kept our mounts contained. Saddles were draped over the rails and I grabbed mine before whistling for my mare, Kismet.

"It wasn't good news, was it?" Emre asked, leaning against the fence as Kismet trotted over and bumped my shoulder with her velvety nose.

"No." I pressed my lips together, my throat tight. I swung the saddle onto Kismet's back and began the methodical process of tacking her up.

Emre was silent, watching me with that knowing gaze that meant he was waiting me out—waiting for my words to pour over like a bubbling pot over a fire. Silence was my enemy, eating away at the guard of my tongue until the words poured like a flooded riverbed.

"They want me to marry," I finally blurted.

"What?" Emre's face paled, and he pushed off the fence. His blue-gray turban covered his hair, but I knew that it was such a deep black it nearly gleamed purple in the sunlight. His brown eyes—almost as dark as his hair—bore into me like a rhinoceros' horn.

"They're bringing eight sinovi from the head tribes for me to pick from." I wrinkled my nose. It felt like the horrid Wife Markets that Inara—Dhamar's wife—had told me existed in Taletha. Only in this case, I was the one doing the picking.

"Do you even want to marry?" Emre asked, his voice low.

Kismet bumped me again, and I stroked her nose absentmindedly. I cut a look at Emre and shook my head. "No, not right now. Maybe someday, when I find the right man. But now, I guess I don't have much of a choice. Otac said that, if I want to be the ambassador to Taletha, I have to be married."

Emre snorted and shook his head. Crossing his arms, he leaned against the wooden slats that made the horses' pen. "You do so much to earn that title of yours."

Is that a shred of disdain in his voice? I bristled. After the comment of me being *too wild* and *too reckless* to be a good princezo, it grated me in the opposite direction. Would I never be worthy? I wasn't a good enough princezo for the tribal leaders, and now Emre thought me too dedicated to the job. Turning away from my friend, I swung up on Kismet's back.

"Where are you going?" Emre asked.

"For a ride." I glared down at him. "I don't want you to come."

He raised a brow, pulling the cloth that hung from his turban up over his nose and mouth. "I don't see that you have much of a choice. I'm your guard."

I ground my teeth together and dug my heels into Kismet's side. She sprang forward, her large hooves pounding against the sandy earth before she gracefully flew over the rails of the fence. I didn't wait to see if Emre was following yet or not. With a shout of ecstasy, I spurred Kismet up the dune and down the other side.

This was freedom. A wild, glorious abandon where I could let the fire that simmered in my chest out in order survive the weeks stuck in the camp. Joy swirled through me, and I let loose another whoop. I could be the perfect šefe. I would be what they wanted me to be. No matter what, I was the future leader of Šeri, and I wouldn't let it go without a fight.

I reined in Kismet as I neared the small oasis about a hundred yards from the camp. We didn't camp *in* it, as most of the oases around the Šeri desert were where wild desert animals came to drink their fill. Rather, our tribes camped a mile or so away, allowing both humans and animals to live amicably.

Hobbling Kismet, I strolled under a palm leaf and over to the small pond of water. A few plants grew around the natural spring, as eager to find liquid in the parched earth as humans were.

I sank down and tugged my knees to my chest, the joy of the ride gone. Emotions swirled in my chest, and I wasn't sure which to address first. My anger? It would take a while to bring that boiling pot back down to a simmer. My grief? The course of my life was being dictated to me by tribe leaders who knew nothing about me but what rumors claimed. If that wasn't reason enough to collapse into a puddle of tears, I wasn't sure what was. But tears were a waste of time, and I wasn't going to let them control me. Because beyond the anger and grief, there was a subtle hint of excitement. What if I did meet my future husband at this contest? I worried the inside of my cheek with my teeth, imagining a million scenarios that would likely never happen.

But what if?

I was so lost in thought that I missed the growl until it was right in front of me. With a gasp of pure terror, I watched as a wiry-haired desert wolf stalked forward. His tawny fur blended into the sands of the dunes so perfectly he was easy to miss. Unlike the wolves of Taletha, these stalked prey during the day. Their coats reflected the sun's heat, keeping them cool as they ran across the desert. But above all, their defining trait was their blood red eyes that seemed to glow with rage.

The wolf rolled back his lip, revealing sharp canines as he lowered itself to pounce on me.

Chapter Two

Emre

"Reckless, obstinate princezo!" I muttered as I watched the dust cloud that was Aysa fly across the desert sand. The woman would be the death of me, I was certain.

I whistled to my mare, Esma, who trotted up with a happy whinny. Shoving the bit into her mouth, I swung up, not bothering with a saddle.

What had I said to set Aysa off? She both astonished and infuriated me. She was life and light, chaos and confusion. She was enough to make the strongest man lose his mind and heart. And I wasn't that strong of a man.

The dust had dissipated by the time I guided Esma out of the gate and relatched it. My anxiety rose as I set off at a steady lope. If something happened to Aysa without me nearby, I'd never forgive myself.

"Even if it was her stubborn refusal to wait for me," I groused to my mare, who tossed her head and knickered in agreement.

I knew exactly where Aysa was going. It was the same place she always went when she needed to reflect—the oasis.

This was Aysa's favorite retreat, but letting her go there alone choked the air from my lungs. While it usually wasn't dangerous, there was always the chance of encountering a wild animal looking for water—many of whom were not as tolerant of us as we were of them.

I urged Esma forward once we reached level ground, flying into a gallop as the palm trees, and green grass of the oasis caught my eye. I couldn't escape the whispered *hurry* that brushed my mind.

Something is wrong, my mind screamed.

But surely not, I argued back. *Aysa has only been gone fifteen minutes at the most.*

I reined in and left Esma by the hobbled Kismet. Both horses huffed an acknowledgement to each other before bending over to chomp at the green grass that signified water was near.

Satisfied that the horses were contained, I dove into the undergrowth of the oasis. Two steps in, and a growl rumbled over the ground, freezing my blood. I knew that sound all too well; had witnessed its carnage before.

I sprung out of the undergrowth to see a desert wolf poised to pounce on Aysa. Its tawny fur was raised in anger, its teeth bared. Aysa had her eyes squeezed closed, her back braced against a tree. Her hands were pressed against the ground as she waited for the inevitable.

With a shout, I leapt in between her and the wolf. Without a thought to my own safety, I drew my sword. It was different from most in Taletha and Šeri, as it was a straight, double-edged sword and about the length of my arm, with a single-handed grip. I favored it to the curved scimitars of our lands due to the advantages it brought against them.

Thankful that my weapon of choice put a good three feet between the growling creature and Aysa, I snarled back at the wolf. His ears went flat when I took a step closer and leaned over his head, gnashing my teeth and warning him back.

Slowly, his tail dipped between his legs, and with a whimper of fear, he turned and fled into the undergrowth.

We waited for a heartbeat, and when no other animals emerged, I wheeled on Aysa. My words came out as a growl. "*What* were you thinking?"

Her eyes slid closed, and a tremor shook her. "I wasn't."

"Obviously." I tore off my turban and wiped my sweat-slicked fore-head with the back of my hand. Sweet Nicar, I'd never been so scared in my life. Not even when I'd stopped the man from assaulting Aysa ten years ago. A desert wolf didn't usually back off so easily. We'd been blessed. Though, I didn't want to press that blessing by lingering. Desert wolves often had packs nearby, and I wasn't eager to fight an alpha. They would be much harder to intimidate.

I glanced back at Aysa. She still had her eyes clamped closed, and she was breathing a bit too rhythmically to be natural.

"Are you all right, princezo?" I asked, cautiously.

"I'm fine." With a final deep inhale, she scrambled to her feet and forced a smile that didn't reach her eyes. "Thank you."

"Aysa—"

"I'm fine!" she snapped. "Let's go back to camp."

"What did I do?" I asked once we reached Kismet and Esma.

Aysa swung up into the saddle. When she looked at me, her lips were pressed thin. "Nothing."

I raised my brow, waiting. Aysa hated silence, and if something was left unresolved for long enough, eventually she'd begin talking. It was hard to stop her once she started, which was something I enjoyed about her. She talked so I didn't have to. She was logical in whatever plans she came up with, and relentless once she'd decided on a course of action. She always found a reason to smile and laugh. Life was never dull with Aysa, and I was thankful to be her guard.

Guard. Hired to do a job. I clutched the reins as we began to head back toward the tribe.

"Why did you say what you said?" Aysa blurted, interrupting my thoughts.

I blinked. What was she talking about? I hadn't the foggiest notion. "You're referring to...?"

"You said 'you do so much to earn that title of yours.' What did you mean by that? Why would you say that?" Her words were biting. Like an abused animal who, scared of being beaten, lashes out to protect itself.

"I said that because you do. You do a lot in the name of being the future šefe." I furrowed my brow. "I meant it as a compliment, Aysa."

"But you had this—this tone to your voice." She looked away, and I could tell she was chewing on the inside of her cheek. "It was scornful."

I snorted. "If it was, it was toward the idiot tribal leaders who are forcing you to marry. It has nothing to do with you."

"Truly?" Her dove-gray eyes held so much insecurity, so much vulnerability, that I wanted nothing more than to shake the fools who'd wounded her. But that would involve high treason against Šeri. I wasn't that furious. Yet.

"Yes, truly." I smiled.

"In that case, I'm sorry about running off." She glanced at me. "Could we keep this little adventure with the wolf between us?"

I chuckled. "I've kept enough of your other near-death escapades from your otac and majka. What's one more?"

She grinned, a real one that sent a spark dancing in her eyes and wrinkled her nose so that I could more clearly see the faint freckles that danced around her tan skin.

I swallowed the lump that had decided to lodge itself in my throat and said, "I want to help you, Aysa."

The horses had reached the base of the large dune, and our conversation paused as we charged to the top. Reining in, we stared out over the rolling sands.

"How can you help me?" She reached her hand up and rubbed at a coin on her necklace. "I have to marry someone I don't love so I can earn the job I want. But even then, I have to travel with the man. He'll become my consort and successor. I may not be the šefe the leaders want, but I know far more than any of the entitled brutes coming over the next few days."

"Perhaps we can find one who's not quite a brute," I suggested.

It was met with an immense eye-roll and sigh. "They're men."

"And?"

She shrugged. "Most men *are* boorishly awful, Emre."

I'm not. I bit back the words and stared down into the desert without replying. I hated this contest—this departure from tradition. We weren't Taletha. Šeri didn't force their women into matches. Yet that was exactly what the tribal leaders were doing to Aysa. She either married one of the eight sinovis of Šeri or she didn't get to be an ambassador. It wasn't fair.

I waited, watching Aysa finger the largest of the coins and nibble on the inside of her cheek. With another sigh that should have left her lightheaded, she gathered up the reins. "I would like your help, Emre."

I smiled and nodded as we kicked our horses for home. There wouldn't be much time left with the princezo. She was getting married. That thought left a boulder in the pit of my stomach. I hated the thought of Aysa leaving—with a man no less—but it was what it was. I was simply her guard. And if her otac knew the direction my thoughts were headed, I wouldn't even be that.

CHAPTER THREE

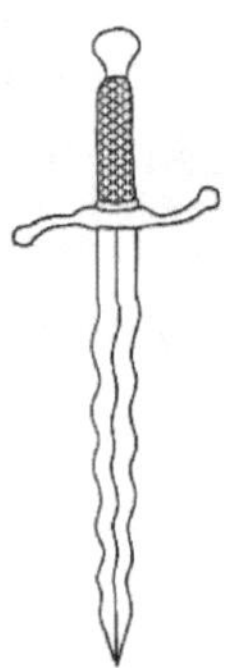

Aysa

I strode toward my sisters' tent as the sun dipped toward the horizon, bathing the desert in reds, pinks, and oranges as the sand gave back the heat of the day. It lit up the multicolored fabrics of the tribes' tents. Spaced a few feet apart, they boasted the personalities of those within. Some were plain—browns and tans with little to no adornments—while others were as vibrant as the sands at sunset.

Throwing the flaps open, I stepped under the canopy that stretched over my sisters' orange-colored tent. A slight breeze chased away the stuffiness the tent had accumulated throughout the afternoon.

"Aysa!" My youngest sister, Zlem, launched herself into my arms with a squeal. I laughed, spinning her around before untangling myself from her grip.

"How's my favorite baby sister?" I asked, tweaking her nose like Majka.

Zlem wrinkled her nose, making her eyes shrink to slits. "Gulya is being difficult again."

"Is she now?" I glanced across the tent to where my sixteen-year-old sister was curled among her pillows and blankets. Her long black hair fell over a yellow pillow she had tucked beneath her head while a scarlet one was cradled to her chest.

A long-suffering sigh said more than words what ten-year-old Zlem thought of Gulya as she shook her head at me. With a final roll of her eyes, my baby sister hurried out of the tent to talk with Emre, who had taken up his position at the flap.

I lowered myself beside my other sister, Dilan, who was busy brushing her waist-length brown hair. "Who broke Gulya's heart this time?"

"Your guess is as good as mine." Dilan shrugged. She was the second born kćerka, and if anything should happen to me—Nicar forbid—she would inherit the title of šefe. It was something she didn't desire in the slightest, probably due to the fact that she had her eye on a certain shepherd boy.

"How long has she been crying?" I asked as I crossed my arms and stared at the still sniffling Gulya.

"All morning. She came in from breakfast with a friend" —Dilan rolled her eyes, dove gray like my own —"and has refused to speak or even look at any of us since."

I raised my brows and tsked my tongue. "She gives her heart away far too easily."

Dilan laughed softly. "And you keep yours in a box, all to yourself."

"I do not!" I rebutted hotly, glaring at my sister. After all the other insults to my character that day, this one stung nearly as much as Emre's.

"You do, too." Dilan slid large golden hoops into her ears before pinning her kerchief in place. "But I cannot say if it's intentional or not. You'll learn." She smiled and patted my arm. "Someday, someone will catch your eye, and you will give him your heart. Every part of it. And he will be very lucky indeed."

Not if the leaders have their way, I thought somewhat bitterly.

Dilan sighed, biting her lip as she glanced at Gulya. "I can't deal with her tonight. I was invited to dinner at Hamid's tent and am already running late."

Knowing what this dinner was about, I smiled. Hamid had asked

Otac's permission to marry Dilan, and I, as the future šefe, had been present when he'd done so. But between the war, the new trade routes being formed to Taletha, and moving the camp closer to the border than before, Hamid hadn't had a chance to ask.

"Have a good time." I enveloped Dilan in my arms and squeezed her. While bitterness brewed in my heart at my own situation, I was happy for my sister. The hardest part was knowing I wouldn't have what she did. I couldn't marry for love. No, it was politics and pandering before love and happiness for me.

But you want to be the ambassador. Hold on to that fact. If you're the ambassador, you'll get to see Inara and Dhamar. I smiled at that thought as I leaned back and squeezed Dilan's shoulders. "I'll talk with her," I said, gesturing to the whimpering Gulya.

"Thank you. Don't get upset with her, though."

"I won't," I promised. Dilan knew me too well. I often couldn't handle the dramatic flair Gulya trotted out when sad, angry, or even mildly upset. She could rival the storytellers of the tribes, enlarging the smallest of details into massive proportions.

Dilan slipped out of the tent after pressing a kiss to my cheek. She greeted Emre and gave Zlem a kiss of her own before her shadow moved down the rows of tents for Hamid's.

I stepped closer to Gulya, who hadn't moved since I'd entered. "What happened?"

"None of your business." She sniffed. "You wouldn't understand anyway."

"Wouldn't I?" I raised my brow when she shook her head.

"You've never been in love." Her voice cracked as she said, "Hadi was kissing one of the shepherdesses."

Anger flared in my gut as I plopped next to Gulya, tucking my legs up under me. Leaning over her, I tried to see her light brown eyes. She screwed them closed; I sighed. "Honestly, Gulya. You're being ridiculous."

"Ridiculous?" She sat up, her voice near a shriek. "You don't know, Aysa. You can't know because you don't care about anything but your stupid title. Hadi said he loved me—that he wanted to marry me—and then he was kissing someone else."

"Gulya—"

"No!" She leapt to her feet, her fists shaking as she clenched them at her side. "You can't know. You don't care about me, so stop pretending to!"

She turned, ready to bolt out of the tent, but then Emre was there. He caught her in his embrace and hugged her tightly, whispering something in her ear that had her tense shoulders relaxing before a sob shook them.

Emre looked up at me, his eyes questioning. I rubbed a hand over my face and tried not to groan. I'd never been good at comfort when it came to my family. I could fake it well enough for those who didn't know me, but my logical thinking was off-putting to my more emotional relations. While I really tried with Gulya, when her emotions spiked, I shut down.

Emre rubbed Gulya's back and whispered something else to her that had her nodding. He smiled, but it didn't reach his eyes. In fact, it looked almost feral.

"Sit with Aysa." He guided my sister next to me before he waved a finger in my face. "Stay put. I'll be back in a moment."

"Where are you going?" I demanded.

Emre still had that emotionless smile on his face and ducked out of the tent without replying.

"Do I want to know what he offered to do for you?" I asked.

Gulya scoffed and wiped her nose with the back of her hand. "Probably not."

I sighed and reached out, trying not to feel the stab of guilt when she flinched. "I'm sorry, Gulya. I only meant that crying wasn't going to solve anything."

"I know." Gulya sniffed, smiling sadly at me. "But crying isn't bad, Aysa."

I scrunched up my nose. "What is the point?"

"It's like—a release. Healing." She raised her brow. "Haven't you ever just cried because you can't handle the emotions anymore?"

I fingered my necklace. No, I didn't do that. With my logical thought process, I was usually able to talk myself out of tears. Once in a while, when life felt truly hopeless, I'd let a few silent tears fall, but never around anyone and not for very long. The last time that had happened was when Šeri had started the war with Taletha.

"I can usually use logic to reason my way out of crying," I admitted.

My sister rolled her eyes. "Now who's being ridiculous?"

A scuffle at the door saved me from another harsh reply. Emre strode in, a young man in his grasp who looked positively terrified of my guard. Hadi's wide brown eyes grew larger still when his gaze landed first on Gulya and then on me.

"Gulya, princezo. I'm—what's going on?" His voice cracked as Emre thrust him forward.

Turning toward Emre, I raised my brow, wanting to know the answer to that question as well.

"The boy has some explaining to do," Emre replied to my unasked query. He crossed his arms and jutted his chin toward Gulya. "And I figured he could do it before all of us."

"Explain what?" Hadi sounded confused.

Gulya, however, had no such tone in her voice. Lurching to her feet, she strode forward until she was nearly nose-to-nose with the skinny boy. Her body fairly shook as she jabbed her finger into his ribs. "You know perfectly well what you did!"

Hadi raised his hands in surrender. "Nicar as my witness, I have no idea what you're talking about!"

This is going nowhere. "Gulya is referring to seeing you kiss another girl today, Hadi. That is what we want an explanation for."

The boy opened and closed his mouth three times before shaking his head. "That wasn't what it looked like."

"You were kissing her!" Gulya all but growled.

"What did you see?" Hadi asked, his voice lowering to a controlled, level tone that impressed me a small amount.

Gulya, red-faced and near-tears again, whispered, "You had your hands around one of the shepherdesses, and you had your head tilted. *Kissing* her."

"Did you see my lips on hers?" he asked.

I met Emre's gaze, both of us wide-eyed at the direction of this conversation.

"No." Gulya crossed her arms. "But it looked like—"

"That was Songl, my sister."

"You were kissing your sister?" I questioned at the same time Emre asked, "Your sister?"

Hadi rolled his eyes. "No! We tend the flocks together. I told her I liked Gulya. That I wanted to—" He trailed off, his cheeks turning rosy before he cleared his throat and continued. "Well, Songl was encouraging me to—"

Kiss. It's not that hard to say. I bit the inside of my cheek to keep the words to myself.

A coy smile tipped up the corners of Gulya's mouth. Gone were the anger and tears from moments before. A pink to match the color in Hadi's cheeks flooded her own as she tugged the shepherd boy forward. Her voice dropped to a whisper as she asked, "To kiss me?"

Hadi cleared his throat, but his, "yes," still came out as a squeak.

"Well, I would have shown you how." Gulya snaked her arms around his neck.

"I *didn't* kiss her," he stated emphatically as his hands settled on my sister's waist.

I grabbed Emre's hand and yanked him behind me as Gulya pressed her lips to Hadi's.

"Shouldn't we stay in there?" Emre asked.

"Five minutes, and then we'll return." I shrugged, then smirked. "Make them truly uncomfortable."

"You're terrible," Emre stated flatly.

"Then why do you spend so much time in my presence?" I elbowed him in the side. "I could do a lot more without you around."

He draped an arm over my shoulders and drummed his fingers against my bicep. "And that, dear princezo, is why. You're still alive because I follow you everywhere."

Visions of the desert wolf flooded my mind, and I shivered. "I guess I'll tolerate you then."

"Why, thank you." He pressed a palm against his chest, chuckling when I rolled my eyes. "Do you have a list of the men coming?"

I blinked, startled at the abrupt change of subject. Looking up at him, I replied, "Not yet. Why?"

"You don't want to marry a brute, right?" When I nodded, he continued, "Well, I want to be knowledgeable on their names and tribes. That will be a start. Besides" —he lowered his voice and leaned closer to me — "I have connections."

His whisper wafted warm air against my cheek, and it was then I realized he still had his arm draped around my shoulders. I shivered, but this time it wasn't from fear. Forcing a smile, I didn't feel, I ducked under Emre's arm and back toward the tent.

"Time to stop Gulya!" I said, shocked when my voice squeaked almost as badly as Hadi's had. What was going on with me?

"Aysa?" Emre's tone had me stopping in my tracks.

"Yes?" I looked over my shoulder, finding him smiling softly at me.

He inclined his head. "Thank you for letting me help you. It means a lot that you are willing to let me do that."

I managed a nod, not trusting my voice again. It was strange, letting him help me, as I often did things alone. It was easier that way. Because when I became the šefe, or even an ambassador, it would be me against the tribal leaders and the kingdoms I was traveling to. I couldn't afford to trust anyone, not even those who were supposedly allies. It was hard but better that way.

No one to lean on but yourself. Perfect little princezo. With a mental groan, I stepped back into the tent to send Hadi home. But Gulya and my future job weren't the only things on my mind. *Why did I react to Emre's touch that way? This can't be good. Can't be good at all.*

CHAPTER FOUR

Emre

I followed a few steps behind Aysa, watching as she skipped between the sunset-drenched tents. She smiled at everyone she met, a gleam in her eyes that spoke of her love for her people. I drummed my fingers against my thigh as she ducked into her otac's tent to retrieve the list of potential suitors. The šefe and leaders were making her marry to secure the ambassadorship, but it felt like a slight against my guarding skills. Yes, a husband would be with Aysa at all times, but I wasn't half-hearted in my duty to protect the princezo.

Even now, I thought as she returned and stepped up to my side with a massive scroll cradled in the crook of her arm.

She glared at it with a furrow in her brow. "This is ridiculous. How much information does my otac have on these men?"

"Enough for you to have a good idea of their character before even meeting them." I tried to keep my voice level and must have succeeded—at least in part—for Aysa sighed and began to trudge toward her tent.

Aysa's tent was much like her. While she was quick when it came to her decisions, they weren't made without logic. Her tent reflected that. A russet orange with golden tassels, one could easily miss the red embroidery around the edges, or the seemingly random runes that spoke blessings over the tent that Aysa herself had sewn into the thick fabric. I brushed my finger over the one that placed a blessing of safety over those who entered her abode before following her inside.

Lighting her oil lamp, Aysa settled on one of the multicolor cushions that surrounded the low table the lamp sat atop. By habit, I scanned her tent. Her pile of pillows and blankets sat in the far corner. The heating pot stood cold by the tent's support pole. I crossed to light it, my footsteps muffled by the red and orange rugs that covered the ground. They kept the sand from getting everywhere and helped the tent feel like a home rather than a dwelling.

"This is going to take forever." Aysa groaned and thumped her forehead against the table. "An arranged marriage is sounding better and better."

I raised my brow at her as the coals caught, and I pocketed my tinder box.

Aysa snorted at my silence, agreeing with my unspoken observation. "No, never mind. Otac *would* pick a brute."

"He did try to marry you off to Dhamar."

She shivered. "Who was married to a perfectly lovely woman at the time."

With a chuckle, I sat beside her and turned the scroll to face me. Scanning the parchment, my brows rose in surprise. "This is thorough."

The list started with the Southern tribes—Tribe Ender and Tribe Hamid—and contained not only the names of the men coming but their ages, interests, personality, and why they were worth Aysa's consideration.

"What do you know about Ulvi from Tribe Ender?" Aysa asked, tapping the first name with her finger.

I thought back to my time of wandering across the Šerian wilderness. The Ender Tribe was known for being a warrior people, and they had been the ones to train me as a fighter. How to protect and defend.

Though, during those years, my defenses had been refined by the boar that was Ulvi. He trampled anyone and anything that got in his way. I was certain he would remember me; the only young man to beat him in a hand-to-hand fight.

"I know enough about him to say you won't like him. Not unless he's changed drastically in the last eight months."

She cocked her head. "Was he here with the other warriors during our war?"

"Yes, and he was just as bad then as he was when I knew him as a boy."

A sympathetic smile flashed on Aysa's face. I hated it. Hated that she knew some of my past and the pain that coated it—though there were some parts that were still too raw to share, even with her. But I also loved that she knew because she treated me the same. I was simply Emre; friend and guard of the princezo.

And that's all you're ever going to be.

Taking my silence as a reply to her unspoken sympathy, Aysa moved to the next name. "What about Kerim?"

"He's from Tribe Hamid, which is a good tribe. They're also one of the wealthiest. Being so near the coast, they export a lot of their flocks to the east. They're also fishermen."

I'd also learned that trade for a year and a half when I was thirteen. While I had loved Tribe Hamid, I hadn't enjoyed the job of fisherman. Truly, I hadn't loved any job until I saved Aysa's life ten years ago. Yet Tribe Hamid had become not only my tribe, but my family; leaving them shattered any illusion of a peaceful life.

"But what about Kerim as a man?" Aysa pressed.

"It's been twelve years since I've seen him. He was a fun boy." I tapped my chin, ignoring the surge of pain the memories brought. Of bright eyes, a flashing smile, stolen moments. I shrugged them away and said, "He was eleven when I last saw him."

"Well, at least his age is close to mine." Aysa pressed her palms into her eyes. "Tell me about the next one."

I rolled the scroll past the parts we'd read and reached the one tribe from the Northeast. "Tribe Zafer's option is Berk."

"What about Berk?" Aysa folded her arms and propped her forehead against them.

"He's a beast." I cupped my chin in my hand and watched her. "He's as brutal as Ulvi and twice as big. He's a fierce protector, and if he chooses to be loyal to you, there's nothing you can do to stop him."

"Great. An overzealous lover." Aysa sighed. "Next?"

I could see the defeat pressing against Aysa's shoulders, so I rolled up the scroll. "What does it matter?"

"I need to know!" Aysa sat up, her gray eyes flashing with a frustration that I found strangely satisfying because she needed to feel *something*. She needed to let herself have emotions and identify them in order to pick a husband. Her logic was clouding her mind and muddying her perception.

"Aysa, is any of this going to help you pick the right man?"

"I—"

I pressed a finger to her lips. "Shut up and listen. Please?"

My tacked-on request did nothing to smooth out her scowl, but she pressed her mouth into a thin line anyway.

"Good," I commended, and her eyes turned murderous. "Now, think about this; marriage is more than just what you see on this parchment. These are facts—cold, hard facts about these men. But you don't know what they feel, what they're thinking, until you meet them. A lot can be said for what your instincts tell you."

Aysa's jaw worked, and I knew she was chewing the inside of her cheek.

"If you meet Berk and something tells you to get to know him better, do it. Whether or not I find him to be a beast, you might just find the man who will be your koca."

The words made my heart ache inside my chest. Because—for all my ignoring—my heart was telling me this was the woman I would always love. She was my best friend—one of my only, if I were being honest. Aysa was the woman I wanted to marry. But I couldn't. Because I was her guard, and she was my princezo. I wasn't a tribal leader. I wasn't someone who would rein in her wildness and impulsiveness. Yes, Aysa was logical, but she was also loyal. Loyal to the point of recklessness. Her fire, her passion for her people, showed so brightly that I'd fallen into the flame. She was the type of woman who loved and loved fiercely. And oh, how I longed to be on the receiving end of that love.

Aysa sighed and tugged off the magenta kerchief that covered her hair. She fingered the knot in the fabric as she thought about my words. "All right, Emre. I'll wait until they start to arrive tomorrow. However" —she pinned me down with her unwavering gaze — "I will want your observations each night about how they behaved around you."

"Of course, Princezo." I inclined my head, struggling to pull my wild thoughts back into line.

She threw her kerchief at me. "I hate when you call me that."

I chuckled and threw the piece of cloth back. "That's precisely why I do it."

Aysa rolled her eyes, but her lips curved up ever so slightly. "Thank you, Emre. You always know the right thing to say."

My heart lurched in my chest as I struggled to my feet and bowed at my waist. "It is my duty and my pleasure, my princezo."

Aysa's smile froze as a terrified look filled her eyes. I blinked, and she was back to smiling as she pushed to her feet and guided me to the tent flap.

"Promise me you won't look at the scroll again tonight?" I asked. My fingers flexed, my heart telling me to grab Aysa's hand even as I curled my fingers into a fist and held them at my side.

She nodded, not looking at me. Worry had her forehead wrinkling, and I allowed myself the small comfort of laying a hand against her shoulder. Aysa looked up at me. "What if I can't find someone?" she whispered.

Marry me. I cleared my throat. "You will, Aysa. You're far too brilliant to be alone forever."

"Yes, but one of these men has to be it. I have to be the ambassador to Taletha, Emre. It's... I have to."

She was still looking up at me, and an overwhelming desire to lean in and kiss her slammed into me. I swallowed, my mouth dry as I squeezed Aysa's shoulder and forced myself to step back. "You will, Aysa. I know you'll find a man in the next few weeks. Eight are coming, and one will turn you head and heart."

And I will have to stand by and watch it happen. I silently swore and forced myself to bow once more. "Sweet dreams, Princezo."

Before she could reply I ducked out and nodded to the night guard as I strode through the camp to my tent.

Tiny by comparison, it was a dingy brown. No embroidery lined the canvas, but Aysa had tied golden tassels to the corners at some point. I ducked in, not bothering to light my own heating pot as I tore off my turban and threw it onto my bed with a growl. Around the support pole, I paced, trying to outrace the thoughts in my head.

You can't have her. So why do you want her? I shoved my hands through my black hair, trying to ignore the thoughts swirling in my head. But they were a cacophony too loud to be ignored. Slowly, they righted themselves into order, and I hated every single one of them.

You want her because Aysa is everything you've been looking for, the reason you quit running all those years ago. She's your home, your family.

I groaned and flopped onto my bedroll with a sigh of defeat. It was true. Protecting Aysa had become the motive to stay put and the reason I had claimed this tribe as my own. I'd found a family here, but now Aysa was the one woman I couldn't have. Couldn't love. Couldn't call my own.

The reason to stay has become the very reason to leave.

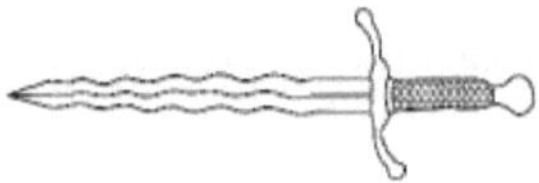

Morning came far too soon. I was accustomed to waking early, determined to be in front of Aysa's tent when she emerged. The princezo was notorious for slipping out without a guard, and I wasn't willing to let her risk her life because of pigheadedness.

But that morning, my eyes felt itchy, my limbs ached, and my head buzzed after my realization last night.

Nicar above, give me strength. I groaned as I rose and dressed, the grittiness turning into a dull throb behind my eyes.

"Sleepless nights and early mornings," I grumbled as I stalked to Aysa's tent. For all I loved my job, this morning I was in a foul mood, and no one had better mess with me.

"Good morning, Emre!" Aysa was annoyingly perky as she skipped from her tent, a smile on her face that usually produced one of my own. But all I saw was what I couldn't have. I couldn't have that smile for the rest of my life. Couldn't hold her, help her, lend my strength when she was floundering.

Yet, I couldn't tell her that, so I forced a smile of my own to my lips. "Good morning."

Her lips pursed as she studied me. "You look awful."

"Thank you," I replied drily before changing the subject. "Are you ready to greet the men today?"

Aysa scowled. "No."

She lapsed into silence, both of us lost in thought as we stood before her tent. My fingers drummed against my thigh as Aysa's jaw worked, proof of her usual nervous habit. "You will be fine," I said at last, breaking the tension that was building up between us. "I will be at your side every step of the way."

Aysa smiled, her forefinger and thumb rubbing at her coin necklace. "Thank you. I think I'll need my best friend to get through all of this."

Best friend. The words slammed into me, making me smile outwardly while inside I was crumbling. Because of course that's how she saw me. The friend. Forever and always.

Memories I wanted to forget flitted into my mind, distorted by years of ignoring.

Feray, a ball of energy and light, laughing as we ran up and down the shores of the Eastern coast.

"Oh, Emre. You're such a good friend," Feray laughed as we splashed in the waves.

"He's my best friend, Otac." She swung our hands back and forth.

Pale and sick, Feray coughed, "You're leaving? Best friends don't leave!"

"You're more than a friend," she whispered, half-delirious.

"Kiss me, Emre. If this is goodbye forever, I want to remember you this way." Shallow breaths, cold fingers and lips. "Goodbye, Emre."

I shook my head, shoving the past back into the recesses of my mind. I couldn't think about *her* right now. Aysa needed my help, and by Nicar, I would see that she had it. Perhaps I couldn't love her the way I wanted to, but I could love her the only way possible—by supporting her until the very end.

CHAPTER FIVE

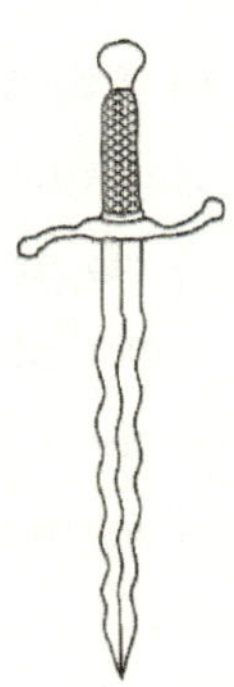

Aysa

My hands felt clammy, the moisture on them begging to be wiped off on my purple kaftan. But that wasn't proper, so I pressed them flat against my thighs, willing my churning stomach to stay put.

Otac stood beside me in his bright red kurta and black salwar, his gaze flinty as he watched the approaching group of men; men who were after me. I'd thought about it long and hard the night before. These men wanted one thing—power. They didn't care about the person I was. Rather, they wanted the advantages of being the husband of the future šefe. The power, fame, and glory that I would bring to a marriage. Yet I would do all the work. I would lead the people, bear the man children, and earn the wealth that would hold our tribes together.

I ground my teeth as the thundering desert mounts approached. I hated them. Hated them all for what they were subjecting me to. I had to choose a husband—the peace with Taletha wouldn't last if an ambassador wasn't sent soon. I had brought this peace to our land. Dhamar and I had fought with word and deed to stop our people from continuing a pointless war. We'd rejuvenate a trade route that had been broken for decades. And I wanted to continue what we had started. I wanted to be the ambassador to Taletha. But none of that would happen if I couldn't find a man to marry among the sons of our tribe's leaders.

"Welcome!" Otac smiled and extended his hands in greeting as the men swung off their horses. All wore turbans and face covers that kept sun off their heads and the sand out of their mouths and noses. They varied in height, but one thing was certain—they all towered over my slight stature.

I wanted to step back, wanted to run to the oasis—although the memory of the desert wolf was still fresh in my mind. But as the young men began to remove their face coverings, bowing and smiling toward Otac, I forced a steadying breath into my lungs.

"You can do it," Emre whispered, his warm breath caressing my cheek, causing my breathing to hitch. "Show them why you are the future šefe."

I nodded and strode forward.

Otac saw me and smiled, gesturing me to his side as he wrapped a protective arm around my shoulders. "Here is what you shall be competing for. This is my kćerka, Aysa—princezo of the Šerian tribes."

My smile turned brittle at Otac's words. *What you are competing for.* As if I were a prize to be won, a medal of honor for whichever man I chose. I didn't want to be an ornament. I wanted to find a partner, a helpmate.

But I swallowed the roll of emotions and inclined my head to the men. "Welcome to the Tribe of the Šefe."

"Thank you." The tallest of the eight men stepped forward. Fisting his hand over his chest, he bowed low. "I am Efe, eldest sinovi of Tribe Neval. It is an honor to be chosen to attempt to win the princezo's hand, oh my šefe."

"I am Ömer, second sinovi of Tribe Neval." This man had to be Efe's twin. Both had short cropped brown hair and dark green eyes that shone like emeralds in their tan faces. When they smiled, the sides of their mouths dimpled. They were handsome, tall and broad chested, and positively terrifying.

"And I am the youngest sinovi." Another man stepped forward. A bow was slung over one shoulder, and while he was shorter than both Efe and Ömer, he was no less muscular. "I am Derin."

"A pleasure to meet the sons of Tribe Neval." I inclined my head. Far above these men in my station, it was the only acknowledgement they deserved.

All three of them smiled at me before stepping to the side. I found myself returning their grins with a small smile of my own. These men seemed friendly enough, despite their looming height.

Another man stepped forward. His skin was dark, which made his teeth gleam brightly in the early afternoon sun. But his dark eyes seemed hard despite his smile as he bowed toward me. "Ulvi, from Tribe Ender."

It was a struggle to keep my serene expression in place. Even though he was behind me, I was certain I felt Emre stiffen. Ulvi's gaze landed on my guard. His smile faded, casting his whole face in hard lines. I wasn't entirely certain what had happened between Ulvi and Emre, but from the blazing fury in Ulvi's eyes, it couldn't have been good.

"A pleasure to meet you, Ulvi," I forced out, drawing the man's attention back to me. His smile returned, but it lacked all warmth.

"All mine, Princezo." He bowed again and strode to stand beside the Tribe Neval brothers.

Otac shifted his ebony staff into his other hand, a beaming smile on his face as the next young man stepped forward. This one I knew. He'd been underfoot frequently when we'd been children; had practically been a brother to me until he'd been adopted by the leader of the Alïm tribe.

"Kagan!" I smiled and hugged him. Probably improper, but I hadn't given myself time to over-think the action.

He laughed and hugged me back. "Well, this wasn't the greeting I was expecting!"

Otac cleared his throat, and I stepped away, still grinning widely. "How are you?"

"I am well." He smiled, and it was the same as ever, too large for his narrow face and causing his eyes to become mere slits. "I am in line to be the leader after Otac passes. I've been studying endlessly for the position. A few of our people don't think I'm ready."

His smile slipped into a scowl, and I squeezed his forearm. "You will be an excellent leader, Kagan. Of that I have no doubt." *Unlike the way I doubt my own leadership abilities.*

"We have three more young men to meet." Otac cleared his throat and gestured for Kagan to take his place among the others. Kagan smiled and bowed to Otac and me before hurrying to follow Otac's order.

The next man oozed arrogance. His smile was as oily as the black hair that hung to his shoulders. Two curved swords were strapped to his back, another at his waist. Along his left side, five daggers were sheathed, and his hands rested on his weapons as he strode forward.

"Princezo." He bowed. "Naz, from Tribe Nidar."

I parroted my response from the others. Already my head was buzzing with all the names, yet I had to continue to do this. I couldn't forget any of them; first impressions were vital in my choosing the right man. I balled my hands into fists and kept my smile on my face.

"Princezo!" The next man to step forward fisted his hand over his heart and dropped to one knee. I raised my brows as he said, "My undying loyalty to you, Princezo Aysa. Forever you shall be in my heart."

A snort sounded from one of the other men, and I had to swallow twice before squeaking out, "Thank you?"

The man met my gaze, the strange blue of his eyes shocking me. It must have shown on my face, for one side of his mouth turned up in a smirk. "I am Berk, from the Tribe of Zafer."

He stood, bowed, and went to stand by Kagan—leaving me feeling quite flustered as the final man stepped forward.

Wariness had his lips pressed thin as he studied the other seven men before turning to face me. His olive skin matched Emre's. He was lean, and his long brown hair was pulled back into a low tail. His sleeveless kurta revealed the faintest sprinkling of freckles down his arms.

He bowed like all the others. "I am Kerim, from the Hamid tribe." He straightened, and his eyes flicked to my guard. "It is an honor to meet you, princezo."

"Thank you, Kerim. I'm glad you accepted the—challenge." The word lodged in my throat, and all I wanted was a cool drink—of water or ale, I didn't care which.

Otac spread his arms wide to the men. "Welcome to the Tribe of the Šefe! We're honored to have you. You may stake your tents on the outskirts of the tribe. There shall be a feast at my tent later this evening where you shall all get a chance to speak more with the princezo and to me. Until then, rest well." Otac turned and offered me his arm, guiding me back toward the tents.

I could hear the men moving, preparing to stake their tents alongside my people. They would join our tribe—however temporary—before one would join me as my husband. Consort. Partner. I couldn't see any of them bending to me, to my leadership. It wasn't that I wanted to lord my title over them. Far from it. But most of the men had appeared...proud. I sighed as we stepped onto the path that wove toward the heart of the camp and my family's tents.

Otac waggled his brows at me as the shade of the tents fell over us. "It appears that Berk is quite taken with you already."

"He was ridiculous and made a total spectacle of himself." I resisted the urge to roll my eyes.

"Well, we can't all be perfect." Otac laughed. "The Neval brothers seemed like nice boys."

But that was just it. They were *boys*. According to the scroll—which, despite my promise to Emre, I had glanced at that morning—Efe and Ömer were only nineteen years old. But despite their ages, all the men had carried themselves with confidence. Even Kagan, much to my surprise.

"Kagan has grown into a competent young man, Otac." I watched him out of the corner of my eye. "He's not the...what did you used to call him?"

Otac visibly squirmed. "A scrawny runt. And no, he isn't."

I chuckled and hugged Otac's arm tighter. "He will be a good friend to have during this search."

Stopping before my tent, Otac tugged me around to face him. "I hope you know that your sisters, your majka, and I all wish to be part of this contest with you. You aren't alone in this decision, Aysa."

Aren't I? I swallowed, unable to meet Otac's gaze. I didn't want to get married, but Otac and Majka were forcing my hand. Because what I wanted was to be the ambassador to Taletha. Yet to do that, I was having to sacrifice my will. My desires.

"Aysa?" Otac tucked a loose curl into my kerchief. "You are my brave, beautiful girl. You will make a wonderful šefe someday."

He pressed a kiss to my forehead, patted my hand, then headed off to his and Majka's tent.

I folded my hands and pressed them up under my chin. Otac wasn't making this easy. No, I felt more confused now than ever before.

Emre stepped up, his hand settling on my shoulder. "Are you all right, Aysa?"

With a deep breath, I rolled my shoulders back, effectively knocking Emre's hand off. When he touched me, it was hard to focus and be logical, which was the last thing I needed right now.

"I'll be fine." I glanced at him over my shoulder. "But I think we need to review my list before dinner."

He crossed his arms over his chest and raised that infernal brow of his. "You looked at the scroll last night, didn't you?"

"What if I did?"

"You promised!" He wagged his finger at me. "You little liar!"

"No." I batted his finger away and tried to stand taller. "I said I wouldn't look at it last night. And I didn't. I looked at it this morning."

He paused, and I could tell he was thinking back to last night. After a moment, he scowled at me. "You knew what I meant."

I shrugged, a real smile tugging on my lips as I said, "You have to be clear with me, Emre. Otherwise, I get terribly confused."

"Aysa!" Emre exclaimed.

With a cheeky smile and toss of my hair, I ducked into my tent, trying desperately to ignore the flip of my heart as Emre's rumble of laughter followed after me.

CHAPTER SIX

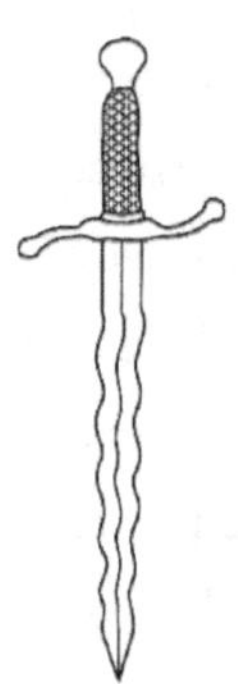

Emre

I stood in the doorway of Aysa's tent as she stared down at the scroll. The names of all eight men who could earn her hand were scratched onto the yellowed parchment. I hated every one of them.

"What did you think about the Neval brothers?" she asked, rubbing her eyes. "They seemed nice, although a little young."

"I don't like them." I crossed my arms over my chest, dipping my chin to hide my eyes from Aysa.

She sighed, the sound long and exasperated. "I think you'd have a problem with any of the men, including Kagan, who is arguably the mousiest man I've ever met. His nose even twitches."

Her attempt to wiggle her nose—which caused her eyes to squint and lips to purse—made me smile unconsciously.

"Besides, of all of them, he's the one I know the best." She sighed again, cupping her chin in her hand.

I tapped my fingers against my thigh, fighting the rising panic. The thought of Aysa marrying any of those men made me want to vomit. "None of them are worthy of you."

"Well, I have to find someone, or Otac will pick one of them for me."

I bristled, dropping my gaze to the floor. "Don't remind me."

This had been a bad idea, helping her pick her future husband. It had been pure torture standing at her side as man after man fawned over her, wanting her affection. It was hard to banish images of them kissing her, holding her, loving her as a husband. My shoulders tensed even thinking about it. *No one* was worthy of Aysa in that regard. Not even me.

"It'll be all right, Emre. It has to be. Surely someone will meet our expectations." She sounded defeated and worried—two emotions I wasn't accustomed to from Aysa—and it caused my head to snap up.

Aysa's arms were crossed, and she stared at the side of her tent, her chin quivering ever so slightly. My heart pinched. This was crushing her; crushing the wild spirit that I loved so much. But she would hide it, force herself through it to be the šefe she thought her people wanted her to be. I hated that she did this to herself. No one expected perfection, yet she forced it onto herself and didn't even realize it.

Ineloquent as I was, I tried to offer comfort to her. "We will find one, Aysa. There's the perfect man out there for you, I know."

"I hope so." Her lips twisted into a grimace.

I sat beside her at the table, daring to clasp her hand that was pressed against the scroll. "Someday, somewhere, somehow, some*one*" —she giggled, her shoulders relaxing— "is going to see how brave, strong, caring, passionate, and absolutely brilliant you are. They won't be frightened by it but will love all of it. Love all of *you* for who you are."

"I'm the princezo, Emre. The future šefe of our people. Those men don't care for who I am. They only wish for the power I'll someday have. They most likely resent me for it." Her chin quivered again, and she looked back at the wall of the tent, her jaw tensing as she forced her emotions back under control.

"Then they are fools. A man should be proud to call his kari šefe." I dared to tuck a strand of her hair behind her ear, earning another small smile. "Today, I call you princezo. Someday, I'll call you šefe. Either title, it doesn't matter. *You* make me proud, Aysa."

"But—" She swallowed, her gaze flicking over my face. "Emre, you hate guarding me."

"No," I whispered, my voice a bit husky. "I've never hated guarding you. Now, the mischief and danger you get into..." I smirked, tapping the tip of her nose and easing away from her, despite my mind protesting. "That drives me crazy. I hate it because it puts you in harm's way."

She huffed a breath of pure exasperation. "They don't *always* put me in danger."

"You let a prisoner sleep in your *tent*."

"He was my cousin!" she protested with a scowl.

My heart lurched. Something about Aysa being angry did strange things to my breathing. Sent my mind down paths better left untrodden.

"You didn't know that then," I refuted, rather weakly.

"But it all worked out." She flipped her hair over her shoulder, effectively ending the argument. "And I'm not worried about the past. The concern at hand is finding me a man that I want to marry and who wants me for more than my title."

Stifling a sigh of pure annoyance, I nodded and motioned back to the scroll. "Well, let's talk about that."

We went through the list. Each name added a new level of tightness to the ache building in my chest. Each name was a potential spouse. Each name produced a new image of a man that wasn't me kissing Aysa, loving her in a way I longed to do. Each name brought another wave of regret, anger, and failure. Although I knew it was illogical, a large part of my mind told me that Šefe Aydin was essentially saying my guarding wasn't enough—that Aysa needed someone better than me. I couldn't curb her enthusiasm and reckless spirit because I didn't *want* to. It was what drove her to lead her people. To love and fight for them.

And because of that, I needed to let her go.

But you knew this wasn't forever. Just like the love you had for Feray wasn't forever.

I ground my teeth as Aysa sighed. "I have to go get ready for dinner.

Dilan is going to help me."

"I assume tonight will be a fancier occasion?" I asked as I offered Aysa my hand and helped her to her feet.

"Yes. Majka had a special kaftan prepared." She wrinkled her nose. "It shows more skin than I like."

That comment sent my thoughts racing, and it took all my willpower to wrestle them into submission. "I'm sure you'll look lovely."

"If it helps me choose the right man, that's all that matters, yes?" She shrugged, curling in on herself with that infernal logic of hers. She was reckless in her loyalty yet, more often than not, could give you a rational reason for why she did what she did. Wild yet sensible. Aysa was a contradiction I wanted to try and solve for the rest of my life.

We strode between the tents side-by-side. The sun was halfway to the horizon, the temperature nearly unbearable. I had been away from the coast for years; I had grown used to the ever-present sweat and the warmth that crawled up from the sands like scorching flames racing across parchment. Yet I didn't know what to do with the all-consuming heat in my chest. It matched the sun in intensity, pouring out without fear of what it would consume. I reined it in, but I knew it would devour me if I wasn't careful. Because what it required to abate its raging fury wasn't mine to have.

We reached the sisters' tent, and Aysa casually tossed her brilliant grin my way. "I'll be out soon."

"Take your time." I returned her smile, despite the lurching in my stomach. "I'll be here to escort you when you're finished."

She nodded and stepped inside.

I breathed a bit easier, rubbing at my chest as if that would ease the discomfort lodged there.

"There you are!" A high-pitched squeal rent the air as Zlem skipped up. She matched Aysa in spunk, but her laughter came easier, her words tumbling over themselves without a thought for what was being said. She grabbed my hand, her tiny fingers dwarfed by my large ones. "I wondered where Aysa was."

"She's getting ready for dinner with your otac and majka."

Zlem wrinkled her nose. "And all those horrid men."

"You don't like them?" I raised a brow as she adamantly shook her head. "Why not?"

"They aren't you." She shrugged as if that were the most obvious thing in the world.

My eyes widened. "You can't say such things, Zlem!"

"Why not?" Her brows furrowed. "I want you for a brother, not any of those stuffy tribal sinovis."

I choked on my inhale, coughing so hard that stars danced in the corners of my eyes. "Zlem..." I shook my head.

"What?" She threw up her hands. "It's the truth."

"The truth doesn't always need to be spoken." I finally managed as my face flushed. "Especially near Aysa."

Zlem rolled her eyes and planted her fists on her hips. "If you told her you cared for her," she dropped her voice to a whisper after I pressed my finger to my lips, "she'd convince Otac to let her marry you."

"The men are here." I shook my head. "I won't dishonor your otac, your sister, nor them by doing that."

"You're ridiculous!" Zlem hissed. "You should do whatever you can to be with her."

The last time I did that, it ruined everything. I bit my tongue and shook my head again.

The flap rustled, and Aysa stepped out, looking like a vision from Nicar. A dark orange kaftan clung to her, swishing with every step. There were no sleeves, and the straps over her shoulders were cinched with golden clasps. If one knew where to look, you could just make out her tattoo on the underside of her bicep. Around her neck was a gauzy yellow scarf. Her hair was down, curling in wild disarray around her shoulders while a golden coronet was nestled over her brow. Each step jingled, drawing my eyes to her bare feet. Golden anklets with tiny bells on them wrapped around her ankles, a strand of the metal covering the top of her foot and wrapping around her second toe. Glittering diamonds were embedded in them, catching the sun. She was breathtaking. Absolutely stunning.

Far too exquisite. I swallowed and bowed. "Tonight you are the most gorgeous princezo in all the world."

Her cheeks turned a pretty pink hue. "Truly?"

"Beyond words." I cleared my throat. "Are you ready?"

"She better be." Dilan huffed as she stepped up, fanning her face with her hands. "It's sweltering in there."

Aysa chuckled. "It's a good thing Otac planned on the feast being outside his tent then, hm?"

Zlem jabbed her elbow into my side. I glanced down, and she angled her head toward Aysa. It was a bad idea, me leading Aysa to the feast. They would all see her on my arm, think there was more to us than there was, more than there could be. But I held my arm out anyway. "May I escort you to dinner, Princezo?"

She smiled up at me and Nicar above, did I ever want her to do that again. It was a heady rush, like the strongest wine imaginable coursing through my system. I would die a happy man if I could spend the rest of my life earning that smile.

But you can't. You won't. So settle for making her happy with the man she chooses.

Chapter Seven

Aysa

I eased closer to Emre as we reached Otac's tent, aware of all eight sets of eyes that swiveled toward me. Green, blue, brown, and black—they bore into me, studying me in a way that made me want to squirm. But I refused to give into that impulse, so instead, I threw back my shoulders and let go of Emre's arm to stride forward.

The sand was warm against my bare feet, and I allowed myself the small pleasure of curling my toes into it as I bowed before Otac.

"Welcome, kćerka." He pressed a kiss to my cheek and then gestured for me to take a seat beside him at the head of the long table. All the men sat straight and tall on their cushions, their eyes riveted on us. I swallowed and reached for my necklace that I had insisted remain around my neck.

Otac thumped his staff on the ground, though not a soul was talking. "Men of Šeri, I know you are eager to prove yourselves to this fine young woman at my side. This challenge shall not be easy. The princezo is a hard woman to please."

It curdled my stomach to see Naz get that cloyingly slick smile on his face, his eyes already undressing me. I shivered and returned to listening to Otac.

"But she will eventually choose one of you as her koca and—once she is the šefe of Šeri—her consort!"

A rambunctious cheer rose up from the men, but my gaze didn't linger on any of them. Rather, it found Emre at the far end of the table. His mouth was set in a grim line as he surveyed the group. As if sensing my eyes on him, he turned toward me, smiled, and raised his brows, attempting to remind me that I was supposed to be poised and happy about this occasion. Even if I wasn't.

With a steadying breath, I smiled at Otac as he sat and patted my knee. "Begin the feast, kćerka."

I stood, hands stretched high. "With thanks to Nicar, goddess of all, we partake of the bounty she has blessed us with. We thank her for those gathered around this table, for the beauty in the land and in each other. May she continue to bless us as long as the sun and moon endure."

"Amen," echoed all around, and then the clinking of dishes being passed filled the silence.

I sat, fidgeting with my necklace as I watched the men laughing and talking. Pressure built at the back of my eyes, but I ignored it. Pushed away all the swirling aches in my chest and the pain in my head. I turned to smile at the man on my left-hand side.

"Why did you decide to join this contest, Efe?" I asked the eldest of the Neval tribe.

He finished his sip of wine and smiled winsomely at me. "Well, I heard of your great beauty and—"

I held up my hand, cutting off his ridiculously flirtatious compliments before they could start, and raised a brow. "No flowery words. Truth is the only thing I welcome in a compliment. You know nothing of me nor my personality. So, do speak plainly."

Efe's grin only grew as he chuckled. "A woman who speaks her mind is a refreshing thing indeed."

I folded my arms and waited for the truth, an action I'd learned from Emre. The tactic worked on me, and it appeared to do equally well on Efe. He cleared his throat and dropped his dark green eyes to his plate piled with kofta, hummus, and falafel. "I am here because our tribe needs the support of the šefe's people."

My brow rose. "In what way?"

"As you know, we are the Western Tribe. The mountain people have been harassing us for quite some time about our livestock that like to wander the ridges. They mean no real harm, but they do eat a great amount of the vegetation."

"Which the mountaineers don't particularly like," Derin interjected with an eye roll. "Our otac has tried everything in the way of making a deal with them, but they refuse. We would simply pull out and find a different place, but our herds are large."

"I am assuming the mountain provides a certain amount of unique flora growth as well?" I questioned.

The brothers nodded in tandem, and I fingered my necklace, thinking. "And how large are your herds?"

There weren't many places in Šeri that could host a small herd, let alone a large one. We were a mostly desert country; though a long time ago we'd owned more land and reached further into what was now Taletha. But hot sand and brutal sun covered most of what we called home. My fists clenched under the table as I glared at my plate. If I were the ambassador, I could work a deal with Taletha where we could graze our animals on their land and, in exchange, they would receive some of our livestock.

"If I'm chosen to go to Mordova as the representative for Šeri, I shall draw up a petition and present it to Malek Dhamar. Perhaps he'll allow you to graze some of your flocks over the border."

Efe's eyes narrowed. "We want nothing from the Talethan dogs."

"We'd rather go to war with the Westerners than take anything from the *malek* of Taletha." Derin spat to the side, his light green eyes narrowing.

I heaved my eyes heavenward. "And pray, why is that? *They* brought us peace. Perhaps they initiated the war, but we were no better. We raided. We killed. They retaliated and rightly so. We would have done the same. Now, I will hear no more disrespect toward my *kinsman's* nation."

At my steady gaze boring into him, Efe ducked his head. "Of course, Princezo."

"Good." I picked up my goblet and took a sip, trying to cool my simmering temper. Over the top of my cup, I dared another glance at Emre. Though he wasn't looking at me, I could see the flickering smile on his face, and I hoped it was from my words.

Completely irrational. I turned my attention across the table. Kagan was grinning like a fool. I always loved his smile. It stretched from ear to ear, taking up a lot of his face. His brown eyes—what could be seen of them—danced in the shadows cast by the twilight and flickering light given off by the torches. "Kagan, tell me about your training to be the leader of Tribe Alïm."

He blanched, the smile dropping off his face like rainwater washing away tracks in the sand. "That's a conversation for later, Aysa."

I pressed my lips together to keep from saying the first thing to pop into my head. Far too often, I spoke first, thought it through later. My random bouts of impulsiveness needed to be tempered in logic. It had to be. If I was ever going to convince the tribal leaders I was ready to lead, I needed to curb my instant reactions. That wasn't how a good šefe responded.

No, a good šefe was my otac. He led with quiet strength and dignity. He never rushed into a decision. He weighed everything, took his time, and came to the best conclusion in complete steadiness. I wanted to be like him. Strove for it, if I were being honest.

"A toast to the princezo!" Berk launched to his feet from further down the table, sloshing some of the wine onto his kurta sleeve. "The most beautiful woman in Šeri! May we all have good fortune in our endeavors to win her!"

Rounds of *here, here* echoed among those gathered, but I couldn't look away from Berk. He still wore the smile, a slightly infatuated look on his face. Emre's warning rattled around my mind. Berk was loyal—to a fault. What would he do to earn *me*? Looking at him in the lengthening shadows, I wasn't all that certain he wouldn't try and seduce me—use me to gain a position of power. And that knowledge shook me to my core.

The rest of the meal sped by in a blur. I couldn't look at Berk nor Naz, whose leering smile soured anything in my stomach. Because of that, I barely ate anything as the conversations swirled around me. Otac laughed at something Kagan said and I smiled, but my ears rang. I wanted away from the table and away from the men; desperately needing a chance to clear my head.

As the torches reached the end of their lives and the baklava was mostly gone, Otac stood. "Thank you for coming to our meal. The princezo will be meeting privately with each of you in the coming weeks to get to know you better. It will be a time of conversation and exchanging of information only. A guard will be posted as her escort whenever she is with one of you to ensure propriety."

Thank Nicar. I thought as Naz, Berk, and, surprisingly, Ulvi all smiled coyly.

"Aysa, who would you like to meet with first?" Otac asked.

I glanced around the circle, my head buzzing like a swarm of gnats. Each face looked at me expectantly, and I hesitated only fractionally as I met Kagan's gaze, panic in the depths of his eyes.

Who can I see myself with? I wondered while scanning down the line. Naz was leering again, Berk looked entirely too eager, and the brothers of Tribe Neval appeared bored.

The two who looked more or less impartial were Kerim and Ulvi. *Both men Emre knows.* Curiosity gripped me, and I gestured toward the latter. "I would like to meet with Ulvi first, if it pleases him?"

Ulvi stood and bowed deeply. His muscles rippled as he crossed his bare arms, the shoulders of his short-sleeved kurta pulling taut. His face, hard but not hate-filled, was impossible to read in the flickers of the lanterns around the table. "It would be an honor, Princezo."

Emre's presence shifted behind me, waiting to escort me back to my tent. I heard him suck in a sharp breath as Ulvi took his seat. The man sent a cold look at my guard as Otac clapped his hands once and said, "Ulvi it shall be then! I shall see you in the morning, kćerka." Otac pressed a kiss to my forehead—more public affection than he'd given me in years—and gestured Emre forward. "Escort the princezo back to her tent."

"Yes, my šefe." Emre bowed and offered me his arm.

I had been around handsome men all day—dined and drank with eight who were fawning over me and trying to win my affections. But it wasn't until my hand rested on top of Emre's forearm that I was able to breathe deeply and relax for the first time since he'd brought me to the meal. He was comfortable—a bit of normal in a sea of chaos and change. I tightened my grip on his arm as he led me through the tents to my own; clung to him like he was the last sane person in the world.

"Thank you, Emre." I muttered, resting my head on his arm once we reached my tent. "I'm exhausted."

"You look it." He laid his hand over mine. "You did wonderful tonight. They were all practically salivating."

I laughed humorlessly. "Not Efe. He's angry that I want to create a trade deal between his tribe and Taletha for grazing grounds. Kagan seemed scared to even look at me all of a sudden. And Berk and Naz—" I shivered, feeling Emre's muscles tense under my fingers at the mention of those two. "I don't want to marry Berk or Naz, yet I fear what they may try if I reject them."

"I'm not leaving your side again." Emre emphatically shook his head.

I don't want you to leave my side for the rest of my life.

As soon as the words entered my head, I pushed them away. It wasn't an option. It wasn't plausible *before* the contest, let alone now. Emre was my best friend and guard, and that was all he could be, whether I liked it or not.

CHAPTER EIGHT

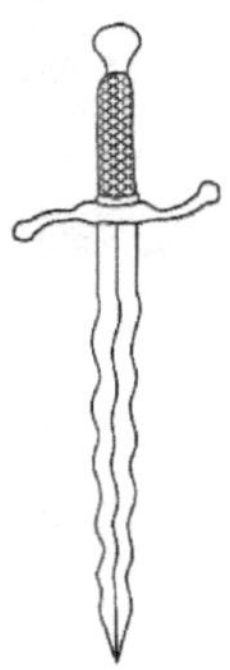

Emre

I didn't want to let her go. With Aysa's head tucked against me, her hand tight on my arm, I wrestled with the urge to step into her tent and never leave. I wanted her. I would love and cherish her, unlike the idiots who fawned over her at dinner. I hadn't allowed myself to watch her, but I couldn't turn off my ears. Her words and laughter had floated between the distance, simultaneously warming and chilling my heart.

The men around her were like desert wolves. Sleek, beautiful, graceful. But all of that hid the cunning underneath, the muscles that were poised to pounce, the teeth and claws prepared to shred her heart into tiny pieces and devour her soul.

"I need to go to bed," whispered Aysa, but she didn't move.

"Must you?" I angled so I could see her eyes. "We could go for a ride. That always helps clear your head."

"But Otac—"

"Aysa, we've pulled off a number of escapes in our day." I pretended to be affronted. "Unless you think I've lost my ability to sneak?"

She chuckled, low and throaty and real. "No, I don't think that. But if Otac finds out, the men will, too. I have to make a good impression. I have to pick one of them."

I ignored that final comment, tugging her to follow me.

"I can't wear this to ride!" she protested, sliding her hand out from under mine. "Let me change."

"But you look stunning in that." I snagged her arm, halting her escape into her tent as a horrible idea bloomed in my head. "Ride with me."

"What?" She froze, her eyes locking with mine while her mouth opened in shock.

I should have recanted my offer, but I didn't want to. I had seen the way Dhamar had ridden with his wife when they'd gone off to face his father. Cradled to his chest, they'd shared whispered conversations as they'd waited to leave. I wanted to do that with Aysa. Perhaps it was foolish, but if I couldn't have her forever, I wanted to savor the moments I still had left.

"Ride with me?" I offered again as the silence stretched.

"I—" Aysa shrugged, a smile teasing her lips. "Why not?"

With a squeeze to her arm, I slid my hand down and interlocked her fingers with mine. Then, we ran to the corrals.

I quickly saddled Esma and swung up. Reaching down a hand to Aysa, I asked, "In front or behind?"

She was biting the inside of her cheek, glancing over her shoulder. "Perhaps..."

Giving into my impulse, I pulled her to sit in front, contentedly wrapping my arm around her waist. Without warning, she nestled against me, and I thought my heart might very well beat out of my chest. Here was Aysa—my Aysa—in my arms, snuggled against me in such a tender, trusting way.

Nicar above, this is pure torture.

With a kick to the side, I urged Esma into a trot, tightening my hold on Aysa as we sailed over the fence and into the night. She didn't speak, content to lean against me as Esma's hooved pounded the sandy ground.

We reached the top of a dune, and I reined in Esma. Asya tuned her head, gazing out over the vast desert. "You can almost imagine Taletha right there." She pointed, one hand still clasping my hand on her waist. Her legs dangled over one side, her body pressed against my chest as she scanned the moonlit dunes.

I swallowed. *This was a bad idea.*

"I want to help my people," Aysa whispered. "But I don't know that I can handle this."

"Picking a koca?" I asked, catching the scent of whatever soap Aysa used. Orangey and sweet. My mouth went dry, and I had to force myself to focus on her next words.

"Choosing someone who doesn't love me. Who doesn't care." Her voice cracked and she sighed, leaning her temple against my shoulder. "I know I don't know them, and they don't know me. But how can I be certain that they're not deceiving me? People can say pretty words for a few weeks and turn out to be nothing like the image they presented."

"You do that," I murmured.

"What?" She twisted around to look at me, hurt and anger flashing across her face before she schooled it into an icy mask.

"There!" I waved a finger at her face. "You did it right there. You pretend, Aysa."

"Well, it's how I survive." She crossed her arms, turning away from me. The moonlight glowed against her sleek hair, and I cursed myself for upsetting her.

"I'm sorry."

She shrugged, still not looking at me. "Now I know what you truly think of me."

I grunted in disbelief. "You really think that's what I see when I look at you?"

"How should I know?" she snapped, reaching for Esma's reins. I tightened my hold on them, and she muttered a curse under her breath. "Nicar above, just take me back to camp, Emre!"

"No." I waited for her to turn her flashing gray eyes at me before I shook my head. "You are an amazing woman, Aysa. I told you that in the tent yesterday, and I meant it. Don't hide yourself."

"The version of me I show you? No one admires her or wants her, so why would I reveal her to the world?" She swallowed, and it took an enormous amount of self-control to not let my eyes follow the motion down the length of her neck. "They want a perfect šefe, so that's what I'll give them. They want a strong leader, so I will become that. They want a woman with controlled decisions and logic, and I will be that for them."

"But what about you? What do *you* want to be?" My hand tightened around her waist, and I found myself longing to hold her forever. To marry her and let her be her wild self. Why anyone would want to stifle the life and light that was Aysa, I didn't know; but it made me want to hurt whoever attempted to do that to her.

"I want to be what Šeri needs."

Not the right answer. I swallowed my words and turned Esma back toward our camp. "Then we'll have to find a man worthy of Šeri and everything you are."

"We're not going to find him in that group, Emre."

"We can try." I tugged her closer as my horse began descending the side of the dune. "And Nicar willing, we will."

Once Esma was corralled, Aysa slipped her arm around mine and leaned her head against it like she had before our ride. "I hope you're right."

"About?" We stopped in front of her tent, and I swung her around to face me.

She wouldn't look at me, something in her posture sagging. "About me finding someone worthy of Šeri. Of me. It seems like wishful thinking most days."

"Aysa, why—"

She shook her head, cutting me off, and turned toward her tent. She whispered, "Good night, Emre," before slipping into her tent.

Silence hung around the camp. Ominously, it promised trouble on the horizon. I tapped my fingers against my thigh as I stood before Aysa's tent, waiting for the evening guard. I was certain I wouldn't sleep well tonight. Not with images of men hovering around the woman I cared about racing through my mind.

With a nod to the night guard, I strode between the tents, pausing when I reached mine. The hair on the back of my neck rose. Something wasn't right. Drawing my long sword, I slipped into my tent. A shadow stood on the far side, barely distinguishable against the dark canvas. He turned, striking flint to a lamp, and illuminating his face.

"Kerim." I sheathed my sword but kept my guard up. This man had reason to hate me. "What are you doing here?"

"I could ask you that question as well." He placed the lamp on its stand and crossed his arms. His dark brown eyes—so similar to *hers*—bore into me with accusation. "Why did you leave?"

"You know why. Your majka couldn't even look at me, Kerim." I pulled off my turban and tossed it onto my bed. "It was better for me to leave."

"For you, perhaps! But what about us? You didn't even let us say good-bye." Hurt was buried in the harsh words, and I couldn't look at him.

"I've seen the wounds goodbyes create. Have felt them. I couldn't put you and your family through another one of those. Not so soon after—" My voice failed me, and I shook my head.

Kerim cocked his head, a lock of his brown hair falling across his forehead. "How long have you lived with the šefe's tribe?"

"Ten years." I unstrapped my belt and hung it on the hook by the door. "I saved Aysa from an unsavory man, and because of that, the šefe offered me a job guarding her."

"So that's all she is to you? A job?"

The way Kerim phrased the question made my body tense. I met his gaze. "No."

Kerim's lips pressed thin, and he stared at me. His look said he knew more than I wanted about Aysa and me. But I don't let him see how much his gaze burned me from the inside out.

"What?" I finally snapped, glaring at him.

"Did loving Feray jade you that badly?"

"Feray was my friend, Kerim. That's all, and that's all Aysa will ever be."

My old friend's brows rose. "If you love someone, you don't just give up."

"Don't you? What if it's what's better for them? Sometimes loving someone means letting go."

Kerim scoffed. "Like how you walked out on Tribe Hamid? Was that really what was best for us, or what was best for you?" Before I could respond, Kerim was at the door, his shoulder brushing mine. "Not everything is well and good in Šeri, Emre. There are other players in this game you know nothing about. Think long and hard about how much you care for the princezo. Her life might lie in your hands." He breezed out of the tent without a backwards glance.

My fingers began to drum once more, my shoulders taut with concern. Had Kerim just warned me about a threat on Aysa's life? Or was he the threat himself?

CHAPTER NINE 

Aysa

Dilan's smile was large the next morning as she helped me braid my hair into a crown on the top of my head. A scarf would cover most of it, keeping the sun off my scalp. But no matter my sister's best efforts, a few of my black curls still escaped.

"Hamid petitioned Otac for my hand, and he said yes!" She squealed in joy and my own lips curved into a smile. "Oh, Aysa! Love is a beautiful thing."

I chuckled but couldn't respond past a lump in my throat. I wouldn't know what Dilan was talking about. Otac was forcing my hand in marriage—thwarting it in love.

No, not Otac. He told me he wouldn't do this if it weren't for the tribal leaders. I needed to remember that. Otac loved me. If I truly wanted it, I could back out of the contest, out of marriage to one of the sons of the leaders. All I had to do was give up my desire to be the ambassador. Otac wouldn't force me if I didn't want it. Would he?

"Where is your mind this morning, Aysa?" Dilan asked as she knotted my scarf over my head.

Oh, if I could only tell her. Emre's face flashed before my mind's eye, and I shook my head. "I'm happy for you, Dilan."

"You didn't answer my question." My sister's brows rose. "What's wrong?"

So very much. "Nothing. I'm fine." I smiled and rose, smoothing a hand over my ruby-colored kaftan. The metal bracelets on my wrists jangled and the light caught on the gems in the earrings that brushed against my neck with every turn of my head.

"You're a horrible liar." Dilan shrugged and stepped toward the door. "But I've learned long ago that I can't pry anything out of you."

Flicking the tent flap open, she jabbed over her shoulder as she smirked at me. "He, on the other hand, has perfected that art."

Emre started, but his face remained impassive as his gaze swept over me. A blush rose in my cheeks, and I ducked my head as I moved to the door. Emre's approval meant much to me; more than the men coming to win my hand.

And therein lay the problem. Why now, after ten years, was I noticing his steady presence, his willingness to listen to me? He understood me like no other, knew when I was happy and sad. He was the first to help me escape, to protect me, to support me.

But you're going to marry one of those eight leaders' sons, and they will have to learn all that about you. Ten years of friendship—gone.

With a swallow, I smiled up at Emre. "What do you think? Will I impress Ulvi?"

"He's a fool if he isn't." Emre smiled, but it didn't reach his eyes. Offering me his arm, he gestured with the other. "Ready for breakfast?"

No, not at all. "Of course!"

I slipped my hand against his arm and followed him toward Otac's tent. The long table was before it, but only three of the men sat around it. They all jumped to their feet when I approached.

Naz's dark eyes met mine, and he bowed. "Good morning, Princezo."

"Good morning, Naz." I inclined my head. "I pray you had a good sleep."

"Tolerable, thank you." He smiled, and I forced myself not to shiver.

Ömer and Efe smiled their matching grins. Efe clasped his hands behind his back. "We slept excellently, Princezo."

"Good." I returned their grins and sat at the table. I could feel Emre at my back, knew he was standing with his hand clenching the hilt of his sword and that cold, hard look on his face that he reserved for those he did not care for. It was reassuring that, until the day I wed, I would always have him at my side.

"Are you eager to begin the meetings this morning, Princezo Aysa?" Ömer asked, his voice softer than Efe's. His green eyes were bright in the light of the new day, and I found that I couldn't help but smile at the man.

"I am. And somewhat wary as well. This is a decision that shouldn't be made lightly. Šeri is depending on me making a wise choice."

"And what about you, Princezo?" Efe popped a falafel into his mouth, his head tipping to the side as he chewed.

"What about me?"

"What about what is best for you? Don't you deserve happiness in marriage? It's not only about the tribes, but about your welfare for which we strive to earn your affections."

Naz scoffed softly, but when I turned to him, he was staring at his plate.

Emre shifted behind me and hummed thoughtfully.

I clasped my hands together and forced a lighthearted grin to my face—though it felt more like a grimace. "I will be happy if Šeri is secure."

"Is that your first duty then?" Naz asked, his voice sharp. "To the country and not your koca?"

The implication of his words had my face heating. "Not at all. My duty as a kari is to my koca; my responsibility as šefe is to my country. When those conflicts arise, it will be my choice as to what comes first."

"So you are over your koca in marriage because you're over him in status?" Naz's eyes narrowed. "That seems heavy handed, even for you,

Princezo."

"And what does that mean, Naz?" Efe leapt to my defense. "Would you not defer to your princezo or šefe simply because you are her koca?"

"I would hope she would listen to my council and choose me over the nation, if it came to it." Naz stood and brushed his hands together. "Good morning."

As he turned his back on us all, Emre leaned closer and muttered, "There is one brute you can cross off your list."

I stifled a laugh, but my mind was racing faster than Kismet's hooves over the dunes. "But what if he's right? What if I have to choose between my country and my family someday?"

"Then I would trust you to make the right decision *if* that time ever came. It wouldn't be easy, but you would handle it with grace," Emre stated.

I blinked up at the two men still at the table. They quickly glanced away, trying too hard to appear like they hadn't been eavesdropping.

"Well, then." I cleared my throat, uncertain how to lighten the now heavy mood. "Thank you for rising to defend me, Efe."

"With pleasure, Princezo." He winked and grinned.

I found myself once again returning it. He was young, but perhaps he would be one worthy of consideration.

But first, I had my meeting with Ulvi.

Emre's presence at my side soothed some of my tension. As he had been the night before, he was silent as we moved through camp, knowing I needed the time to gather my words and order my thoughts.

We rounded the corner to my tent. Someone—probably Dilan—had spread rugs and pillows beneath the canopy that had been stretched over the tent flap. A low table with a teapot and mugs was situated in front of the doorway. Ulvi sat on a cushion before it, appearing completely at ease with his arms crossed and his dark eyes scanning each person to cross his path.

Emre gripped my arm before the large man noticed us, pulling me to a halt in the shadow of my neighbor's tent. "Tread carefully, my princezo. He doesn't care for me, and while I don't think he'd take it out on you, I can't be certain."

"Can you still best him, Emre?" I asked.

His brown eyes moved to look over my shoulders, hands falling to his side as he sighed. "I don't know."

I swallowed at his admission and stepped away. "I have to speak with him at some point. I need to know that you can come to my aide against him in the need arises."

He nodded once, crossing his arms across his lean, yet solid chest. "Go. I'm at your back, Princezo."

Hands shaking, I turned and forced my smile to my lips as I settled onto a cushion across from Ulvi. "Good morning, Ulvi. How are you this fine morning?"

The man stared at me for a long moment before replying with a mere shrug of his shoulders.

My smile faltered, and I cleared my throat. "Wonderful."

A strained silence settled around us. I ran my tongue over the calloused skin of my cheek, wondering what I was supposed to say to a potential spouse. *There should be instructions on how to do that,* I thought sullenly.

Emre cleared his throat, directing Ulvi's hard gaze toward him. The man's dark brow turned down into a V, and he scowled.

"Do you have issue with my guard, Ulvi of Ender?" I asked, folding my hands and placing them on the table before me.

His head snapped in my direction, but his eyes never left Emre. "Yes."

Getting this man to speak is like trying to move a stubborn mule! I swore under my breath. "And what, pray tell, is the issue you have with Emre?"

"He humiliated me."

My eyes widened, not so much by the revelation—one I already knew—but by his use of three words. I tapped my thumbs against my folded hands and cocked my head to the side. "Wasn't that humiliation nearly thirteen years ago?"

"Humiliation is humiliation, Princezo." Ulvi shrugged, finally turning his full attention to me. "I don't let go of grudges easily."

"How on earth did Emre embarrass you that badly? From what I heard, he merely won a sword fight. A fair fight by all accounts."

"He made me surrender." The words were snarled between clenched teeth, and I leaned back from Ulvi, disgusted by the man's arrogance. "I surrender for no one!"

I pushed to my feet, sliding my hands along my red kaftan with a sniff. "Then I won't ask you to lower yourself by marrying me. You and Naz have something in common, Ulvi. You are both far too arrogant to be my consort. Whomever my koca will be, he will both support and defer to me. I see now that that won't be possible for you. Unless" —I gestured with my palm facing up, a small smirk pulling on my lips — "you are able to prove me wrong in the coming weeks."

I turned, glad when Emre fell into step at my side. I waited until we rounded the corner and were out of sight from Ulvi before sagging into a crouch.

"He was terrifying!" I shuddered, trying to calm my frantic heartbeat.

Emre chuckled, hand on his sword hilt as he watched for threats. "Not much has changed in twelve years, that's for certain."

"And you truly beat him?" I glanced up, feeling a tad steadier just by hearing Emre's laugh. It unwound the fear and tension in my chest and mind.

Wrapping me in the light of his dark brown eyes, he smiled for me alone. "I did indeed. But like I said earlier, I'm not certain I would be able to best him now."

"Have a little faith." I stood once more, trying to stifle a sigh. "And to think, I have seven more such visits!"

"It appears that way." Emre chuckled, resting his hand on my shoulder for a brief moment. "You'll be fine, Aysa. One of them will sweep you off your feet."

He was always saying things like that. Emre seemed confident that we would find the right man for me to marry among the eight that strode through our tribe like preening peacocks. They were strong, sure, and handsome. But with each hour that passed, every minute spent in their company, I found myself more and more uncertain that I would ever find the man my heart longed for. One who saw me for me, who loved the chaotic woman who beat in my chest more than the beautiful future šefe. If I wanted to be myself, that's who I needed to find. Yet I feared it would never be possible.

Chapter Ten

Emre

I stood in front of Aysa's tent in the midday heat as she napped prior to the first challenge that evening. Her otac had announced at the noon meal that it was to be a battle of wits, though what that entailed, no one knew.

My fingers drummed a beat against my sword hilt as I watched for danger, subtly aware of Zlem sprawled across the rugs laid outside the tent flap, reading a scroll she'd borrowed from her otac. Her chin was nestled in her hand, and her tongue stuck half-way out of her mouth as she slowly read the document.

"What are you reading?" I asked in a whisper, glancing over her shoulder but not able to decipher the words scratched to the page.

"This is the language of the north!" Zlem's whisper was loud, and I winced, shushing her. She rolled her large brown eyes and lowered her voice with a huffed, "Fine! Better?"

"Much." I chuckled at her sass. "But where did you learn the northern language?"

"From one of our guards! He's from there originally, you know."

"I didn't know." I hid my smile with my hand. "What's his name?"

"Jerome. He's nice to me. Doesn't shush me like some people!" Zlem stuck her tongue out.

"I only shushed you because your sister is sleeping."

Zlem tipped her head to the side, her dark hair falling across her forehead. Unlike Aysa's wavy curls, Zlem's were tight and coiled into springing locks that refused to be tamed. Though, not from want of trying; Zlem simply didn't sit still long enough to let anyone style it.

She studied me, now, like she had the scroll. I stood, trying to ignore her probing gaze.

"Emre?" she asked after a moment, her voice loud once more.

I grabbed her arm and hauled her around the side of the tent. Waking Aysa was always a terrible idea.

Zlem wrinkled her nose as she yanked her arm free. "You *love* Aysa, don't you?"

She'd hinted at me marrying her sister a few days before, said that if I cared I'd do whatever I could to be with Aysa. But to ask me to my face if I loved her...that was dangerous territory. Territory I might not survive if I navigated incorrectly. Clearing my throat, I replied, "That is my business. Whether I do or don't, it doesn't truly matter."

"It does matter." Zlem huffed again and tucked the rebellious curl under her orange kerchief. "But I know you won't tell me the truth anyways."

"If you knew that, then why did you ask?"

"Because it's fun to rile you up." She giggled as she gathered the scroll into her arms. "Besides, your reaction to the question tells me much more than the answer."

She winked and waltzed back through the tents. I shook my head. Zlem had Aysa's spirit without the crushing weight of leading an entire people. She was free to be fiery and bold—the parts Aysa kept locked up inside.

My heart picked up its pace as I thought about Zlem's words.

You love Aysa, don't you?

Yes, but I shouldn't.

How could you not love her? She's brilliant, gorgeous, funny. She knows how you wandered for years and doesn't reject you like so many others. She's strong and bold, not afraid of a fight even if she's not certain she can win. And she's the šefe's kćerka which means she'll never be yours.

I settled in front of Aysa's tent once more, an uncomfortable knot in my chest. Zlem had picked back a scab I'd thought healed over. But I could see now that I was wrong. It was still festering, oozing out as I watched Aysa talk and laugh with the eight leaders' sons. Her beautiful gray eyes that focused on the others, seeing them on a deeper level than they realized. She was special. She deserved someone who valued her for that uniqueness.

My blood chilled as a muffled shriek sounded from inside Aysa's tent. For a moment, I couldn't move. Couldn't breathe. Another shriek and I had my sword drawn and sprang for the door.

Aysa was thrashing on her mat as a figure hunched over her, his hands clamped over her mouth and around her throat. A growl ripped from my chest, startling the assailant. He jerked back from Aysa. A mask covered his nose and mouth while a turban shaded his eyes from view. Coupled with the shadows of the tent, it was impossible to tell the tone of his skin.

I lunged for him. He drew a dagger from his boot, avoiding a jab from my sword. I cursed the tight confines of Aysa's tent as the man darted to the side. He slashed at my leg, nicking it with the tip of the dagger and causing me to step back. He turned, his back to the tent flap. As I advanced on him, he ducked out.

I followed but the man had disappeared. Swearing, I stepped back into Aysa's tent, pulling my turban off my head and swiping my sleeve across my brow. Aysa had pushed herself up, shaking as she folded her arms across her chest. But they weren't tremors of fear.

"Who was that?" she snapped, her gray eyes flashing with rage. "How dare he attack the princezo in her own tent!"

A word slipped off her lips that would have made her majka wash her mouth out with soap. I raised a brow at her, but she waved away my questioning look.

"We should tell Šefe Aydin." I lowered myself into a crouch, wincing at the cut on my calf.

Aysa's brows knitted together, and she stood. "Sit. You're hurt."

"It's only a scratch." I shook my head but moved to obey her when her fists went to her hips in stubbornness. There was no use arguing with the princezo sometimes.

She fetched a small bag from a peg in the support post. Withdrawing a jar of ointment, she pulled the leg of my salwar up. She studied the slice, her eyes missing nothing while her fingers were gentle against my flesh. A shiver worked down my back, and it took far too much effort to remain still.

Going to a pitcher by the door, Aysa wet a rag and cleaned the cut. She uttered nothing, a feat considering Aysa's constant desire to fill the silence with words. Her lips were pressed thin. Something was bothering her besides my fight with her would-be assailant. I waited for her to finish cleaning my cut, the sweet scent of the ointment filling the space, before I spoke.

"What's wrong?" I asked, grabbing her wrist when she tried to finish her task.

"Nothing. I just—" She looked away, her chin quivering ever so slightly in the dimness of her tent. "This was the first time I've had to watch you stop a threat—a human threat—in ten years."

"And I stopped him." I cupped her chin, stilling the tremor of it. My thumb slid against the soft skin of her cheek of its own accord.

"You could have died!" she retorted, her terror-filled eyes meeting mine for a heartbeat. Then, she yanked free of my hand, pulling a roll of bandages from the pack.

I leaned back on my hand, relishing her touch, even if I knew I shouldn't. "Would it have bothered you, if I had?"

"Had what?" Her words were sharp, like the tip of a knife poking soft flesh.

"If I had died."

She scoffed, tightened the knot on the bandage, and sat back on her heels. "That's about the most ignorant thing I've ever heard you say."

"That's not an answer, Aysa." I bit back a smile as she scowled at me. "Would it bother you if—?"

"Yes! Yes, it would bother me! You're my best friend, and if I lost you, I'd—" She shook her head and turned away. Her arms crossed over her chest while her shoulders hunched. Her body trembled as she drew in a breath to calm herself. "Otac doesn't need to know about this attack."

"Aysa—"

"No." She slashed her hand through the air as she wheeled around to face me. "Otac doesn't need to know. I'm fine. You're fine." Her eyes flicked to my leg before meeting mine. "He doesn't need to know. Promise me you won't tell him."

My throat tightened. The image of the man standing over her, hand pressed against her mouth, soured my stomach. But I had scared him off. I tapped a beat against my knees. The blankets beneath me smelled like oranges and earth—like Aysa—clouding my ability to think clearly.

"Emre, please? If he knows, it'll only worry him. You'll be beside me for the rest of the trials, and we can watch for any clue as to who the attacker was."

I sighed and stood, looking down at her. She was so close. Her scent wrapped around me, even stronger than the blankets. Like the woman it belonged to, it was heady, strong, and bold. I wanted desperately to pull her to me and hold her close. I tightened my grip on my sword and gave her a short nod. "For now, I'll keep silent. But if more threats arise then—"

Aysa wrapped her arms around me, pulling me into a hug I didn't know what to do with. "Thank you, Emre."

Slowly, I relaxed, leaning my cheek against the top of her head, relishing the silky strands of her hair as they brushed against my skin. This was right. In my arms was where she belonged. Where she needed to be. I sighed. "Don't make me regret it, Aysa."

"I won't," she whispered. "You'll keep me safe."

But who will protect my heart? With another sigh, I stepped back. "Are you ready for the first challenge?"

Her nose wrinkled. I laughed. But inside, my heart was breaking into a million pieces. Try as I might, I couldn't seem to banish the image of this brown-haired, gray-eyed beauty from my thoughts.

CHAPTER ELEVEN

Aysa

Thankfully, my attacker hadn't left any bruising on my face or neck. I dressed in a kaftan the colors of the sunset, the expensive silk feeling itchy against my skin, despite its coolness. I didn't want men fawning over me. I wanted to be alone, free to race Kismet across the dunes, Emre at my heels. I wanted to climb the dunes and watch the sunset.

Yet even if this marriage wasn't hanging over my head, those things would still be illusive. I was the future šefe. When that role settled on my shoulders, any freedom I currently had would be stripped away.

I still don't have to like this marriage, though. I slid my slick palms against my hips, smoothing the wrinkles from my kaftan before I turned and stepped out into the twilight. *Nicar take the council and this idiotic contest.*

Emre glanced over at me, and a small smile quirked his lips. "You look lovely."

I shrugged, crossing my arms as I stared between the tents toward Otac and Majka's.

"Aysa?" Emre's hand brushed my elbow, the contact sending sparks shooting through my stomach. "Are you certain you're all right after...?"

The attack. He didn't have to say it for me to know. To recall the suffocating pressure of a palm against my nose and mouth. The dark shadow leaning over me in the shadows of my tent.

I sucked in a lungful of air and nodded. "I will be."

Emre's brows lowered, but he nodded, beginning to guide me toward Otac and my horde of suitors. My stomach churned, and I wasn't certain I would be able to eat my dinner.

"Breathe, Aysa," Emre whispered. I forced myself to inhale, feeling a bit dizzy. I swayed, and Emre gripped my elbow to keep me from crumpling to the ground.

"I'm all right." I pulled on every ounce of my pretend calm that I could, rolling my shoulders back as I breathed deeply. Sliding a serene smile to my lips, I declared, "It will be fine."

Emre's grip loosened though he didn't step back. "If you need to leave, signal me and I'll be by your side in an instant."

"Thank you." I smiled up at him, forever grateful for my faithful guard. He'd stood by me through some of my wildest schemes, always ready to jump in to defend me. I'd taken him for granted. Now, after he'd protected my life and gotten injured in the process, something in my heart had shifted. I didn't want to lose the constant presence at my back. But I would. With a sigh of resignation, I slipped my mask back into place and turned the corner to my otac's tent.

The men all stood to their feet and bowed in my direction. Fisting my hands in the folds of my kaftan, I inclined my head.

Nicar above, keep me calm. I swallowed back bile as I glided toward the table and settled onto a cushion by Otac.

"Are you well, kćerka?" He clasped my hand in his, his gray brows furrowed. "You appear a bit pale."

My mind flashed to my talk with Ulvi—if one could call it that—then to the attempted murder in my tent. No, I wasn't well at all. The wretched tears were far too close to the surface, but I managed a smile for Otac's sake and nodded.

Efe stood, raising a mug of cider high and grinned. "Seeing as how

Berk blessed the princezo last evening, it's only fitting for me to do it tonight."

"Of course, it is." Kagan scoffed, but a smirk played around the lines of his mouth.

"To Princezo Aysa," Efe continued, ignoring the interruption. "The most gracious, beautiful lady in all Šefi. While she may discount this as flattery"—he winked as I rolled my eyes—"it is the truth. May Nicar bless you and yours!"

"Here, here!" his brothers cheered. Naz and Ulvi looked sour but raised their glasses in polite salute. Berk, who was sitting at my left, grabbed my hand and planted a kiss to the back of it. It was cold and wet. With a yank, I extricated my hand, subtly wiping it against my leg as I stifled a shudder.

"Thank you, Efe." I smiled as Otac stood and blessed the meal.

I barely ate. Rather, I pushed the food around my plate with a piece of pita bread. The men laughed and joked; Berk was overly attentive at my side. Otac kept sending worried glances my way, and I could feel Emre's gaze against my neck.

Weariness pressed down at me. I was tired of the competition (though it had only been a day), frustrated that I had to politely entertain eight men (all of whom fell short of my standard for a husband), and the largest part of me was terrified of returning to my tent. To face the darkness and the memories of my assault that night.

Perhaps I can get Dilan to spend the night with me. Or maybe Emre will stand guard tonight. I took immense self-control to not turn and look at Emre. Where had he gone that afternoon to allow a stranger access to my tent? There were a number of the men whom he knew. Was he in league with my would-be assassin?

Where are these thoughts coming from? I pressed a hand to my cheek. *He defended you! Got injured in the attempt, for Nicar's sake! You're getting overly suspicious, Aysa.*

Otac raised his hand, signaling for silence among my eight suitors. He smiled conspiratorially as he placed the mouthpiece of his hookah between his teeth. He pulled a draw from the hose, holding it before he blew the fruity scent around us.

"A riddle I give to you. One answer shall rise above the rest." Otac's voice was low, commanding attention from all who stood around us. "What is more precious and dazzling than jewels, has a spark that is brighter than any flame, and is stronger than a dozen men? The one who holds this will have the greatest treasure in all Šeri and shall be greatly blessed."

Brows lowered, eyes grew vacant, many of the men muttering under their breaths as they attempted to find the answer—an answer even I didn't know. I glanced at my otac, but he had his eyes closed, inhaling the smoke from his hookah as he waited for someone to solve the riddle.

I felt Emre's presence as he leaned over my shoulder. His breath tickled my ear as he whispered, "It's you, Aysa."

"What?" I hissed back. "I'm no jewel! Nor am I a flame!"

"But you're worth more and shine brighter than either of those."

I turned to Otac, who had opened his eyes as he studied Emre with approval. None of the men seemed to have heard, much to my relief. It was a bit embarrassing, truly, to be the solution to such an outrageous riddle.

Emre ghosted back to his spot behind me, and I fidgeted with the sash of my kaftan. Who would figure it out?

Efe or Kagan. Please let it be them. Would the goddess of all even care who got the riddle right? She had to. This was my future; my happiness hung in the balance.

My breath caught in my throat as Kerim rose, his gaze hard as he met Otac's. "I believe I have the answer, my šefe."

"Do tell, Kerim." Otac's smile was hard, his gaze unwavering as Kerim bowed at the waist to both of us.

"What is more precious and dazzling than jewels, has a spark that is brighter than any flame, and is stronger than a dozen men? The answer, Šefe Aydin, is your kćerka, Princezo Aysa. The man who weds her will truly be the most blessed in all Šeri."

Silence thick as honey—but not nearly as sweet—hung around the table. Every gaze flicked from Otac to Kerim and back. I shifted, wanting Kerim to be wrong, but knowing that he wasn't. Otac drew one last puff of his hookah, set the hose down, and grinned. "Well done, Kerim. Yes, the answer to the riddle is Aysa."

Heat flooded my face, but I kept my smile in place as Kerim inclined his head once more. Otac gestured between us. "As reward, you will be next to have a meeting with the princezo."

"It would be an honor, my šefe." Kerim lowered himself back to the cushion. "I look forward to tomorrow and the princezo's company."

I smiled, but it felt brittle. Like Ulvi, Emre had a history with this man. Some innate part of me didn't trust anyone—not like how I trusted my loyal guard. Wrapping my arms around my stomach, I turned to Otac. "May I please return to my tent?"

Otac's brows lowered, and he nodded. "Sleep well, kćerka."

I forced my smile to remain in place as I pressed a kiss against Otac's cheek and turned toward my tent. The crawling sensation of nearly a dozen pairs of eyes against my back had me quickening my pace, practically running once I was out of view. Did I even want this? Any of it? Was this worth being ambassador? I was miserable, utterly exhausted with the pretense of perfection. I'd thought my love for my people was worth sacrifice, but now I wasn't so certain.

"Aysa." A hand grabbed my wrist and I turned, nearly smacking the person in the face. "Aysa, stop, it's me."

Emre. I calmed, willing away the tears with the realization that I was safe. I was fine. Emre was here, holding me, and no monster lurked in my tent.

"I'm sorry." I sagged against him, weariness pressing against me once more. "I can't keep this façade up."

"Why are you pretending?" Emre asked, his grip loosing from my wrists as he rubbed my arms. "Be yourself, Aysa. Like your otac said tonight, you are beautiful and fiery and the most glorious thing to behold."

"I haven't been that girl for ages," I whispered, breathing in the sweet and spicy scent of Emre.

"I've seen her. Recently, as a matter of fact." He chuckled, the sound vibrating his chest and warming my frosty heart. "She's a beautiful firestorm, braver than most men, short in stature but wild and fierce."

"No one wants a wild woman, Emre."

"I do." I blinked up at him, leaning back to look into his face. He smiled sadly, dropped his hands from my arms, and gestured for me to move forward. "You need rest, princezo."

"I—what did you say?"

"You need to rest." He chuckled when I scowled at him.

I let him guide me to the entrance of my tent, too tired to press the issue tonight. Emre checked the interior before allowing me inside. "I'll stand guard tonight."

"Not all night, yes?" I grabbed his hand, forcing him to stop in the doorway. "I want you with me tomorrow when I speak to Kerim."

"I'll be there." He reached up as if to brush his fingers over my cheek, then fisted his hand and dropped it to his side. "Sleep well, Aysa."

"Good night, Emre." My heart roared in my ears, my eyes aching with unshed tears as Emre sent me one final smile and ducked out the door.

I crawled beneath my blanket, thankful that the vision that swam before my eyes wasn't of my assailant, but rather of being wrapped in my best friend's warm embrace.

CHAPTER TWELVE

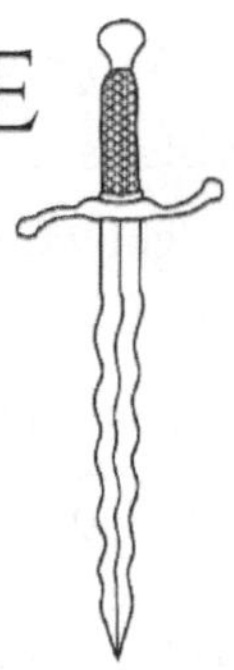

Emre

My eyes felt as though I'd rubbed handfuls of sand in them as I stalked between the tents the next morning. I'd stayed in front of Aysa's tent long into the early morning hours, only relinquishing my detail when a seasoned guard I trusted insisted I get a few minutes of sleep. But it had been fitful, filled with the terrifying image of a man leaning over Aysa, choking her, killing her. It was a constant reminder of my failure—one I wasn't planning on repeating.

The guard bowed to me as I took up my position once more, no words exchanged but plenty said through the action. I could hear Aysa moving around inside as she readied herself for breakfast and her meeting with Kerim.

My stomach knotted. What would he ask her? What would he want to know about her life? About me? I tapped my thumb against the pommel of my sword, anxiety swirling through me. Though I'd shared much, Aysa didn't know everything about my past. Most, but not all. Some memories were too precious to bandy about carelessly. Such was the case with Feray.

"Emre? Are you out there?" Aysa's question jerked me from my dismal thoughts.

"Yes." I leaned closer to the flap. "Are you all right?"

"I'm fine, but please come in for a moment."

Everything in me warned that this was a bad idea—especially in broad daylight. But Aysa had me wrapped around her finger. If she wanted a pocketful of stars, I would have leapt into the heavens to obtain them. Which was why I found myself walking into her tent.

"What do you think?" she asked, turning to face me in a dark green kaftan the color of the palm leaves at the oasis. The silky material fluttered around her ankles, while a bright yellow kerchief was knotted over her loose, black curls. "Do I look presentable?"

She looked more than presentable. She looked ravishing. My palms slicked with sweat, everything in me wanting to pull her close and—

And what? my brain screamed at me. *You can't have her! You won't ever have her, so you best wrap those thoughts up tight and bury them.*

Clearing my throat, I nodded. "You look beautiful as always."

Aysa smiled, and my heart skipped several beats. I was in way over my head. I could feel the water filling up my lungs, and I knew it was pointless—I was drowning in my love for the princezo.

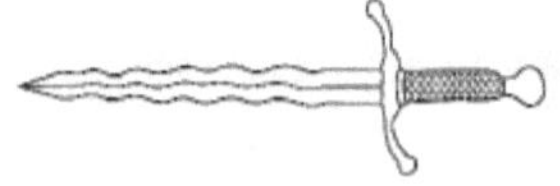

Thankfully, breakfast was uneventful. The men laughed, talked, and flirted with Aysa, but she appeared to be lost in her own thoughts.

Much like I was lost in mine. Since I couldn't be with her, my prayer was that I could find a man out of the eight present who would value and treasure her. See her spark and joy that drew me like a moth to a candle flame.

Make a way for us both to find happiness, I prayed. Deep in my heart, part of me tacked on the addition of *together.* But why would Nicar allow that? The tribal leaders would have a fit. There was the chance that Aysa could be disowned, cast out of the šefe's tribe and be forced to wander as I once had. Who would except the woman who'd given up a place of power for a common guard? Aysa deserved to have the position of ambassador and someday rule as šefe in her otac's stead. She couldn't have that with me, and I wouldn't ask her to give it up.

Her laugh echoed around the small clearing where she ate. Kagan sat beside her, clasping her hand in his as the princezo covered her mouth with the tips of her fingers. Her eyes found me, and her smile grew, a hidden secret in her gaze.

Sweet Nicar, I'm in trouble. I swallowed and forced myself to return her smile, though deep in my chest, my heart was slowly crumbling away.

Kerim stepped to my side, his hands clasped behind his back. His eyes narrowed when he caught sight of Kagan's hand on Aysa's, but he turned toward me without commenting. "What does she know about you?"

"Enough." I tightened my grip on my sword. "The past is best left alone, Kerim."

"Perhaps. Or perhaps you're just too scared to tell her the truth. That there was someone else in your life before her."

His words hit too close to the truth, one ring from the center of the target. Because I had almost failed Aysa. The image of the man choking the princezo caused the breath to stall in my lungs. She could have left me. Left me like Feray did. My vision swam.

Kerim shifted, unaware of the power of his words. "But be that as it may, the princezo won't hear the truth from me."

I swallowed the bile in my throat and asked, "Won't she?"

"No." His flinty gaze met mine, no affection or warmth in them—this man I'd once called brother. "Some of us still have a shred of respect for *family*."

With that, he turned and strode off between the tents.

My chest ached. Kerim and I had once fought together, trained together, lived together. He knew much about my past, who I was and why I had wandered the Šerian desert for so long. My grip on my sword hilt tightened. Kerim had thrown all that away after I made one mistake. Granted the foolish request of the one person I couldn't say no to. I glanced at Aysa. And I was right back in the same position.

I waited for Aysa to be ready for her meeting, dreading what it could mean for my friendship with her. Moistening my lips with my tongue, I tried to think of something—anything—that could keep me sane in the coming days.

Her hand landed on my arm, startling me from my wandering thoughts. She cocked her head to the side. "You look awful."

"Thank you for that," I replied drily. "It's what everyone wants to hear in the morning."

Ignoring my sarcasm, she asked, "Did you sleep at all?"

"Not much."

"Why? Surely there was a guard who—"

"I promised to stand guard, and that's what I did." I raised my brow at her. "I don't go back on my word."

She shook her head with a tiny sigh. "No, you don't go back on your word, but you are stubborn."

I chuckled as she began marching toward her tent and the meeting with Kerim. "*I'm* stubborn?"

She nodded. "That's what you are."

"Then what are you?" I asked, bumping her shoulder with my arm.

"An angel from Nicar." She smirked and I laughed, unable to hold it back. Some of the tension released, and I thanked Nicar for Aysa, for her joy.

My good mood evaporated when I saw Kerim seated before Aysa's door. His arms were crossed over his chest, his eyes watching for us. My grip tightened on my sword as Aysa stalked forward with her back straight and her small, regal smile on her lips.

"Good morning, Kerim."

He stood and bowed. "Good morning, Princezo."

I stood behind Aysa as she lowered herself to a cushion. She tucked her legs under her, folded her hands on the table, and stared at Kerim.

He met her gaze straight on. "Do you have questions for me, Princezo?"

Aysa picked up a cup, pouring coffee from the steaming pot into it with the tempered grace of her position. She was in control. I bit back a smile as I watched my old friend's reaction.

Kerim cleared his throat, nodding when Aysa held up the pot to him. Finishing her serving, Aysa cradled her cup and eyed Kerim over the brim.

"Why do you wish to marry me?"

Kerim nearly choked, having just taken a sip of the drink. Clearing his throat several times, he looked at Aysa in bewilderment—a look I'd rarely seen on him. "I beg your pardon?"

"Why do you want to marry me?" Aysa plunked her cup down, her shoulders tense. "You don't know me, so you can't say it's my personality. You've never seen me lead, so you can't say it's my sharp mind. All you can say is how pretty I am, the perfect adornment for your arm; or perhaps the other way around. You're handsome, therefore you'll be doing me a favor by standing at my side—an imposing figure for the future šefe of Šeri."

Kerim's mouth parted, but no words came out.

Aysa tapped a finger against the table. "But what benefit do you bring other than appearances? What do I bring other than status?"

Kerim shook his head, breaking the trance Aysa's tirade had put him in. "I'm a warrior, one of the best in my tribe. I do have a quick mind; I hope to use it to better Šeri as a whole. And while it's true I do not know you well, I am willing to learn more about you. You are a vision, Princezo, but I truly desire to see and understand the inward beauty as much as the outward."

I held my breath, waiting for Aysa's reply. Unfortunately, I could see the sincerity on Kerim's face. He meant every word. He was handsome and sharp-minded, able to see many angles of an issue at once. He would be a good candidate for Aysa's husband. I swallowed back the bile that realization caused.

Aysa's head tipped to the side. "Why are you upset with my guard?"

Kerim couldn't hide his reaction quickly enough. He jerked back, his flinty gaze locking with mine. "That is between him and me, Princezo."

"I disagree," Aysa said. "There is a grievance between you; that much is clear. And seeing as how I've known Emre far longer than I've known you, I'll take his side in the matter until you are proven trustworthy."

My chest swelled at her words. She trusted me. That meant more than anything in the world. I knew her otac trusted me—as much as he was able to trust anyone—but to hear that Aysa did as well, that meant the world to me.

"Then I suppose," Kerim pushed to his feet, "you'll not be choosing me. My grief is with Emre, not you, and it's no one's business but our own." He bowed to Aysa and then glared at me over her head. "Good day, Princezo."

After he'd disappeared around the corner, Aysa let out a frustrated growl. "He's a most impossible man."

"He'd keep you on your toes." I sat in Kerim's vacated seat with a chuckle, but it lacked any mirth. Part of me had almost wanted Kerim to tell Aysa the truth about Feray. Then it wouldn't fall on my shoulders to do so. "He does desire to know more about you."

"Yes, and once he does, he'll turn tail and run." Aysa leaned her elbows against the table. "Or he'll already be married to me and stuck." She turned and looked at me. "I think that's almost worse than abandonment. Resentment still causes a person to leave, even when you're together. It's the rejection of the heart rather than the body." Her head drooped, and she stared down into her coffee cup. I'd never seen her so weighed down in my life. Did her otac not see the pressure that being a ruler was heaping onto Aysa's shoulders. She was a fine leader, an excellent one, in fact. She had sway, respect, and support of most of the tribe. But the crushing burden of being a *good šefe* was destroying her.

"Aysa." I clasped her hand, forcing her to raise her gaze to meet mine. "You'll find the right man."

"You keep saying that." She laughed harshly. "But I don't know if I believe you anymore."

"You've only talked with two of the candidates!" I managed to banter back, squeezing her hand. "Take your time."

"I just want this to be over," she whispered, not taking the bait. "I want to pick someone and have it finished."

"Don't rush this, Aysa." I swallowed back the whirl of emotions that clamped around my throat. "Time is precious. Each moment is a memory you'll have forever. Don't run past it to get to whatever lies on the other side. Savor it. Learn from it. Rest in it."

"It's so hard."

"I know. But it's good. There is a time for everything. There's a reason for each season we go through. A season to rest, to plant, to water, to grow, to harvest, to enjoy."

Aysa scoffed. "The season of resting is awful."

"Growing also takes patience." I moved to pull my hand free, but Aysa tightened her grip on it. "But someday you'll harvest the reward, and it will be so very good."

But would it be good for me? Because for Aysa to harvest the joy of marriage and love would mean my heart would be left shattered on the floor.

CHAPTER THIRTEEN

Aysa

Another new dress. Another fancy hairstyle. Golden bracelets graced my wrists, dangling earrings brushing my neck.

Dilan finished buttoning up my magenta gown. Then she poked a brooch through a yellow scarf and pinned it to my shoulder. "You look dazzling, Aysa."

"Thank you."

You are a vision, Princezo, but I truly desire to see and understand the inward beauty. I shook Kerim's words out of my mind.

Dilan arched a brow. "Are you all right?"

"No." I smiled, but it felt wobbly. "I hate this."

She pulled me into her arms, and I hugged her back tightly. My sister was strong but in a different way from me. She was strong by being soft, by cooking and cleaning. She was a caretaker, a minister to the needs of others, and an empathetic soul.

"You can do this. You have a goal you're trying to reach." She smoothed down the bits of hair that had sprung free from the braids. "Remember what you want."

I want to be...loved. I closed my eyes. *But I also want to bridge the gap between Šeri and Taletha, and to do that I need to marry who the council wants.*

I smiled at Dilan, forcing down the swirling mass of emotions that wanted to spring forth. While I knew Ulvi wasn't the man for me, perhaps Kerim was. Would Emre tell me the truth of their animosity? Perhaps then I'd know if I could trust the leader's son.

With a final smile, I headed toward dinner. Majka would be there tonight, judging the next round of the competition.

Dancing. My stomach soured as I thought about swaying through my people's dances with each of the eight.

There is a season for everything. Emre's words floated through my head, unwinding a bit of the tension in my neck and shoulders.

"Are you ready?" he asked now as I turned toward him, forcing a smile to my lips.

I gave him the same answer I'd given Dilan. "No."

He stepped forward, glancing around to make sure we were alone before leaning in closer. "Do you wish to practice?"

Flutters erupted in my stomach. He wished to dance with me? Tipping a nod before I overthought it, I swallowed the dryness that coated my tongue. Emre stepped closer, bending his arms at the elbow with his hands up, in the way that was custom for our people. I mirrored his stance. My heart raced against my chest, not in fear but in exhilaration. I wanted to dance with Emre.

He began to hum a common tune, crossing his feet and hopping as he began to circle me. I twisted my wrists in circles and moved to follow, keeping the space between us. Emre smiled, and I found myself returning it. Around we went, changing direction, clapping, adding hops and spins where we should. And I found myself drifting closer, until I turned and my back was next to Emre's chest. I looked up at him, my heart beating so hard it hurt. He gazed down at me, longing that matched my own in his eyes. Still, he didn't touch me, even as the tune died on his lips. My eyes flicked to them, and I eased closer to him, my back brushing his chest.

It broke the spell. Emre stepped away, clearing his throat with a smile.

"Time for dinner, Princezo."

As my heart returned to its normal pace, I tried to shake away the longing flooding through me. For a moment—one gloriously foolish moment—I had hoped that Emre would kiss me. Nicar above, I wanted him to kiss me.

He's your friend. Your best friend! And best friends don't kiss each other.

I pulled on my serene smile, determined that no one would know what had just happened—not Otac, not Majka, and certainly not the eight young men who wanted to marry me.

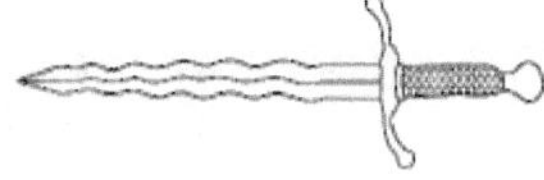

My dancing was horrible. I fumbled through the turns with Berk and Ulvi, nearly slammed into Kerim and Efe, and turned the wrong direction when dancing with Ömer and Derin. I only danced smoothly when I was with Kagan. He talked as we danced, calming my anxious thoughts, and making me smile. Filling the silence was something I always did. Kagan knew that and obliged me.

After the dancing finished, we returned to the tables for baklava and wine. I fingered the flakey pastry, nibbling on it but not really tasting it. The smell of smoke blended with the roasting meats of the cook fires. The heat of the day was lessening, a cool breeze whistling through the tents.

And my thoughts strayed to dancing with Emre yet again and the haunting realization that I had wanted to press my lips to his.

Otac cleared his throat, rising to his feet with Majka by his side. Silence descended, the popping of the fire the only sound. "All of you are warriors. You dance the dance of life and death with your sword. Yet in marriage you will dance a different kind of dance. One of love and tenderness. Your skill on the battlefield is little use in winning the heart of your future bride."

Chuckles sounded, and sourness coated my tongue. I would much rather join the dance of the sword than the dance of love. In fact, I could dance with a sword far smoother than with my feet. Though with my present company, I'd probably only win against Kagan and maybe Derin. Maybe.

"Tonight," Otac continued. "There was only one man who danced in time with the princezo. Who glided with her and did not push his path upon her. That man was..."

Otac turned to Majka, who smiled serenely and said, "Kagan."

I nodded, knowing he would have been the choice. He's the only one I hadn't tripped over.

"Kagan, you shall have your talk with Aysa tomorrow." Otac smiled fondly at my childhood playmate. "Well done."

Kagan stood and bowed, pride in his gaze as he smiled at me. That one look speared me with worry. I bit the inside of my cheek as I realized I didn't fully recognize the man standing before me. He'd changed, and I wasn't entirely certain it was for the better.

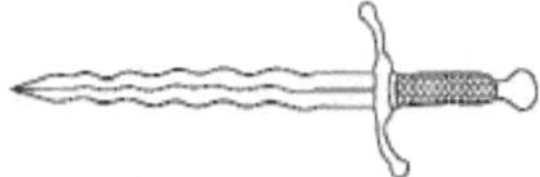

The next morning, I swallowed as we reached my tent, my breakfast unsettled in the pit of my stomach. It rolled as I caught sight of Kagan. He sat on the same cushion as Ulvi and Kerim, fidgeting with the edge of his kurta.

"He's nervous," Emre noted, his voice giving away nothing. "He seemed fine with you last night."

I wished—not for the first time—that Emre would show me what he was feeling. Had our dance bothered him at all? Or was I the only one struggling to stop the fluttering in my stomach whenever he was near? Clearing my throat, I forced humor into my words as I said, "Well, we'll just have to put Kagan at ease."

Emre scoffed. "*You* can do that if you wish. I rather like making your suitors squirm."

"Like you did with Ulvi and Kerim?" I couldn't help the chuckle that escaped, and though his lips never rose, Emre's eyes sparkled with pleasure. He always enjoyed making me laugh. He would say and do things with the utmost solemnity—even the most outlandish of tasks—simply so that I would collapse into laughter. How had I failed to appreciate that before?

We reached my tent and Kagan turned and bowed at the waist. "Princezo."

My spine stiffened hearing him address me so properly. I waved him off, lowering onto a cushion as Kagan shifted from foot to foot beside the table. "There is no need for formality, Kagan. You've known me longer than most. Even Emre."

Kagan inclined his head to my guard who took up station at my shoulder, hand on his sword. Emre's presence seemed to cow Kagan while it offered me a steady assurance that I wasn't alone in this daunting task of choosing my consort.

"Now, you made mention at our first greeting that there is something amiss with your tribe. What seems to be the trouble?" I reached for the pitcher on the table, the warm scent of spiced wine tickling my nose. But Kagan beat me to it, his hands shaking as he poured a mug for me and then himself.

He cleared his throat, twisting the cup around in his hand as he stared at it. "The elders do not see me fit to be the tribal leader."

The hierarchy of Šeri was such that the šefe ruled over all the tribes. Each tribe was guided by their tribal leader who was also on the šefe's council. The tribal leaders were advised by the elders—the head of each prominent family in their respective tribes. Some tribes had three elders, some ten. It depended on the size and the wealth of the tribe.

I began to chew on the inside of my lip, irritation flaring at the fact that once again politics were dictating lives. Mine, Otac's, Kagan's. All of us were caught in the web of expectations and traditions. And like the insects caught in the spider's snare, all of us would have the life sucked out of us eventually; it was only a matter of time.

"Why do they not see you as fit?" I asked, taking a small sip of my drink and wrinkling my nose at the flavor. I had never been fond of spiced wine.

"Because I'm not my otac's child." He slammed his cup on the table, making me jump at the sudden sound. "I'm adopted, and unlike my sisters, I do not have the 'presence of mind' to lead our tribe. They want Ajda—Otac's first born daughter—to be the next leader of our tribe."

I winced, taking another sip of wine while I thought through my response. I well understood Kagan's frustration, but the fire in his gaze told me that sympathy would not be accepted by my friend. "Perhaps they only need to see you leading."

"Perhaps." Kagan met my gaze, his hazel eyes full of emotion. "Or if the princezo of Šeri happened to choose me as her spouse, that would give me more standing too."

Swallowing a gulp of wine, I tried to sort through my hazy thoughts. "I—I don't know, Kagan." *Are my words slurred?* I glanced at the wine, suddenly feeling nauseous. "This is not a decision to be made lightly. There are still five men for me to meet with and…" *Why is it so hot outside already?* I reached up and dabbed at my forehead with my sleeve, feeling dizzy.

"But you could choose me now." Kagan leaned forward, his face turning serious. "As you said, you've known me far longer than the rest. I would be a good koca."

"Kagan…" I shook my head, bile racing up my throat. Something wasn't right. "Emre, I think—"

I gagged, choking on the vomit insistent on spewing from my mouth. My guard yanked me up and hurried me around to the back of my tent. I leaned forward and vomited, heaving as my breakfast and what little wine I had drunk came back up into the sand. I groaned as I finished, glad to feel Emre's arms still around me, supporting me as I rose on shaky legs.

"Thank you." I spat out the vile taste in my mouth and whimpered. "Must have been my nerves."

"Perhaps." Emre's brows drew together. "But you are nervous often and have never gotten ill."

"The heat then?" I shivered, cold despite the beaming sun.

Emre's lips pressed thin. "I'm wondering if someone tampered with your food or drink."

"Do you mean poison?" I gasped when he nodded. While it was true that I had never gotten sick from stress before, it seemed like quite the jump from that to poison... "What makes you think that?"

"You were fine until breakfast and drinks with Kagan." Emre shrugged as I started to tremble harder. "It is only a theory, Aysa."

My stomach churning, I managed to croak, "I need to lie down."

"Of course, Princezo." He pressed the back of his hand to my forehead, his brows furrowing. "I will send for the healer as well."

I nodded; there was no fight left in me. Exhaustion pressed heavy on my shoulders, and it frightened me. I'd never felt so feeble before.

The only thing holding me upright was Emre. Despite my weakness and pain, his hand on my hip blazed warmth through my body. His scent soothed my fuzzy mind, and all I knew was I didn't want him away from me. "Emre," I whispered, tears pressing against my eyes as my stomach twisted in pain again. "Please don't leave."

"I won't, Aysa." His brows lowered further, and he tightened his hold around my waist. "I won't."

With Emre's support, I managed to get into my tent. He called for another guard and shared a hushed whisper with him. Then he returned to my side. I grasped his hand, wrapping my other arm around my cramping middle.

"Did you drink much wine?" Emre asked, eyeing the open door and the table sitting there.

"A few mouthfuls." I bit back a groan as another pain speared my stomach. "Why?"

Instead of answering me, he asked, "Did Kagan drink any?"

I searched my memories, but all I drew up was his comments about the elders and leaders. "I don't know," I moaned.

"It's all right, Aysa." Emre looked up as a shadow crossed the door. "Healer Rafal is here. I'll be back after he looks you over."

I nodded, not wanting him to leave, but propriety meant he had to. "Don't go far?"

Pathetic sounding, even to my own ears. Yet Emre smiled softly and nodded. Then he said something to Healer Rafal—that I couldn't hear over my groan of pain—and stormed out the door.

Healer Rafal asked me questions and poked and prodded my stomach. He sniffed the little wine left in my cup and his forehead scrunched in confusion. Moaning, I rolled onto my side, wanting the agony to stop, all the while wondering who would do this to me.

"Princezo, did any of your food taste odd at the morning meal?" Rafal asked, placing a cool cloth against my forehead.

"No. But I was a little distracted with my suitors, so perhaps it was…" I blinked back tears of pain. "Who would do this to me, Rafal?"

Rafal's full lips pressed thin as he studied me. He was young, as healers went. Yet he had trained with the best and was knowledgeable in the healing arts. He set his hand against my abdomen, his brow furrowing when I gasped. "I don't know, Aysa. But I do know it wasn't by accident. Someone was trying to poison you."

Chapter Fourteen

Emre

I forced myself to pause and breathe when I reached Šefe Aydin's tent. Going in angry would not help the situation at all. Part of me wondered if it would be better to go confront our eight visitors first, but no. Šefe Aydin deserved to know about Aysa.

Besides, I had a plan. A plan that would keep me sane and help Aysa in her endeavors to pick a husband.

"Emre to see the šefe," I stated to the guard.

The guard ducked into the tent. I tapped my fingers against my bicep, trying not to be sick myself. Aysa had looked so pale as I hurried out of the tent. If something happened to her, I would never forgive myself.

Naz and Ulvi seem disgusted by Aysa. The thought of bowing to a woman still goaded some of the tribes' more delicate egos. But was that a reason for murder? Besides, there were three other women below Aysa who would take her place should something happen to her.

Then there was Kagan's strange behavior. He hadn't followed us behind the tent when Aysa had gotten sick. Rather, he'd left; at least, I hadn't seen him when I'd helped the princezo into her tent. Where had he gone?

Kerim's words drifted through my thoughts. *Not everything is well and good in Šeri, Emre. There are other players in this game you know nothing about. Think long and hard about how much you care for the princezo. Her life might lie in your hands.* There wasn't only that barely veiled threat, but he'd also been agitated at her questioning our feud the day before. But was that reason enough to kill her?

Regardless of who, someone had put poison in Aysa's food or drink. And the question teasing my mind was this—was it meant to kill her or scare her? And how was I supposed to keep her safe if these were the tactics the enemy was using?

I was jerked away from my thoughts as the guard stepped out of the tent. "Enter."

Inclining my head in thanks, I ducked inside and bowed to the šefe. His staff was clutched in his hand, and his eyes narrowed when I approached further. "Is something amiss, Emre?"

"Šefe Aydin..." I swallowed, fear bubbling in my chest and I couldn't me the šefe's gaze. "Aysa's sick, my lord."

"What?" He lurched to his feet. "What happened? She was fine this morning!"

"I know, my šefe. Rafal is with her now, but I think it was poison."

"Who would do such a thing?" There was a wild light in the šefe's eyes. A fear lay there that I'd never seen on him. He was scared for Aysa—perhaps more than I was.

My idea fluttered on the fringes of my mind even as Šefe Aydin moved toward the door. I stepped in front of him. "With respect, my šefe, there's more I must share.

"Is my kćerka all right?" His voice broke, and I swallowed back my own worry about Aysa.

"I believe so." I pinched the bridge of my nose. "But this wasn't the first attack on Aysa's life."

"What?" The šefe's voice lowered dangerously.

"She was attacked two days ago by a man in her tent." Shame pushed down on me. "She asked me to keep it to ourselves for the time being. I've been by her side every waking moment since, but this…this was a stealth attack."

"One attack open, one in secret." Aydin scratched at the side of his cheek. He paused and leveled a gaze at me. "Nicar forbid it, but should someone attack one of my kćerkas again, I want to be informed of it—immediately."

"Yes, my šefe." I bowed again. "And I fear this won't be the final attack to her person."

"Why would anyone attack the princezo? The food I understand. But as for the attack in her tent, how could anyone get past you? You've stopped more threats in the last ten years than many of my veteran guards."

The words warmed me, reinstating my pride in my ability to protect the woman I cared about. "I don't know, my šefe, but I have a feeling it has something to do with the men here."

"Why?" Aydin's brows lowered. "Why would anyone want to harm Aysa? They have a chance to become the consort to the šefe of Šeri!"

I blinked. The šefe was not that blind, surely. Or did he simply think so highly of his daughters and his people that he was missing the obvious? "I am aware of that, my šefe. And that could be the point. They might want her out of the way. It could have something to do with the peace with Taletha. Perhaps she's too close to one of the other contestants, and they want them gone. Today's meeting was with Kagan. She told me she's known him since they were babes, and her greeting toward him wasn't exactly subtle."

The šefe stroked his beard then nodded. "All of this is true, yet you speak as if you have more thoughts. Don't hold back, Emre. You know you've more than earned your freedom to speak in my presence."

You wouldn't say that if you knew my heart. I swallowed. My fleeting thought from earlier snapped into focus as I tapped out a pattern against my thigh. I met Aydin's gaze. "I propose we get the men away from your kćerka.”

He shifted his staff to his other hand. “Explain.”

“I’ll take the eight men away, into the desert. There is an oasis about a day’s ride from here.” I looked away, hating the thought of leaving Aysa in the little time we had left. But if my traitorous heart wouldn’t listen, perhaps this was how I kept both of us from heartbreak. It would be worth it. *I think.* “We can both develop some challenges for the young men. I’ll document the winners and report back to you where you’ll share this information with Aysa. It will keep her away from the men while also giving us a chance to see their character apart from trying to impress the princezo.”

“And I can look into the threats from here.” He passed the staff between his hands, gaze distant as he thought. After a moment he shook himself back to the present with a nod. “A wise suggestion. Now, let’s go check on my kćerka and make sure all this planning is necessary.”

He said it in a light voice, trying to ease the terror of the situation. I hoped that I was correct, and that Aysa’s body had expelled the food and drink, leaving very little of whatever toxin had been in her body. But I had to cross my arms to hide the tremble in my fingers as the šefe and I strode back to Aysa’s tent.

Rafal was stepping out as we approached, his brows furrowed in confusion. Or grief. I couldn’t tell and that terrified me.

Please be all right, Aysa. Nicar above, protect her.

“What news of my kćerka?” Šefe Aydin asked, his words warbling. His knuckles were white where they gripped the ebony staff, and he leaned heavily on it.

“She’s resting. Your kari is with her now, my šefe.” Rafal slung his bag over his shoulder. “I must admit though, I am puzzled.” He paused glancing between the two of us before his gaze settled on me. “You said she only drank a bit of the wine?”

“Yes,” I managed. “About three sips.”

"It should have killed her." Rafal shook his head. "But her expelling it from her body as quickly as she did must have protected her from ill effects."

Thank, Nicar.

"She should be fine, given time to rest." Rafal chuckled. "You'll have plenty to keep you busy, Emre; the princezo must remain in her tent for at least three days to see her body healed from the damage the poison inflicted."

I tapped my fingers against my thigh. "You're certain it was the wine that was poisoned? Not her food?"

He nodded. "It was the wine. I could smell it on the goblet. It's a wonder Aysa didn't notice something was wrong."

"She doesn't care for spiced wine. She rarely drinks it." I shook my head, turning toward the šefe who was eyeing the tent flap. His face had paled, and his brows lowered in concern. My heart ached for him. I knew well the terror of watching someone you loved succumbing to death. "Would you like to go in, Šefe Aydin? I can finish talking to Healer Rafal."

"I—yes, thank you, Emre." Shoulders hunched, he slipped into Aysa's tent.

"Will she really be fine?" I asked.

Rafal fingered the strap of his satchel, his brown brows still furrowed. He was young—a few years above my twenty-five—but he was blessed by Nicar with the gift of healing. He'd brought a young child who'd been bitten by a viper back from the brink of death last year, and since then, he'd been the only healer to tend to the šefe and his family.

"She will be. She's strong, which is a good thing." Rafal pressed his lips together. "Emre, who would do this to our princezo?"

I shook my head, not ready to divulge my fear that it was one of the eight men within our midst. Not ready to think ill of our people. "The šefe will look into it."

"And you too, of course." At my raised brow, Rafal laughed. "Honestly, are you the only one who doesn't see that Aysa—"

Sensing where he was going, I cut him off. "She's my friend. A good friend, and that's all. Honestly, Rafal. You are as bad as Zlem!"

He chuckled and shrugged. "None of us would be upset if you were the one Aysa chose to wed."

I waved him off and stalked to the flap. "Speak no more of this, Rafal. I would like to have a home here after the contest is finished."

"Is any place truly home if we don't have the ones we love around us?" Rafal smiled and chuckled when I glared at him. "All right! I'm off."

I didn't wait to see which direction he turned before I ducked into Aysa's tent.

She was curled on her side, holding her otac's hand. Her majka was by her shoulder, smoothing her hair off her forehead. Aysa still had one arm protectively covering her stomach, and her eyes were squeezed closed.

"How are you faring?" I asked, crouching beside her and the šefe.

"I feel like Kismet is kicking my midsection, but otherwise I'm fine." She didn't open her eyes, and she sounded exhausted. "How long am I to be imprisoned in my tent?"

"I'm glad to see your humor is still there." Šefe Aydin chuckled, some of the tension leaving his shoulders. "And Rafal said you must remain in the tent for a few days to ensure you're fully healed."

"Have you figured out what happened?" Aysa popped open one eye, meeting my gaze. "Was it my wine?"

"Yes." I wanted to reach out and take her hand. Wanted to feel her chest rise and fall, reassure myself that she was fine. Alive. I turned away, squashing those feelings beneath my heel as I did so. "Are we agreed then?" I asked the šefe.

Šefe Aydin startled from staring at his eldest kćerka. "Hm? Oh, yes. Challenge them in their fighting—both with weapons and hand-to-hand. Survival, perhaps?"

I nodded. "I'll also observe their interactions with each other and the comments they make about the princezo."

"Are you leaving, Emre?" Both of Aysa's eyes snapped open. When I nodded, she pinned me with a look I didn't know how to interpret. Was it hurt? Fear? Anger? Yet it wasn't like her normal expressions of those emotions. "Where are you going? With whom?"

"Emre is going to take the men here for your hand out to the desert for a week or so and do some challenges with them." The šefe squeezed Aysa's hand. "We think they may have had something to do with your attacks."

"You told him?" Aysa snapped. "I told you not to."

"After this attack, he needed to know," I stated.

Aysa huffed, wincing as she said, "I'm fine."

Her otac shook his head. "You are not *fine*. You nearly died! Emre is leaving with the men, and that is final, Aysa."

"Please, Otac?" Aysa bit her lip, her eyes glassy. "Don't send him away."

"*Him?*" Aysa's majka asked, her brows raised. "You mean *them*, yes?"

"Them, of course." Aysa's cheeks colored, and she closed her eyes again.

"It's to keep you safe," I said, though it lacked conviction. Because what if I was wrong, and the person intent on hurting Aysa was still in the camp? What if something happened and I failed to protect her because I wasn't here?

"Emre's right. You had no threat until these men arrived. There is evil afoot in our tribe." Šefe Aydin's brows lowered as he studied his kćerka.

"It's probably Naz." Aysa mumbled, her breathing slowing as she began to drift off to sleep. "Or Ulvi."

Šefe Aydin turned to me, brows raised. "Naz? What about him?"

"He became a little agitated at breakfast a few mornings past." I shook my head. "I'll admit, I wondered about him for the attack in her tent. But then Aysa dismissed Ulvi a few mornings past as well as Kerim." There was also Kerim's threat and Kagan's odd behavior around Aysa. Both had me more concerned than Naz. Someone was pulling strings, playing us like instruments. I was going to figure out who it was and why they were doing it. Before, I had been powerless to protect the woman I loved. This time I wasn't helpless, and nothing would happen to Aysa.

I swear I'll keep you safe. I swear on the sun, the moon, and all the stars.

CHAPTER FIFTEEN

Aysa

Otac and Emre slipped out not long after I pretended to fall asleep. But I couldn't sleep. I kept feeling Emre's strong arms wrapped around me while I was sick; felt him holding my hand as the pain twisted my gut.

He's leaving. Possibly with the man who wants me dead, and I have to let him go? Yet, I couldn't marry him, so perhaps it was better this way. If he left with the men, he wouldn't be on my mind. I could learn to survive without my friend and protector. I had to.

"You can stop pretending now." Majka moved from my head to my side, picking up the hand that Otac had been holding before he sailed off to prepare for the men's departure with Emre. "What's wrong, my kćerka?"

"Nothing."

Majka let out an unladylike snort. "Don't lie to me, Aysa. I know when you're upset. Besides," she squeezed my hand, "you nearly died. One isn't usually fine after that."

I smiled weakly. "It was terrifying. I'm thankful it wasn't worse."

Majka pressed her lips into a thin line, waiting for me to tell her what was on my mind like Emre did so often.

Emre. My eyes itched, but I pushed the tears away. I wouldn't cry in front of Majka. Perhaps after she left, I'd let a few fall, but not now. Not when people were around.

"Aysa, what is Emre to you?" Majka's light brown eyes studied me, and I resisted the urge to squirm.

"He's my friend and my guard." I laughed, hating how nervous it sounded. "What else should he be?" *Could he be?*

"I've lived forty years, kćerka, and in all those years I've learned a few things." She smirked, her expression holding far too much of Zlem's impishness. "First, I've learned that kćerkas are a gift from Nicar. They bring joy and laughter. Heartache and sorrow. I wouldn't trade the four of you for a dozen sinovis. Besides, I will get them by marriage—men my kćerkas love and who love them."

"Except for me." I pressed lips together so hard, they ached. Why had I said that?

Majka's smile softened to one of near pity. "Aysa, your otac and I aren't forcing this on you. It's your choice. You can choose one of the excellent young men who are here for your hand and become the ambassador to Taletha. Or you can let go of that dream for another one. Perhaps a better one?" Her brows raised, and she smiled knowingly.

"I want to continue to build our ties with Taletha, Majka. If that means marrying simply to appease the council—" I shrugged, stubbornness flaring. The tribal elders knew how much I wanted to be the ambassador. They were playing me to get their hooks into me. To control me. I gritted my teeth, refusing to show my hurt and anger to Majka. "It is what it is."

"Aysa, look at me." Her words were firm yet gentle, spoken as only a majka could. I dragged my eyes up to her, and she cupped my cheek. "Love means sacrifice. We can't have everything we want in life, as much as we petition Nicar for it. You have a desire to serve your people and Taletha. That's noble and good, and I'm so proud of you for that, kćerka. But know this—love is worth the cost. To love and be loved is the greatest treasure of all. If you are having doubts about this contest, if you see something in someone you think you can't live without, latch onto that. Be brave enough to let go of one dream for another one. Perhaps an even *better* one."

"A new dream?" I smiled wistfully when she nodded. "But I've wanted to be ambassador since *before* we formed the peace with Taletha, Majka."

"I know." Majka smoothed my hair out of my face. "And if that's what you truly believe Nicar has for you, then she'll reveal one of the young men to be your koca. You'll learn to love him, and he you."

"Like Dhamar and Inara? How they fought to love one another?"

Majka nodded. "I believe there's someone out there that is perfect for you, kćerka. Don't let him go."

Her words conjure Emre's face to my mind. My eyes burn, and I roll onto my back, staring up at the orange canvas of my tent.

Emre. My protector. Shadow. Best friend. Could I give up my dream of serving as ambassador for him? I wasn't certain. All I knew was I couldn't be all the council wanted, yet pride meant I would keep trying. Keep pushing. Even if that meant I couldn't pursue a life with Emre.

I closed my eyes and moaned. Why was love so hard?

"Aysa?" Majka tightened her hold on my hand.

"I'm fine." At least, I would be after I figured out the swirl of heat and pain in my chest. Although, I was beginning to suspect that it had nothing to do with my poisoning and everything to do with my handsome friend who was starting to invade my thoughts far too much.

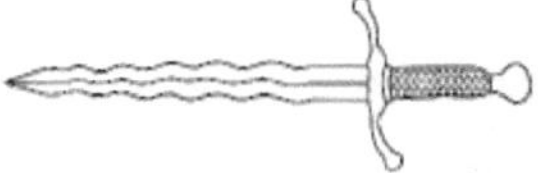

"May I enter?"

I looked up from my scroll, smiling as Emre ducked into my tent.

Having slept most of the day before—which Healer Rafal promised was normal after a near death experience—I was feeling particularly fidgety today. My family had been in and out almost constantly that morning to try and entertain me. Otac, Majka, Dilan, and Gulya had each spent an hour with me. Zlem had only just skipped away after thoroughly trouncing me in a game of King's Ransom—a game played on a board with different pieces opponents attempted to capture with their own. Having time on my hands, I had pulled the list of men out of my trunk to search for clues as to who would want me dead.

"That better not be what I think it is." Emre jabbed a finger at my scroll and rolled his eyes when I shrugged. "You're supposed to be resting."

I spread my arms out. "I'm in bed."

He leveled a glare at me. "And reading stressful material."

Chuckling, I rolled up the scroll. My smile hurt like my lips were not used to curving up anymore.

"Good girl." Emre's smirk flipped my heart into a frantic pace.

"What are you doing here?" I asked, fingering my coin necklace as Emre leaned against my support post.

"I can't come see my favorite princezo?" He raised a brow when I rolled my eyes. "What?"

"I'm the only princezo." A weight settled on my shoulders. This was why I couldn't let go of my role as ambassador. If I cavalierly gave that up, would the leaders see that as another wild choice and remove me from the line of šefe? While Dilan had the quiet strength and care that would aide her in leading our people, the constant demands would cause her to wither from the strain. I couldn't do that to my sister. I loved her too much.

Emre reached out like he had done so many times in the last week, but I quickly drew back. "What's wrong?" he asked.

"Nothing. Why does everyone think something is wrong with me all of a sudden?"

"Because you're being defensive." He shrugged when I glared at him. Pulling off his gray turban, he sat with his arms wrapped around his legs. He looked far too comfortable beside my bed, his eyes dancing like mirages against the sand. "Are you doing all right since yesterday?"

"It still hurts at times." I pulled my lips in. "But it's not the stabbing pain it was after drinking the wine. Did Kagan...?" A lump choked the words off, and I dropped my gaze to my hands in lap.

"I don't know, Aysa." Looking up through my lashes, I watched Emre run a hand over his face. His jaw had the shadow of a beard against it, and his dark brown eyes were troubled. "I leave tonight with the men to head to one of the northern oases."

"Do you *have* to go with them?"

"Your otac thinks it's best. As your guard, I know much about you." He smiled at me. "And as your friend, I want to make sure you have a good marriage."

I smiled sadly. "Me too."

He scooted closer. "We will catch whoever did this to you, my princezo. By the sun, the moon, and all the stars, I vow this to you."

It was a binding vow, one that could take his life if he failed to complete it. Though, I would never demand it of him. Perhaps he knew that. But the passion and vehemence in the words had me flinging my arms around his neck and hugging him. He was solid. Steady. Comforting. I buried my nose into his neck and held on, afraid that this moment wouldn't last. Could I find a man as sure and confident as my Emre? Someone who would love me no matter my faults.

"Aysa?" Emre's arm curled around my back. "I—"

Steps approached the tent, and I leaned back, smiling at Emre as the flap snapped back as Berk, of all people, strode in.

"Princezo Aysa, I have heard about the grievous attempt on your life. I am here to swear my service to capture the bas—" Berk hesitated as Emre slanted him a glare. "The scoundrel who attempted it."

"Many thanks, Berk, but I trust my otac and Emre to catch him. Or her." I furrowed my brows at that thought, then smiled. "I hear you are off on a grand adventure."

"Yes, yes! A challenge to prove ourselves worthy of you, our beautiful princezo." He dropped to a knee, scooped up my hand, and pressed another long and lingering kiss to the back of it.

I glanced at Emre over Berk's bowed head. His shoulders shook, his lips twitching with barely suppressed laughter, and when his eyes met mine, they sparkled with mirth.

My heart flipped. Stopped. Started to race. Butterflies fluttered in my stomach. What was this?

I pulled my hand from Berk's and folded both in my lap with as demure a smile as I could manage. "Well, I hope you enjoy it."

"Our only regret is that your beauty will not grace us on this trip." Berk's eyes glassed over, and he sniffed dramatically. I dared not look at Emre, and it took effort not to laugh at the poor man.

"I'm certain you'll manage just fine, good sir."

Berk sniffed again, though less dramatically, and bowed. "I am sure you are correct. Now, pardon me. I must go pack for this journey. Good day, Princezo."

He sailed out of the tent with far too much flair. I shook my head, turning to Emre who was chuckling with a shake of his head. His laughter had me falling back against my pillows and giggling.

"He is ridiculous." I wiped a tear off my cheek, still laughing between gasps of air. "Honestly, you would think I was someone worth fawning over."

"You are." Emre's laughter cut off, and he cocked his head at me. "Do you still doubt your value?"

"They value me for my position. My power. Not me. Emre" —I held up my hand and shook my head when he tried to argue— "stop. Don't placate me. I am princezo first, woman second."

His jaw worked. "You're wrong."

"Well, we shall see, I suppose." I laughed, but this time it was hard and detached. I wasn't wrong. The men wanted me for my title and to satisfy their basic need. Heirs, perhaps. But they didn't *see* me. See the woman who longed to be more than titles, politics, and perfection. And I doubted they ever would.

CHAPTER SIXTEEN

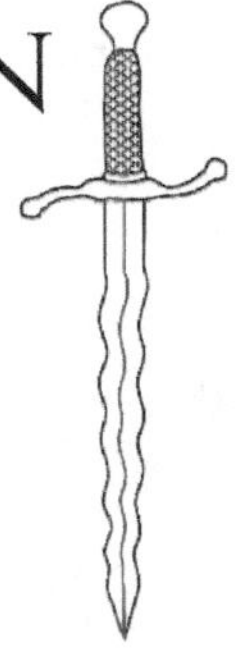

Emre

I tightened Esma's bridle and sighed, leaning my forehead against her neck and trying to pull myself together. The men were milling around, laughing and talking as if it were perfectly normal to be packing up and heading off into the middle of the desert.

My conversation with Aysa hung over me like a storm cloud. She thought herself a pawn in a game. Only worth her title and position. Perhaps that's what she thought others saw. Or maybe it was a bit of both. I looked around at the men, my jaw aching as I ground my teeth together. Already I loathed this trip. Regretted suggesting it. I wanted to stay with Aysa and protect her. What if the murderer wasn't one of the men?

No, we're not thinking that way. Besides, you vowed you'd catch him, and you will. That thought brought to mind Aysa's hug, the way her arms had tightened around me as her breath tickled the crook of my neck, the way her body nestled perfectly against mine.

I swore, kicking the sand. Esma shook her head and snorted, irritated with me for ignoring her. Scratching her neck, I whispered, "If only Aysa was coming with us. Then it wouldn't be completely unbearable, eh?"

Esma sighed and wagged her head, almost as if she agreed with my assessment. But it didn't matter—for the horse nor the human. Aysa wasn't coming. She wasn't even seeing us off.

With a sigh, I swung up into my saddle and clicked my tongue. Esma turned away from the corral and trotted toward the assembled group of young men.

Šefe Aydin stretched his arms out and smiled at the men. "May Nicar be with you all in the week ahead. May she guide your feet, your hands, and your hearts as you strive to win the love of Princezo Aysa. May good be in your right hand, faithfulness in your left and deceit far from you. Go with Nicar, my sons, and return ready to win the love of my kćerka."

I caught sight of Aysa standing in the shadow of a tent, her arms crossed over her stomach. Already she'd slipped her guard. I had half a mind to drag her back to her tent and berate her new guard for all he was worth. But Aysa met my gaze, a stubbornness resting in her eyes that dared me to challenge her, and I knew it would do no good.

The men cheered and turned their steeds toward the rolling dunes. The sun glared and I wanted to scream. Duty over desire. That had always been my way. The one time I'd let desire win was the day I regretted most out of my twenty-five years of life. The day I lost my family.

Sending a disapproving look toward Aysa, I followed after her eight suitors, certain that this was going to be the longest week of my life.

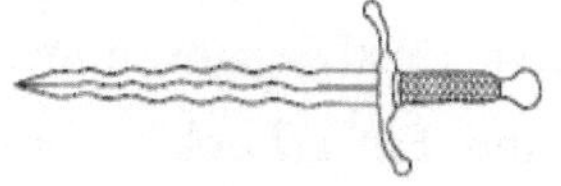

Sweat trickled down my temple as I reined in Esma and surveyed the land before us. The oasis was only a short ride away from where we stood. A shadow lay against the sand, growing longer as the sun began its downward descent.

Efe rode up to my side. Like all the men, he was comfortable in the saddle. His sharp green eyes looked around, and he nodded. "Pitch camp?"

I grunted my acknowledgement, frustrated at the resentment in my chest toward my traveling companions. It was likely that none of them even had a choice in being here, vying for the princezo's approval. We were all tools in the hands of the more powerful members of Šerian society. Whether or not they married Aysa shouldn't have stoked my jealousy. The odds of me marrying her had been slim to none in the first place.

"We're stopping here?" Naz dismounted his massive stallion, eyeing the spot with a critical air that had the muscles in my neck coiling.

"Yes." I swung off Esma and went toe to toe with Naz. I was half a head taller than the man and leaning over him with a glare brought me a petty surge of satisfaction. "The šefe placed me over these challenges, and if you have a problem with it, you can return to Tribe Nidar. Understood?"

He nodded once and moved around me to unload his horse. It probably wasn't wise to aggravate the man with an armory on his belt, but he had to know that I meant what I said. They all needed to know—I wouldn't be easily cowed.

Kerim stepped up to me with crossed arms and a raised brow. "Where are we setting up camp?"

I gestured behind me. "Not too close to the oasis. We don't want to deal with the wildlife."

Kerim eyed me as if I were a rabid desert wolf. "Are you all right?"

"Fine." I ground out between clenched teeth, sounding anything but.

Kerim stepped back as I stalked to my mare and gathered my tent and bedroll. I'd volunteered, I was here, and I would help Aysa find the love of her life.

Even if it destroyed me in the process.

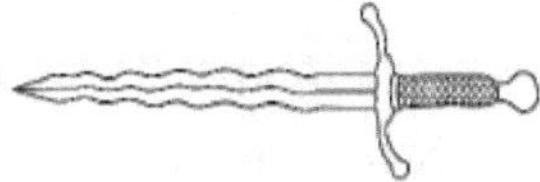

I finished hammering the final stake into the ground a few paces from our camp. A rope looped around the top of each, marking the sparring ring. Brushing my sleeve across my brow, I surveyed my work with a small measure of pride. I liked working with my hands. Always had. Fishing with Kerim and his otac was one of the happier memories from my youth, a skill I still performed in my dreams some nights.

"What's this for?" Kagan loped over, his hand resting on his scimitar as he eyed the circle. It was about ten yards across, plenty of room to swing our swords in practice matches.

"Sparring," I stated as I moved back toward the tents the others had assembled in my absence. I wasn't looking forward to the fighting matches. I knew for certain Kerim and Ulvi would not take it easy on me, and while all the men had packed their fighting leathers, I prayed to Nicar that no heads would roll because of a bout.

"We're sparring?" Efe asked, looking up from whatever he'd been cooking over the fire. It smelled good, but I was wary after Aysa's poisoning.

"After dinner." I gestured over my shoulder. "You will each fight, and I'll document your skill to be sent back to the šefe and the princezo."

"Why you?" Naz asked, a sneer curling his lip "What makes you so great as to be lord over us?"

I crossed my arm and returned his glower. "Because unlike you, I am not competing for the princezo's hand. I am a neutral party." *Or as neutral as I can be when I am in love with Aysa.*

"I think the šefe has brought you out here to find our flaws." Naz leaned his elbows on his knees. "I think you were the one to poison the princezo to get us here. Alone. Tell me, Emre, are you going to murder us one by one?"

Efe scoffed. "Come off it, Naz! You've been so childish these last few days. Why don't you just accept that Princezo Aysa doesn't care for you?"

"I haven't been given the chance to show her my qualities!" Naz nearly roared.

"What, your surliness and temper?" Ömer rolled his eyes and fell into a fighting stance when Naz turned on him with a snarl. "You're proving my point!"

Naz's teeth were grinding so hard I could hear the squeak of them. Kagan's eyes were about three times their normal size as Berk and Ulvi moved to Naz's side and Efe and Derin moved to Ömer's. This was getting out of hand, but anything I might say would have them all pouncing on me.

Kerim stood on my right with his arms crossed, brows raised in questioning. "What are you going to do, Emre?"

"Let it play out," I replied in a low voice. "I can see their fighting without getting injured myself."

Kerim grunted as one side of his mouth quirked up. "Perhaps you're smarter than I give you credit for."

"You're going to let them thrash each other?" Kagan asked, looking up at me from where he sat on a cushion.

I lowered myself down beside him with a chuckle. "That I am."

The two groups circled each other. I studied them both. While Naz and his men were more muscular, the brothers of Neval had sheer height on their side. They also appeared lither than the burlier crew, lending to swifter movements.

Naz struck first, lunging at Ömer and starting the scuffle. Efe charged forward, ducking a blow from Berk, and getting up close to the stronger man. With his left foot, he smoothly pivoted, tripping Berk, and causing him to tumble into Naz. Efe leapt to Ömer's side, and both stood over their fallen opponents to make sure they stayed down.

My gaze swiveled to Ulvi and Derin. The younger man was hopping around like a desert hare, keeping Ulvi moving. I could tell already that the burly man was tiring, and when Derin barraged him with a series of jabs, one landed solidly on his nose. The crack was audible, and blood trailed down Ulvi's face as his eyes watered.

I stood, clapping slowly as Naz and Berk pushed to a sitting position. Both men glared at me with narrowed eyes.

"I can see the brothers of Neval know how to fight hand to hand quite adeptly," I stated.

"It wasn't fair!" Berk protested with a little wail of dramatics. His gaze cut to Kagan and Kerim, and it darkened like a storm cloud.

Interesting. I raised my brow. "Three on three seems plenty fair to me. What do you think Kerim? Kagan?"

They both nodded, smirks firmly in place at the downfall of the bigger men.

"The fact that you are heavier and stronger also plays a part. The brothers won fairly, pure and simple. Now, are we going to eat or not?"

There was no more grumbling that night. Everyone ate, Kagan and Kerim joining the brothers as they laughed, sang, and enjoyed the comradery of men in arms.

I sat on a cushion, looking up at the stars as they twinkled, and penned that day's observations to Šefe Aydin. I paused, my heart aching like Derin had punched it instead of Ulvi's nose. Because I knew it wouldn't be me, but one of the five laughing men sitting around the fire, who would soon be Aysa's husband.

CHAPTER SEVENTEEN

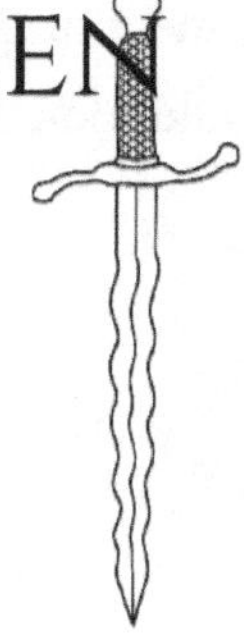

Aysa

The day after the men departed, I paced the length of my tent, hands clasped behind my back. Worry for Emre clenched my middle, making it ache nearly as badly as when the poison had been in it.

I knew I shouldn't be this concerned. Emre had held his own against my first attacker, he was strong enough to survive my suitors. But still I paced.

Dilan and Gulya sat on my bed, watching me with raised brows that spoke what they were thinking far more than words. And I knew they were reading my agitation in much the same way.

"What?" I finally snapped, propping my fists on my hips and glaring at my sisters.

"Wow!" Gulya turned a falsely sweet smile on me. "I think Emre is onto something with that silence thing. You can't stand it, can you?"

Instead of replying, I huffed and flopped onto my bed roll between them. Laying on my back with my arms crossed, I stared up at the orange canvas of my tent.

Dilan stretched out on her side, cradling her head in her hand as she stared down at me. "Does this agitation have anything to do with said guard?"

"No, nothing whatsoever." My cheeks warmed. It wasn't possible that they knew what my heart had just figured out…was it? Nicar above, was my family that observant?

Gulya smirked, confirming my worst fear. "You've been smitten with him for as long as I can remember."

"You were six when he came into the tribe. We're friends, that's all."

Dilan patted my cheek. "You're cute when you're in denial."

I sat up and buried my burning face in my hands. "He's my guard, and I have to marry one of the leaders' sons. Even if I wanted to feel something for him, it's improper at best and grounds for him to be cast out at worst!"

"Misery or love." Gulya shifted her hands up and down before shrugging. "Seems like a clear answer to me."

I shook my head. "You don't understand."

Dilan's light touch settled on my arm. "No, we don't. That's why you have to choose what's right for you, Aysa. But if this *is* love, why are you hesitating?"

"I have duties, Dilan." I looked at her. While it was common knowledge that she was next in line if the worst were to befall me, no one—not even my sisters—knew my fear that if I chose to marry Emre, it was likely the tribal leaders would strip me of my title as well. Dilan *would* become the princezo and then the next šefe.

I didn't voice those fears as Dilan chuckled. "It seems pretty clear to me what you have to choose."

Frustration welled up. She didn't understand, and yet she was speaking as if this choice were easy. It was either my happiness or hers. My love or hers. And she hadn't a clue. My words stumbled out before I thought them through. "Do you realize if I do this, there is a chance that your petition to marry Hamid will be revoked? That *you'll* be forced to marry one of the leaders' sons? I won't do that to you, Dilan. You'd become princezo and the future šefe. I can't be selfish."

"Or perhaps none of that will happen. Perhaps the leaders will let me marry whom I will. Perhaps you'll get to marry Emre, and then you can be happy." She was voicing my own thoughts, and as Dilan pressed her hand against my cheek, the selflessness that had been her way since she was a babe poured through her eyes and touch. It warmed the ice part of me that was afraid to dream of something else. Of *someone* else.

"No." I lurched to my feet. "I have to pick one of the eight. I have to." I bit hard on my cheek, shoving the hope down. What good was hope when the future laid out before me already? "This makes the most sense and doesn't hurt anyone."

"Except you." Gulya crossed her arms and shook her head, her green eyes flashing. "Why do you do what's best for everyone except yourself, Aysa?"

"This is what's best for me." I scoffed and shook my head. "Best for me and for Šeri."

My sisters shared a look, and Dilan sighed. "All right, Aysa. If you say so."

"I do." I smoothed my hands across my kaftan and stood straighter. Shoving all the inconvenient emotions down in my chest, I turned a cheeky grin on my sisters. "I do wish I knew what was going on at the camp though."

Gulya laughed. "Too bad you're not a man."

"If she were a man, she wouldn't be wondering, now, would she?" Dilan huffed a strand of her brown hair off her forehead.

Gulya shrugged, conceding the matter to Dilan.

Too bad you're not a man. I tapped a finger against my lips, my mind racing through the logistics of what I was about to suggest to my sisters. *Should I even mention it? But I will need help to pull it off.* My fingers moved from my lips to my necklace as I became lost in thought.

"Oh dear," Dilan said. I blinked down at her, and she giggled nervously. "You have that look."

"What look?"

"That look that means you're thinking through a plan. You had it after you captured Dhamar, and you have it again now."

"It's rather terrifying to be honest." Gulya leaned back, twirling her black hair around her finger.

"I resent that." I rolled my eyes with a small laugh then sent them a conspiratorial glance. "However, I do have a plan. But I'll need your help with it."

Gulya raised a brow. "That will depend entirely on what this plan is."

"Is it dangerous?" Dilan's brows lowered. "I refuse to get on Otac's bad side because of you."

"You can plead ignorance." I shrugged, settling down between them again. When they leaned in, I whispered, "I'm going to disguise myself as a man and sneak into Emre's camp."

"Aysa!" Dilan pressed both of her hands against her mouth. "You can't do that! It's not proper!"

"Oh, to the stars with propriety!" I protested. "Otac and Majka won't know, and if I'm a man, the others in the camp won't think anything of it. I'll be able to learn all I can about my suitors while I'm there, too."

"But none of those men will be so ignorant to think you are a man." Gulya gestures to my chest and my ample assets. "Even if you manage it, there's no way you'll be able to breathe!"

"And Emre could get in trouble for this," Dilan argued. "You wouldn't want that!"

No, I didn't. But this wasn't how I wanted to choose my future husband and consort. I wasn't one to sit back and let chance have its way. I was going mad sitting in my tent, awaiting word of what was happening. I had to see for myself and know what I was walking into. And then there was Emre. What I felt...I didn't want it left unresolved. I had to see him again, even in disguise. Perhaps then my heart would finally listen to my head.

"I'm going. With or without your assistance." I stood, unknotting my kerchief and flinging it onto my table. My hair tumbled down my back and I fingered the strands, smiling over my shoulder at my sisters. "Dilan, dear. Do you know where I can acquire some shears?"

Her eyes widened, and she lurched to her feet. "No! Absolutely not! You are not cutting your hair like a sheep!"

"Not that short." I rolled my eyes. "Honestly, I've thought this through."

"Really? Because it seems like you're making it up as you go along." Gulya stood and brushed a lock of my hair. "Something I heartily approve of, by the way."

"A bit, perhaps." I winked at Gulya, who laughed and clapped her hands. "But it will work, I'm certain."

"This is insane! You're going to get caught, and your reputation will be ruined!" Dilan shook her head, but she also fingered a lock of my hair.

"Dilan. I have to do this." I gripped her shoulders. "Please?"

I couldn't convey all I was feeling in that single plea, but Dilan must have seen something in my gaze. Her eyes flicked back and forth between my own before she sighed. "Fine. I'll go get my shears. Although let it be known, I'd be a much more willing participant if I knew you were actually going after happiness."

Gulya clapped her hands again and squealed. "I'll go get some men's clothes!"

"I'll gather my knives and other things I'll need." I bit my lip, excitement thrumming through my muscles as I began to pack.

I grabbed a piece of parchment and began to pen a letter to Emre. In twenty-four hours, I would get to see him again. Get to be in his presence for our final days as friends. *There will also be the leaders' sons. Don't forget them. You do remember them, right Aysa? One of them is your future koca, not Emre.* But try as I might, I couldn't picture a life where my guardian and friend wasn't there, protecting and loving me.

Chapter Eighteen

Emre

"Good. Good." I called from outside the ring, watching Kerim and Kagan spar hand-to-hand.

"What happened to holding back?" Efe muttered, his brows raised in surprise, as Kerim landed a solid punch to Kagan's stomach. The thinner man doubled over, gasping as Kerim's other fist landed a blow to his cheek. Kagan fairly arched backwards as his feet left the ground before he landed hard enough to knock the wind out of him.

"Good fight!" I called out. "Derin, can you help Kagan get cleaned up?"

The younger man nodded and helped Kagan to his feet. Kagan swayed but remained standing as he followed after Derin.

I studied the man in the ring as he grinned at me. The wild light I well-remembered from our childhood gleamed in his gaze, and I couldn't help but chuckle. He was still full of energy, but it was tempered with restraint now. As much as I hated it, Kerim was growing in my esteem.

Shaking away the thought, I gestured to Efe. "Efe, your turn against Kerim."

I'd been pitting the winners against the next challenger, rotating through the men, and seeing who the top hand-to-hand fighter would be. Kerim had taken out Ömer and Derin already before thoroughly trouncing Kagan. This next fight would be interesting.

Efe stripped off his kurta as I double checked the stakes of the circle. Both of these men were solid, obviously used to fighting with more than just scimitars. They crouched low, feet wide, ready to spring the moment I spoke the word.

I hesitated, watching them. Both grinned. They seemed to know this was for fun, unlike the fight last night. Their eyes sparkled, and I was taken back fifteen years ago to Tribe Ender and to a less friendly fight. To Ulvi, to sparring and being beaten to a bloody pulp by the end. Fighting hadn't been enjoyable until I joined Tribe Hamid. Then, it was for fun. Kerim and I had sparred after the workday, Feray watching and cheering both of us on. A lump formed in my throat at the memory.

"Are we starting or not, Emre?" Kerim's sharp words jarred me from my thoughts.

"Sorry. Begin!"

They lunged, laughing and goading each other on as they went. And all the while, the lump in my throat grew tighter and tighter. Had I been wrong to leave the family I had found in Tribe Hamid? Would life be different now, had I remained there? Yes, pain and loss blanketed my life. But would it have been bearable with Kerim and his family?

You'll never know. I thought as Kerim pinned a laughing Efe to the sand, winning the spar. *Because it's starting to look like all you know how to do is let go and run away.*

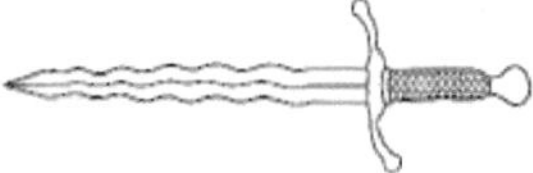

"Rider approaching!" Berk called out as I stirred our dinner over the fire the third night of our challenge. We'd finished most of the hand to hand and had moved on to challenges with the blade that morning. I sported a cut on my arm from Berk, the big man not happy to have lost the hand to hand our first night here. Now, his voice matched the confusion stirring in my mind. We weren't expecting anyone.

Had something happened to Aysa? Was the šefe calling us back to defend her in some way?

I rose, shading my eyes as the rider rode toward us with the sun at their back. It was a lone rider, small and on a dappled mare. He pulled up, a turban on his head and a scarf covering his face from the sand.

"Missive for Emre." He sounded young, but I didn't recognize the lad's voice as he thrust a folded parchment toward me.

I took it, and the boy dipped his chin to his chest. The hairs on the back of my neck rose. Something about this was off.

Glancing at the paper in my hands, my apprehension rose as I caught sight of Aysa's seal in the wax. Breaking it, I read the note. Then reread it.

My gaze rose to the boy's, whose chin was still pressed to his chest. "What's your name?"

He jolted, like he'd been stung by a scorpion, then mumbled, "Cafer, sir."

The cadence of his voice, the way he was avoiding my stare. *Please tell me I'm imagining things.* I tapped the edge of the letter against my chin. "Princezo Aysa sent you to me to aid in this challenge?"

"Yes, sir."

I stopped talking, watching as Cafer shifted on the mare. After a few seconds, his gaze rose to meet mine, and I silently cursed. I'd know those eyes anywhere.

Staring back at me, with a defiant glint in her gaze, was Aysa.

CHAPTER NINETEEN

Aysa

Nicar above, he knew. Emre knew it was me, and there was nothing I could do about it but continue my charade and hope he wouldn't call me out.

Emre's brow rose, and he motioned me off my borrowed mare. "Come, Cafer. I want to discuss this letter with you."

I gulped, my hand rising to my necklace that was no longer around my neck. I fisted my hand over my heart, a general sign of difference across both Šeri and Taletha.

Emre's other brow sprung up, and he smirked. "This way, *Cafer.*" The way he said my name had me bristling, but I followed.

The sun was casting watery illusions across the sand, the sky a brilliant display of oranges, reds, and yellows. But what I noticed was the bead of nervous sweat trailing down my temple and the moisture on my upper lip as I followed my friend. He was going to be beyond angry. I could see it in the tautness of his shoulders, the white-knuckled grip he had on his sword, and the beat of his fingers against his thigh.

He stepped around the back of his tent and whirled around to face me, his voice a hiss as he asked, "What are you doing here?"

I tugged the scarf away from my mouth and rubbed the callous on the inside of my cheek with my tongue. "I wanted to get to know the men for myself. I can't really do that when they're a day's ride away from me, now can I?"

"It was for your own safety," Emre bit out through clenched teeth. "Someone tried to poison you, for Nicar's sake!"

"So?"

"*So?*" Emre gripped my biceps. I'd never seen him this angry. His eyes flashed, his jaw rippled, but he didn't shout. No, when he spoke, it was in a controlled whisper. Somehow that was worse than the shouts of outrage I'd imagined. "Do you know what it would do to your family if something happened to you?"

I couldn't look into his smoldering gaze.

"Aysa, do you know what it would do to *me,* if you were injured or killed?"

Squeezing my eyes shut, I whispered, "I'm sorry."

His grip loosened, his hands sliding up and down my arms. After a long moment, he sighed in resignation. "I forgive you. And since you're here..."

I bit my cheek and looked up through my lashes. "Yes?"

"You can stay." He gazed at his tent. "But it will be a tight fit."

My mouth dropped open. "I'm staying with *you*? In your tent?"

"Unless you'd rather stay with Naz?" He raised his brow, and my mouth snapped closed with an audible click.

"That's what I thought." Emre smirked, and if he wasn't the only one standing between me and returning to Otac for a hefty punishment, I would have punched him. Rather, I let him step back and study me. Finally, he gestured to my face with his finger. "Put your scarf back in place. We have to figure out a way to disguise your features so that others won't recognize you."

"Dirt?" I asked with a shrug.

"No good." To prove his point, Emre wiped his forehead with his sleeve, removing a layer of dust along with the sweat on his forehead.

"Well, the others don't really know me all that well." I shrugged and tugged off my turban. My newly shorn hair would have fallen to my shoulders in gentle curls, but I had tied most of it back with a leather strap. A few stubborn strands wouldn't stay in the tie, and I had tucked them into my turban. Now, they sprung free and brushed against my temples.

"You cut your hair." Emre looked stricken. His eyes turned glassy, and he blinked rapidly as he met my gaze. "Why would you do that?"

"No one would believe I was a man with my long hair." I fingered a strand and shrugged. "Besides, it's freeing this way." I pulled out the leather strap and shook my hair loose. "See?"

Emre's lips twitched in the ghost of a smile, but the frustration didn't bleed from him.

"Emre! Food's ready!" a voice called. Emre glared at me. "Keep quiet and keep your head down."

I obeyed, placing my turban back on my head as I followed Emre out to the fire.

Settling onto a mat beside him, a bowl of boiled lamb was shoved into my hands as all eight men studied me curiously. The only one of them who might recognize me was Kagan, so I planned to stay as far away from him as possible.

"I'm up to sword fight tomorrow." Efe grinned as the others grumbled. With a shrug, he defended himself. "That's what Emre said, not me!"

"But that will leave the rest of us without anything to do for hours at a time while we wait." Berk complained, his eyes narrowing as he all but glared at Emre.

"Aw, what's the matter, Berk?" Efe rolled his eyes as he fingered a piece of flatbread. "Still sore Kerim won the wrestling bouts today?"

"I made him bleed," Berk retorted. "That's more than you did before he knocked you on your—"

I attempted to ignore the vulgar word that slipped so easily from Berk's mouth. I'd heard such things before, but it was never any less startling. Especially among the more cultured of our people.

A few more voices rose with Berk to grumble. It seemed that Efe, Derin, Ömer, Kerim, and Kagan were in support of Emre's leadership while Berk, Naz, and Ulvi were against it. It surprised me to see Kerim on Emre's side, but I was glad. Six against three seemed to be slightly better odds if something drastic were to happen.

I lowered my voice, trying to make it sound gruff and rough when I asked, "You are not popular here, are you?"

Emre slanted a glance my way. "No, I'm not."

Kagan glanced at us, his brows furrowed, and I ducked my head, continuing to eat my food silently.

Finishing my last bite, I sighed and leaned back on my hands. Twilight was my favorite part of the day. Tuning out the bickering, I listened as the insects began to hum from the oasis, loud even from the distance we were at. The stars began to wink and blink above us as the last vestiges of sunlight slipped behind the horizon. A desert wolf sent up a howl, its pack answering it with feral glee at the moon's appearance. It was magical, the coming together of day and night, a complicated dance of light and dark. Small and large, everything seemed to be awake at twilight, praising Nicar for another day—whether rising to enjoy the night, or bedding down to rest.

Emre stood, and I scrambled to his side, head bowed in difference as he met the gaze of each man. "Sleep well. You will need it tomorrow."

I followed two steps behind him as he strode toward his tent. How had I never noticed how confident he was? He was quiet, but he strode with purpose, shoulders back, head high. My palms moistened as he pulled back the flap to let me enter first.

I stepped inside and froze. Heat crept into my cheeks. The tent was far too small. The blankets were piled on one side, rumpled with the signs of Emre sleeping there the night before. A small satchel sat on the other side, leaning against the yellow fabric of the tent. There wasn't enough room for the two of us. We would be mere inches apart, and with my new awareness of my friend, that wasn't nearly enough space.

"Are you going to let me in?" Emre's voice asked, his breath tickling my ear and sending butterflies erupting in my stomach.

But I wouldn't let him know that. Straightening, I said, "No."

He laughed, the air brushing against my neck now. Darting like a jack rabbit, I moved toward the pile of blankets.

Emre ducked in after me, shifting his satchel toward the door. "Changed your mind?"

"I'm tired." I swallowed, cursing my foolish idea for coming to the camp. I was learning, but about me rather than my suitors. *Apparently neither my head nor my heart is to be trusted.*

"If you're tired, then sleep." He gestured to the pillow and shrugged, as if he truly didn't mind me stealing his bed.

He was being too nice. Too thoughtful. I had thought if he recognized me that he would send me straight back to Otac with a disapproving scowl. He'd done it enough times with my other ideas. But this time he was keeping me near, protecting me himself instead of entrusting me to my otac. I shook my head, thoroughly exhausted and confused.

"What is it, Aysa?"

I sighed and glanced up at him. "Why are you letting me stay?"

Emre tugged off his turban and ran a hand through his black-brown hair. "To keep you safe."

"But I can take care of myself. And I would probably be safer with Otac and the tribe."

"True, but I—" He hesitated, then shook his head.

"But what?" I crossed my arms and dared Emre to lie to me.

"But nothing. I simply worry, Aysa. I haven't been able to sleep at night knowing you almost died from that poison. The only reason you didn't was because you threw up. And the idea of letting you head back across the desert alone while I sit here would drive me mad. I'd rather have you here with a horde of men oblivious to your identity than wandering the desert alone."

I will not show him how sweet I find that. I moistened my lips with the tip of my tongue. "As excuses go it's not...terrible. But I could handle it."

Emre threw his hands into the air. "Do you want to leave? Because I can expose you to the men and send you home right now."

No, I don't want to leave. I simply expected it to happen once I was caught.

"I want to stay here with you." I bit my cheek again and looked away. Did I dare tell him the real reason I'd wanted to come? It wasn't only because of the contest. It wasn't my stupid pride. No, if I were being honest, the reason I was here was because Emre was here. Sitting across from me, our knees nearly touching in the small tent, he was staring at me like I was someone special. Someone worth protecting. Stars above, it was intoxicating.

And you can't tell him a thing. I growled and flopped onto the pile of blankets. Glancing over at Emre, I asked "Do you want a blanket?"

"Perhaps one," came his reply.

I stood, hunching over due to the low ceiling, and grabbed one of the larger blankets in the pile. But my foot was tangled in the folds of the fabric. My arms flailed as I fell forward, crashing on top of Emre. His hands caught my sides, but he still tipped back, sprawled out on the rug covered ground with me on top of him. I gasped, scrambling to move back but his grip tightened.

"Aysa." His voice was gruff, his eyes burning with an emotion I'd never seen before and couldn't name. Slowly, he reached up and cupped my cheek. For just a moment, a single breath of time, I thought he might kiss me. His gaze flicked to my lips, longing etching itself on his face. Then he blinked, and the spell broke. He took hold of a strand of my hair and ran it through his fingers. "I like your short hair."

I couldn't seem to find the words to reply, battling the disappointment that beat a steady rhythm in my chest. Finally, I scrambled off him, and he let me go. Turning my back on him, I pressed a hand to my burning cheek, willing myself to breathe. I shoved the blanket at him, not daring enough to meet his heady gaze again.

"Good night, Emre," I said, willing my tone to be light. Rolling up into a blanket of my own, I placed my back to him.

"Good night, my princezo."

But all night I could hear him. His steady breathing, the shifts he made as he slept. I replayed the moment I fell on top of him over and over. Committed to memory the intensity of his face and the solidness of his hands on my waist.

After hours of tossing and turning, I groaned and rolled over to face Emre. He was on his side facing me. Moonlight filtered through the canvas, lighting my friend's face with its silver beams. His dark lashes fluttered as he dreamed, and he clutched his blanket under his chin.

What would it be like to fall asleep in your arms each night and wake up to you every morning? I swore, wanting to slam the door on that thought. Because I couldn't have Emre. It was impossible. But like a wedge keeping a door from closing, a crack remained in my thoughts, allowing the *what ifs* to slip in and dance in the corridors of my mind; and all the while they taunted me with what could never be.

CHAPTER TWENTY

Emre

Oranges and the earthy scent of the oasis tickled my nose as I woke the next morning. Something warm was pressed up against my back. I didn't move, feeling the weight of an arm wrapped around my waist, hugging me close.

The smell, the presence, the hug...I knew who it was. And while I knew I would curse myself later, I let Aysa hold me as she slept, content to take the moment for what it was.

I knew from years of guarding her that Aysa was a restless sleeper. She was a dreamer, and an active one at that. Often, she would roll and thrash, cry out as she slumbered deeply, and twice I'd had to follow her as she walked in her sleep. This sleep-induced hug meant nothing. At least, not to Aysa.

To me, it was a reminder of everything I would never have. I wouldn't wake to Aysa cradled in my arms, to good morning kisses and smiles. One of the eight men outside would wed her. They would receive all the love and kisses and smiles from the day they vowed to Nicar to love and cherish Aysa. And try as I might, I couldn't banish the self-pity that was trying to swallow me.

Aysa shifted, her arms tightening as she slowly woke. I tried to breathe evenly, hoping that she would remain asleep a bit longer. But she startled, a hiss slipping through her lips as she yanked her arm away.

With a slow exhale, I rolled over and smiled as she blinked the sleep dust from her eyes. "Good morning."

"Good morning." She looked everywhere but at me, and I couldn't help the chuckle that rumbled out of me.

"What's wrong?" I asked a bit too innocently.

"How long—when did—?" She met my gaze and swore under her breath. "You were awake, weren't you?"

She can tell that by my eyes? I always thought I was fairly good at hiding what I was feeling, but Aysa could apparently read me like an unrolled parchment. Did she know the depths of my feelings for her? No, if she did, she would have confronted me on them long ago. Because I had loved Aysa far longer than any of her family realized. Far longer than was probably considered proper.

"Are you ready to face the day?" I asked, sitting up and stretching as best I could.

She laughed nervously and said, "No. I'm not nearly as confident about hiding from these men as I was yesterday."

"We'll manage." I smirked. "Besides, this was your idea."

"Don't remind me." Aysa ran her fingers through her hair and chuckled. "Do we pray that Nicar aids us in our deception? Somehow that seems wrong."

I shrugged, pulling my boots on. "That's your choice to make."

Aysa rolled her eyes and tugged on her turban. It was strange, seeing her cover her head in anything other than her colorful kerchiefs. She tucked her scarf in place and pulled on her boots, her eyes flicking to me every few moments as she did. Finally, she growled, "What?"

I shook my head, confused.

"Why are you watching me like a desert wolf stalking a hare?"

"I—sorry."

Heat flamed in my face, and I quickly ducked out of the tent.

The sun was peaking over the horizon, casting the sand in rainbows. A bird soared high above the rolling dunes, wings straight and unflapping as it rode whatever currents wove across the heavens. The air was dry as the heat was pulled up from the ground and into the cloudless sky.

I pressed my hand against the small of my back, and a series of pops sounded, easing the tension resting there.

"Good morning, Emre!" Efe's cheerful voice carried over to me from the firepit. A skillet of shakshuka sat over the flames; the savory scent of onions and basil wafting on the breeze made my stomach growl.

Efe laughed, his green eyes twinkling in the morning light. My mind traitorously conjured an image of Aysa wrapped in his arms. His eyes would sparkle like that right before he kissed her.

I wasn't hungry anymore.

"Food ready?" Kerim stalked out of his tent and over to the log, sending me a knowing glance that twisted my stomach further. His tent was next to mine. Had he heard something last night that he shouldn't have? Or was that simply my own guilty conscience playing with me?

Soon all eight men—plus Aysa as Cafer—were settled on the mats around the fire, plates in hand as we ate our breakfast. Aysa kept her head down, pushing her shakshuka around her plate and only popping a bite in her mouth when no one was looking at her. Every muscle in my neck coiled tighter and tighter. Swallowing was impossible. Pain throbbed behind my eyes, and I stood abruptly, nine pairs of eyes swiveling to look at me.

"I'm going to check the ring for fights today," I stated.

Derin sent a side glance toward Aysa. "Can Cafer duel?"

Her head snapped up, eyes narrowing as she pitched her voice lower. "Is that a challenge?"

No, no, no! My heart began to race, my hands growing sweaty. But I schooled my features into being calm. Denying 'Cafer' the right to fight would raise questions—questions I couldn't answer without endangering the one person I wanted to protect. But throwing her in the ring with a man wasn't exactly safe, either.

Derin raised a brow. "Yes. It is. I challenge you, Cafer, to a duel."

Aysa rolled her shoulders back, and I could see the sparkle of defiance in her eye.

This is really, very bad.

"I accept."

Derin grinned, Kagan's eyes narrowed, and my heart dropped into the pit of my stomach.

"What are you thinking?" I hissed as Aysa followed me to check the ropes of the training ring. "Derin is twice your size and weight! He's going to win."

"But I'm small and fast, and he doesn't know my skill." Aysa tugged her scarf down and sucked in a lungful of air as she glared at me. "Besides, I couldn't reject a direct challenge."

It irked me to no small degree that she was right. "I could send you back with a message to the šefe."

"Don't you dare, Emre!" She poked my chest. "I can beat him."

Of all the men to challenge her, Derin was the most equally matched to Aysa in fighting skill. I'd watched him duel the day before, and he was only a bit behind Aysa in terms of skill. Yet the fear of scimitars and fists flying toward her face was enough to make me hyperventilate.

I tore off my turban, running a hand through my hair in the process. "Promise me you won't take unnecessary risks."

"I promise." She laid a hand on my arm, a smile teasing her lips. "Careful, or I might start to think you care about me."

More than you know. I swallowed and looked away. "Do you have a scimitar?"

Aysa nodded. "But you know I fight better with knives."

"Kagan already suspects something. If you fight with a knife, he'll figure it out." I stared out at the sand, the sun already warming the earth to an unbearable temperature and adding to my discomfort. "And he is the last person I want knowing you're here."

Aysa paled and glanced over her shoulder. "Do you think he's the one who tried to poison me?"

"I don't know." I couldn't look at her. If I did, I would come undone. I would swoop her up and ride far from this place—these men—tell her the truth, the depth of my feelings, and that would ruin everything.

Aysa's hand settled on my arm again. "You'll keep me safe, though. Right, Emre?"

I nodded, words fleeing my mind as I wrapped my hand around the hilt of my sword.

We stood in silence for a moment before I whispered, "Go get ready for your duel."

Aysa hesitated, her eyes studying my profile before she tucked her scarf back over her nose and headed for our tent.

Nicar above, give me strength, I prayed, even at the weight of responsibility for Aysa's life tightened its grip on my soul.

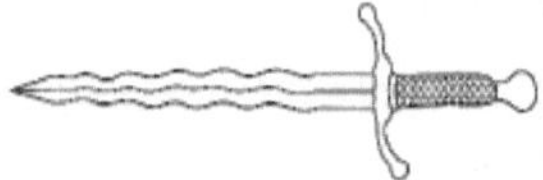

Aysa stood in the ring, shoulders thrown back and eyes narrowed as Derin leapt over the rope and landed lightly on his toes. The other men circled the fighting ring, varying levels of intrigue on their faces.

Derin grinned, his light green eyes sparkling as his gaze swept over Aysa's defiant stance. "Didn't think you'd show up, little boy."

His brothers laughed; their arms crossed as they stood at my side.

Naz scoffed. "He would have been wise to run back to the šefe's tribe with his tail between his legs."

I bristled but kept my lips clamped shut as Derin drew his scimitar and stalked around Aysa, who held her scimitar in one hand and a knife in the other.

Stubborn princezo. She'd insisted the knife would give her an edge and who was I to deny her that? It was her own neck she was risking. My throat tightened at the thought.

Derin laughed and thrusted with his blade, swiping toward Aysa's midsection. She caught the blade between her dagger and scimitar and sidestepped, knocking Derin off balance. But the young man recovered and turned.

Aysa followed him with a jab of her dagger, stabbing at his thigh with her scimitar in the same motion. Derin leapt back to avoid the attack and stumbled. Aysa pounced, her blade whirling through the air as she pressed her advantage. Her eyes sparkled in the morning light, her feet dancing to the tune of metal against metal and the panting of breaths.

Despite Derin's youth and strength, Aysa's offense had him retreating, and soon he lost all semblance of control over the duel. With a final blow, Aysa knocked the scimitar from her opponent's hands, winning the bout. To finish it off, she pointed the blade at Derin's neck, her chest heaving as she ordered, "Yield."

"I yield." Derin grinned, no malice lying in his gaze. But I wondered what he'd do if he knew it was Aysa who had just beaten him. "Well fought, Cafer."

Aysa inclined her head and then strode toward me and the other men. Her eyes flicked over them all, her posture growing rigid. "I'm going for a drink."

Everything in me wanted to go with her, but I had duties with the men. My heart yanked me toward Aysa, but I reined it in, only offering her a nod in reply.

"Efe and Naz, it's your turn." I motioned for the ring as they stripped off their kurtas, trying very hard to focus on the task at hand even as my heart was moving toward the oasis.

CHAPTER TWENTY-ONE

Aysa

I ripped the mask from my face as I stepped into the cool shade of the oasis. The pool, large for the middle of the desert, gurgled happily as I knelt beside it and splashed its refreshing liquid onto my burning cheeks.

My heart still thundered with adrenaline as I sipped the water, refusing to believe that I had done it—I'd beaten Derin. I nearly laughed, some of the adrenaline wearing thin, before tears pricked my eyes. I didn't need a man to defend me. I'd just proven I could protect myself.

Yet you have to marry one of them. Marry an arrogant sinovi of Šefi in order to be an ambassador to Taletha. I sighed, staring across the pool as I worked to gather my composure and return to the camp. For the first time, I didn't know what I wanted. What I dreamed of. The desire to serve Šeri was still strong, but I wasn't so sure it was by traveling to Taletha anymore. Was there another way to serve my people—a way that didn't involve a loveless match? I sighed and wiped the lingering sweat off of my forehead.

"I thought there was something odd about you, *Cafer.*"

I whipped around to see Kerim leaning against the palm tree, a smug expression on his face.

Pitching my voice lower, I asked, "What?"

"Stop playing me for a fool." He pushed off the trunk and sauntered forward. "It's our dear princezo."

Panic choked me as I stood, hand gripping the hilt of my scimitar at my waist as I backed up from Kerim. A million of Emre's warnings rang in my ears, but I couldn't pick one—couldn't focus as the man advanced on me.

"Relax. I'm not here to hurt you. In fact, I want to help." Kerim stopped a few feet away, arms still crossed over his chest like he didn't have a care in the world.

"Help me how?" I asked warily.

"You like Emre." It was a statement, not a question, and heat rushed into my face. "I want to help you win him."

"You know nothing about my feelings, Kerim. I have a duty to Šeri, and that means I have to marry one of *you*." Far too much bitterness coated the final word and I looked away, toward the water.

"And don't you sound so pleased at that prospect." Kerim chuckled. "I know for a fact that a few of us would rather our future šefe be happy than married to one of us."

"Oh, have the eight of you had a heart to heart, then?" I raised a brow, sarcasm thick in my words.

"I said a few of us. Not all." Kerim scoffed. "Besides, what if there is a chance you can have exactly what you want?"

My throat closed off. He couldn't know how hard his words hit me. They offered the one thing I wanted—hope. But hope was a slippery thing. A dangerous thing. It meant lighting a flame and praying, against all odds, that it wouldn't burn you in the end.

"Why should I trust you? Someone tried to poison me, and it could easily have been you. Give me one reason to listen to a word you say?"

"I was once Emre's closest friend." His eyes, normally so hard and cold, softened for a bare moment. "He believed in me. Trusted me. Now, I'm asking for you to do the same." He leaned closer to me, lowering his voice to a whisper. "Things in Šefi and Taletha aren't as peaceful as you wish them to be, Aysa. I've seen things. Heard things. I want to help keep the peace, but I need you to trust me."

I met his gaze, my lips pressed thin. Did I dare trust this man? His words rang sincere, but there was still tension between him and Emre. But neither man would tell me the truth. Neither would admit to what was bubbling right below the surface, threatening to destroy them both.

"Perhaps I will trust you." Some of the tautness in his shoulders bled out until I pointed my finger at him. "But only if you'll tell me what happened between you and Emre. Why do you hate him so?"

Kerim mumbled a curse, turning to look at the blue green water with a dark expression on his face. "Eleven years ago, he was an honorary member of my tribe."

"Tribe Hamid."

Kerim nodded. "A tragedy befell my family, and before it was fully...resolved, Emre had left, taken to being a wanderer yet again. It was only recently we heard he had become your personal guard."

"What was the tragedy?"

"That's something you need to talk to Emre about, Aysa. I won't betray that trust, no matter his disloyalty to my family."

Dread coiled in my stomach. Was the answer truly that awful that Kerim didn't feel he could tell me? I crossed my arms and turned away from him.

"The question still remains though, Princezo. Will you let me help you? Let me assist in protecting you as you do your faithful guard?" He pushed a loose strand of his brown hair behind his ear. "He is a good man. A loyal man, despite my thoughts to the contrary years ago. And he lo—"

A low growl rippled across the small pool of water, cutting off Kerim's words. My blood froze in my veins as I turned, drew my knife, and fell back into a fighting stance. Kerim shifted at my side, and I heard the ringing of his blade as he prepared to face the beast on the other side of the water.

A desert wolf.

Saliva dripped from his mouth, his red eyes bright with anger as he stalked around the pool. He was easily twice the size of the one Emre had scared off a scarce week before. The ruff on the back of the wolf's neck bristled. He gnashed his teeth as slowly he hunkered down to spring at us.

"Emre scared one off by screaming at it," I hissed to Kerim.

"I'd rather end this one."

I flinched as the wolf growled again, his whole body coiled to spring. Fumbling with shaking fingers, I drew my scimitar right as the wolf leapt. Kerim and I dove to opposite sides, and at the same time, the wolf landed and whirled around. The beast shook his head, then glanced at Kerim. Sniffing the air, he growled and paused. His red eyes landed on me before he began to stalk forward. My whole body shook as I raised my blade. The wolf's eyes glowed with the promise of pain. Kerim shouted, but the wolf didn't even flinch. With a yip of feral glee, he ran toward me, his teeth bared as he coiled his massive hind legs and slammed into me.

Hot, searing pain ripped across my right shoulder as the wolf's teeth sank into my shoulder. I felt his claws scrap down my arm even as a gurgling sound cut through my ringing ears. I struggled to breathe under the weight crushing my chest, and my head ached from being slammed into the hard-packed earth.

The weight shifted, and the dead wolf was pushed off me. I gasped, coughing as Kerim helped me to my feet. My vision swam, and I stumbled into him. He caught me by the waist, easing me back with a divot in his brow. "You're bleeding."

"Am I?" I shook my head, but that made the world spin worse than before. "Oh."

"I'm taking you back to camp."

"No!" I stepped away from him and promptly fell onto my backside.

"I can't be seen being helped into camp. They'll know I'm not a man."

Kerim scoffed. "Every warrior who's fought and been wounded has been helped into camp, Aysa. And you're bleeding badly."

I looked down at my shoulder. It was red with blood, some of it trailing down the coarse brown material of my kurta. It hurt horribly. Logically, I knew I needed it cleaned and tended too. Animal bites of any kind were dangerous, but a desert wolf's was one of the most deadly. Swallowing a curse of pain, I reached back and touched the knot on my head. It pounded, making it hard to think. With a sigh, I relented. "Fine. Help me to Emre's tent, then go get him."

"Does this mean you trust me?" Kerim asked as he helped me to my feet. His arm slipped around my waist, but unlike Emre's arms, it felt uncomfortable. When Kerim's breath tickled my ear, I wanted nothing more than to pull away.

As we moved toward camp, I managed a weak scoff. "Send my guard to his tent, and I'll let you know."

Kerim chuckled, a bit of his icy veneer fading with the sound. I looked up at him, wondering if, perhaps, there was more to this brooding young man than met the eye.

Chapter Twenty-Two

Emre

I was watching Berk and Ömer spar when Kerim stepped to my side. Wet dirt coated his pants. In the span of one heart stopping moment, I knew he'd followed Aysa to the oasis. What had happened? I barely kept my expression blank as he leaned close and whispered, "Emre, Aysa's in your tent and needs help."

His face gave nothing away as I turned stormy eyes on him. "What did you do?"

"Nothing." Kerim's gaze swung out over the rest of the men. "Don't make a scene, but you need to trust me."

Ten years of guilt gnawed at my conscience, and so I ordered the men to get a drink and followed Kerim toward my tent.

"What happened?" I asked as I stalked at my old friend's side.

"I followed Aysa. Well, Cafer, but then she took her mask off to take a drink and I realized who she was." Kerim raised a brow. "Risky move, keeping her in your tent."

I didn't grace that comment with a reply.

"She was angry with me, but I want to help the two of you." Kerim tugged at a strand of his hair.

"Help?" I stopped abruptly, wheeling on him as my own frustration burst to life. "Since when have you ever wanted to help me? You've been nothing but antagonistic since you stepped into the šefe's camp, and now you suddenly want to help me?"

Kerim's face morphed into the irritation I knew so well. "Let go of your pride for a moment, Emre, and see that perhaps this is me extending the olive branch."

"What?" I gripped the hilt of my sword so hard my knuckles cracked.

"I've held onto my anger for too long." Kerim stepped around me and toward my tent. "It's hurting me, who I am, and I'm finished letting it rule me. Aysa said she would try to trust me. Will you?"

Everything in me rebelled at this change in my old friend. As much as I wanted it to be true, something in me told me it wasn't—that it couldn't be. But Kerim's brown eyes begged me to accept this peace he was extending. I hadn't seen him so open in years. Not since before Feray fell ill.

Swallowing past the lump of anger and fear, I nodded once. "Let me see her."

Kerim's body seemed to lose some of the fight that had been coiled in it as he pulled back the flap of my tent. I ducked inside and nearly yelped in surprise.

Aysa sat facing the tent wall. She had her kurta off, her shoulders bare and one of them coated in blood. A thick band of material was wrapped around her chest, and I felt my face heating as I cleared my throat.

"Good. You're here." Her voice was thick with pain, and her eyes never seemed to focus on me. "Kerim, can you fetch a bucket of water and some rags?"

"Yes." He dropped the flap, leaving Aysa and me alone.

"What happened?" I asked, fear and anger coiling in my gut at the blood still dribbling down her arm.

"Desert wolf." She gritted her teeth as I eased closer and began poking at the deep slashes and gouges that peppered her shoulder and arm. "Kerim and I disposed of it, but it got ahold of me before we did."

I swore. "He knows who you are."

"He does." Her hand clasped my arm, drawing my gaze to her face. "And I trust him."

"He said you did, but I wasn't sure I believed him."

"What happened between you two?"

A shadow fell over the door, saving me from answering. Kerim's brows furrowed as he caught sight of Aysa's arm. "Do you have salve?" he asked.

"In my bag." Aysa pointed to her satchel by the door, and I wanted to yell at Kerim to get out as he rifled through Aysa's clothes and belongings. There was something personal about it. Something...marital. I fisted my hand at my side, willing my temper to cool as he brought the jar over to me. He quickly looked from me to Aysa. "Anything else, Princezo?"

She shook her head.

Kerim hesitantly turned his focus back to me. "She hit her head when the wolf slammed into us. I think it could be muddling her thinking a little."

"It is not!" Aysa protested, but her gaze flicked over my face with a dazed look.

The insufferable man smiled at both of us before chuckling and ducking back out.

The flap settled into place as I wrung out a rag. Panic roared in my ears, and I wanted to run away. Away from the worry, pain, and frustration that being near Aysa produced. I cared for her but couldn't have her. Wanted her as much as a starving man wanted a scrap of food. Yet being near her was the same as smelling a feast and being denied. It made my stomach ache but didn't satisfy.

Aysa hissed as I dabbed at the wound.

"Sorry." My throat was tight. Anxiety about what could have happened to her swirled in my chest. A few paces off, a better-timed jump by the wolf, and her neck could have been snapped by its massive jaw. Her face could have scars rather than her shoulder. A million scenarios ran through my head, and I sucked in a breath only after my vision began to blur.

"Emre." Aysa's voice pulled me back to reality. She cupped my cheek. Her gaze was still slightly unfocused as it flicked to my lips then settled on my eyes again. "I'm all right."

"I know," I whispered, feeling the intimacy of this moment far too keenly. "But it doesn't stop me from worrying."

She chuckled. Her hand slid from my cheek to my shoulder and then down my arm, igniting fire wherever it went. She tangled her fingers with mine and said, "Worry is paying for tomorrow's possibilities—whether good or bad—today."

I smiled at her majka's saying and finished wiping up both dry and wet blood from her shoulder. Scooping up some salve, I wiped it against the scrapes. I tried not to think about Aysa's smooth skin beneath my fingers, about the way the muscles in her shoulder tensed at my touch. I was tending a wound, that was all. Forcing all my mental focus onto her shoulder, I watched the blood that still oozed from one of the gashes. It looked deeper than the others. My finger stroked extra salve over it and Aysa shivered.

"This one might need stitches." Bile coated my tongue at the thought. "I'm not sure I can do that."

Aysa's eyes slid closed "Can Kerim?"

My jaw tensed at the image of Kerim touching Aysa. Caressing her shoulder to tend the wound. I pressed a clean rag to it, applying pressure until Aysa sucked in a sharp breath.

"I'll do it," I finally whispered.

"Emre," she sighed, her hand trailing over my own. "It's all right to let Kerim do it."

No. No, it isn't. "I can do it."

Aysa watched me, her eyes half closed. "I'm tired." I flinched as she leaned her forehead against my shoulder and shivered. "And it hurts."

"I know."

Voices murmured outside, and I swore. Aysa peeled her eyes open and looked at me. "Sew it up."

"But—"

"Emre." She leaned close, her earthy scent stronger from being in the oasis. "I trust you. Not Kerim, not Kagan, not anyone else here. I trust you to help me heal."

Her words were slurred from the pain and the bump on her head. But they filled me up and gave me strength. "Lie back on the blankets."

She obeyed, her hand clutching mine. Her eyes squeezed closed, and I knew she was chewing on the inside of her cheek.

"I'll be back in a minute."

Aysa nodded, a sheen of perspiration on her forehead. I smoothed a few strands of hair away from her face before stepping out to the fire. The men sat around it, eating dried meat and pita. All looked up at me as I stepped to the fire and put the needle into the flame.

"How is he?" Kagan asked.

I glanced at Kerim, who raised a brow. I had to guess what he'd told them.

"Cafer was attacked by a desert wolf. One of the puncture wounds needs stitches, but he should be fine in a few days."

"Good." Efe smiled. "He's a brave lad, helping to slay a desert wolf."

The others nodded, but I shivered, fear of nearly losing Aysa yet again tightening the vice around my heart.

The needle hot and sterilized, I hurried back to Aysa.

She slept, looking tranquil despite the blood seeping through the thin rag. I knelt beside her once more, my hand holding the needle shaking at the thought of running it through Aysa's skin.

"Nicar above, steady my hand. Please...help me keep her safe." My voice caught, and I tipped my head up to look at the tent roof. "I don't know what to do anymore. I can't protect her. I can't."

Her hand slipped onto my knee. I felt her thumb rub, and when I looked down, she smiled sleepily at me. "I trust you."

Her words helped the shaking subside as I leaned over her shoulder, pressing the tip of the needle against the edge of the wound. At the last minute, I handed her a rag. "You might want to bite this."

She shoved it between her teeth and nodded at me.

With a steady breath, I pushed the needle into her skin.

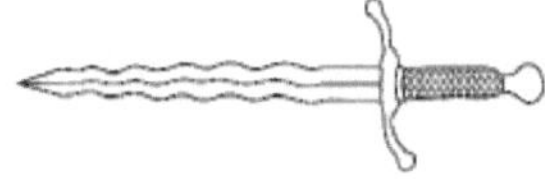

Aysa passed out halfway through me sewing up her wound. Remarkably, she didn't cry out before that, gritting the rag between her teeth as tears of pain trailed down her cheeks. Now she slumbered somewhat peacefully as I wiped salve over the stitches and wrapped a fresh bandage around her shoulder.

The men had gone to spar together to prepare for their next challenge. They were still over at the ring, and I took the moment of silence to sit beside the dying embers of the fire and think. Resting my elbows on my knees, I pinched the bridge of my nose, wishing the roaring pain behind my eyes would lessen. Wishing that, for a moment, I could catch my breath. Leading was exhausting.

Was this the pressure Aysa felt? A crushing weight of never reaching the goal? Always being a step behind where you needed to be?

I wiped my sleeve across my brow and stood. This was just further proof that I needed to get the men away from her. Give her a chance to think before making her choice. She could chase after us, but I wouldn't let her rush the decision itself.

Tomorrow, the men would leave on a challenge of epic proportions. I would look after Aysa for a few days, give her a chance to let her shoulder heal, and, perhaps, get my traitorous heart under control once and for all.

CHAPTER TWENTY-THREE

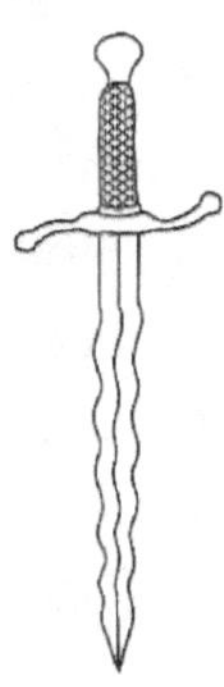

Aysa

My shoulder hurt. My head throbbed. What time was it? I smacked my lips together and forced my eyes to open, though they felt as if they were sewn shut. The tent was cooler than it had been. Twilight, perhaps?

My injured arm tucked to my chest to limit the chances of hitting it, I forced myself to sit up, willing the tent to stop spinning as I crawled to the flap and peeked through.

The men sat around the fire, shoveling food into their mouths as they talked and laughed. Well, most of them laughed. Berk, Naz, and Ulvi glowered from the far side of the fire, their faces cast in dancing shadows that made them appear even grimmer than before.

"What's the challenge for tomorrow?" Derin asked between chews.

Emre took his time in answering the men. They all leaned forward, waiting but pretending they weren't. I stifled a chuckle and shifted to sit cross-legged by the tent entrance.

"We're going to have a race," Emre said at last.

Ulvi scoffed in disbelief. "That's it? That's all you're going to share?"

"For now." Emre smirked, meeting the gaze of each man.

They all went back to eating, grumbling among one another.

A few more minutes passed, every single one of the men glancing at Emre at least once as they ate, hoping for a clue to the morning's race.

But my guard gave nothing away.

The moon bathed the world in its cold glow when Emre stood. "Rest well men. You're going to need it."

"For a race?" Naz rolled his eyes.

"But it is no ordinary race." Another smirk flashed on Emre's face as he inclined his head. "Good evening."

He moved toward the tent, his strides long and sure. I dropped the flap just as he pulled it back, brows raising when he saw me huddled by the doorway. "Eavesdropping is unbecoming."

"Good thing I don't care about that."

He chuckled and stepped over me. My traitorous mind reminded me of the hazy moments when Emre was cleaning my wound—his gentle fingers prodding the injury, wiping away the blood, smoothing the cooling salve. Heat flamed in my cheeks as I imagined curling up at Emre's side tonight, safe from the desert wolves who were stalking my dreams.

Emre shook me from my thoughts when he asked, "How's your shoulder?"

"Fine." I swallowed and crawled to my bed, curling up on my good side. Unfortunately, that meant that I was facing Emre. I winced. "It's still a little sore."

"Does it need more salve?" He sat up, reaching for my pack.

"No!" I nearly shouted the word and Emre jumped. The thought of his fingers on my skin sent heat racing through my body and had me blushing. "It'll be fine."

Slowly, Emre laid back down. His brown eyes stared up at the tent's roof, his fingers interlocked and resting on his chest. "You scared me today."

"I'm sorry."

"I kept imagining what would have happened if Kerim hadn't been there." He turned his head, meeting my gaze. "You could have been killed."

I grimaced. "Or I could have killed the wolf myself. Why does everyone see me as weak because I'm a woman?"

"Wait, that's not what I—"

"You, the council, the men out there, my otac?" I shook my head, rolling onto my back to get away from Emre's gaze. "Everyone thinks I need someone to keep me safe. Well, I handled myself fine today in the ring against Derin."

"You did. I was proud of you for that."

His praise evaporated a bit of my anger.

"I worry, Aysa, because I...well, I care." He sighed, and I barely heard the whispered words that accompanied it, "Even if I shouldn't."

Ignoring the ache of my heart, I changed the subject. "You're sending the men away tomorrow?"

"Yes, on a hunt of sorts."

"Where to?"

"You'll hear tomorrow, same as them." His voice held his smile in it, and I could picture his face, full of mischief and pride at his challenge.

I closed my eyes, willing back the tears as I always did. I didn't need tears, nor did I have time for them. With a shuddery breath, I rolled onto my side and whispered, "Good night, Emre."

"Good night, my *princezo.*"

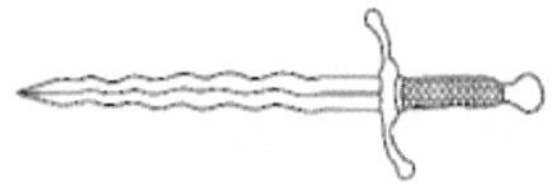

The morning came far too soon. Emre was already up when my eyes fluttered open. The pain in my head and shoulder was a dull throb that accompanied every movement, and I cursed the foul beast as I buttoned up my kurta and struggled to situate my turban and scarf with one hand.

Efe was once again bent over the fire, pulling off manakeesh with za'atar on it. He grinned at me as I gingerly lowered myself to a mat, cradling my bad arm to my chest to keep from pulling on Emre's stitches. "Good morning, Cafer! How are you feeling?"

I shrugged my good shoulder with a noncommittal grunt.

He handed me a plate with the manakeesh. "Well, I'll pray to the goddess that you heal quickly." He winked good-naturedly. "I want to spar with you next."

I forced a smile I wasn't feeling as Emre sauntered over and sat across from me. His gaze was full of questions, but I looked away, feeling far from amiable. My thoughts warred with one another—duty and heart both wanting to be first in my mind. My head ached from slamming into the ground the day before, and all I wanted to do was curl up in the tent and go back to bed.

"What route are we taking today?" Kagan asked between bites, his chewing grating on my already frayed nerves.

Emre licked his lips before smiling at the men. "You will go to an oasis that lies to the east. There is one that is known for its pistachio groves. You will harvest a bag of those nuts and return."

Kerim scoffed, the sound like a hammer to my temple. "There are at least ten oases in that direction. How are we to know which has the pistachios?"

Emre shrugged. "This event may take several days. You are not allowed to receive help from anyone. If you do, you will be disqualified."

"How do you know if we do or don't?" Berk asked, his bright blue eyes hard. "Eight of us, spread out across the Šerian desert, means you cannot possibly check up on us."

"Nicar will reveal all." Emre's fingers curled into a fist on his knee. He clearly wanted to tap them but was holding himself in check. "This challenge was created by the šefe himself. I cannot ignore it."

Grumbles rumbled around the circle, but the men hurried to finish their food and saddle their horses before the day grew any warmer. I stood and moved to Emre's side as we cleaned up breakfast and then strode toward the mounted men awaiting his signal.

"Go with Nicar. May she favor you and shine fortune upon the one she most desires for Princezo Aysa."

Kerim eyed me, his eyes flicking between Emre and me. He was the last to mount and before he did, he stepped to Emre's side. "I'll keep an eye on them. If anyone cheats, I'll report it."

Emre's gaze narrowed, and Kerim's voice dropped further as he uttered one word. "Trust."

Then he was striding across the sand and swinging up onto his desert mount. His gray horse pawed the ground and tossed his large head, ready to be off.

"For the love of the princezo!" Emre shouted and I flinched as it stabbed into my head.

The men whooped as Emre's arm fell, their horses stirring the sand into the air as they galloped off into the blazing sun.

I waited until they were mere specks on the horizon before pulling off my scarf and turban. Swiping my good arm across my brow, I declared, "These are so hot! I don't know how you bear it."

Emre chuckled but didn't respond, worry divoting his brow as he stared at me.

I wanted to go to him, wrap my arms around his waist and breathe in his spicy scent. I needed Emre, more than anything. Desire to say the sacred vow and bind myself to him for forever welled up inside me, but my duty was being terribly inconvenient.

"Are you all right?" Emre's hand landed on my arm, and it took everything in me to keep staring at the dots that were my suitors rather than at him.

"My shoulder pains me still, but otherwise I'm fine. Why do you ask?" I forced a smile, still not meeting his gaze.

Emre crossed his arms. "Why are you hiding who you are?"

I blinked at his abrupt change of subject. "Because you said to."

"No, not right now." He squinted up at the sky. "I mean the other night at dinner. You let Dilan dress you up and you acted so...perfect. Why do you do that?"

"Because it's what people expect of me." I shrugged my good shoulder, pretending yet again that it wasn't important that I was being forced to be someone I wasn't. When had that started to bother me? I couldn't name a time nor a place, but the longer I was stuck in this contest, the more I saw how much I bent to the whims of others. "They want me to be a certain way as their princezo and future šefe. So, I become what they desire."

"That's a sorry excuse." Emre's glare burned into the side of my face, goading me. I bristled at his words. For years, he'd stood by and kept silent about my façade. Now, when I needed it most, he was telling me how he felt about my feigned perfection. I was whatever I needed to be. A chameleon that blended into the background, a hero who shouted from the dune tops, the princezo that rose to expectations, or failed simply because people said she would.

Emre's turned me to face him. "You could simply be you, Aysa. That's a beautiful thing all on its own."

I scowled at him, his words cutting deep. Humiliation from getting injured, the hazy memories of him tending my wound, his fingers against my skin, all of it blended with the pain of him insulting my leadership—just like the tribal leaders and elders. It heightened my embarrassment, tinting everything red in the morning light.

"Don't tell me what to do!" I snapped, jabbing him in the ribs, though it seemed to hurt my finger more than his solid chest. "I'm doing what's best for my people. For Šeri! Don't you understand that, Emre? I want to be what's best for them!"

"By not being yourself?" He flung his hands out wide, his jaw flexing as he ground his teeth. "By sneaking around and manipulating people?"

"What? No! Manipulating?" I scoffed. "That's what you think this is?"

"What am I supposed to think, Aysa? You've been hiding your fire. That burning passion you have for Šeri. This anger" —he gestured between us — "is more real than anything you've shown those eight men in the last week."

"What about my spar with Derin? That was me! I helped slay a desert wolf. I'm strong. If hiding is what makes me so, then I'll embrace it. I'll be whatever is needed for Šeri's sake. Besides," I scoffed. "If the men saw the real me, they'd think that I'm a headstrong, little—"

"Stop." Emre slapped his hand over my mouth, suddenly very close. He smelled like cinnamon and that special aroma of clothes dried in the sunshine. He froze, as if realizing what he was doing. Slowly he pulled his hand away, letting the back of his fingers brush against my cheek as he tucked a strand of my hair behind my ear. A fire ignited in my chest as he whispered, "Don't call yourself that."

"Why not?" My words were breathy, and I couldn't focus as he cupped my cheek, his fingertips skimming the back of my neck. "The tribe whispers it. They think I don't hear it, but I do. I'm—"

"Wonderful. Passionate. An amazing future šefe." He leaned his forehead against mine and squeezed his eyes shut. "Stars above, woman. Why do you never listen to me?"

"I—"

Emre's eyes snapped open, serious yet soft. Heat that had nothing to do with the morning sun blazed through me as he whispered, "You will never obtain the level of perfection you're striving for, Aysa. And you don't have to. There's beauty in mistakes. Grace and mercy. Are you above errors, Princezo?" He raised his brows, his free hand running down my arm.

"No." *I think I'm about to make a very large one right now.* "Anyone can make mistakes."

"Good, maybe you have been listening." He smiled.

All rational thoughts fled my mind. All logic. The memories of Emre's gentle fingers on my skin rushed through me. Now, standing before him, close enough to feel his chest rising and falling, there was only one thing I wanted to do—needed to do. Standing on my tiptoes, I twined my good arm around Emre's neck and kissed him. It was reckless, desperate, but I needed to feel it. Needed to see what it was like. My head turned, my lips teasing Emre's to follow as I let myself get lost in his presence. Emre's arm slid around my waist, mindful of my injury, and he followed my lead. His nose brushed against mine as his fingers cupping my cheek rose and dug into the shortened strands of my hair. Slowly, he began to lead the kiss, catching the corner of my mouth as he pulled me closer still.

A tear slid down my cheek, and I whimpered as he jostled my shoulder. Pulling back, I buried my nose in his neck. "I'm sorry."

"For what?" His words were husky, and he hugged me to him. "This will be a moment I treasure forever. The princezo's first kiss was me."

I laughed, but it held no mirth. In fact, more tears were very near the surface. "I just used you. I'm little better than Naz. I know he only wants me for—" I trailed off; the thought too uncomfortable to finish.

Emre chuckled, but it sounded sad. "Aysa, if you only knew how long I've wanted to kiss you, you wouldn't be apologizing."

"What?" I stepped back but kept hold of his shoulder. "Why would you want to kiss me?"

His face flamed red. "I—I've been in love with you almost since the day I rescued you."

"I was ten!"

He looked away. "Hence why I didn't tell you until this moment."

I heard him, but my mind caught on one word.

Love. He said he loves me.

Emre tipped his head to the side and eased back. "What's wrong? Is your shoulder all right?"

"It's fine, but—" My breath caught in my chest, my head spinning as I stared at him.

He smiled, brushing back my hair as he waited for my swirling thoughts to fall into place. Emre, my faithful, steady friend.

Who shouldn't—couldn't—love me.

Tears pressed against my eyes. "Why would you tell me this now? I can't—"

"Shh." His hands moved from my waist to cup my cheeks. "Perhaps it was cruel, but I felt as if you should know. And you did kiss me first." He smirked, but sadness lingered in his gaze.

"Oh, Emre." I couldn't help the sigh that slipped out. "I shouldn't have done it."

"Do you regret it?" His forehead furrowed, his lips tipping down in a frown.

"No." I shook my head, gingerly wrapping my arms around his waist and leaning my cheek against his chest. "But it makes me sad."

A sigh of his own rumbled through his chest and he hugged me back. "I know."

We stood like that for a long while as the sun beamed down on us. This was our moment. I knew it was improper, but I couldn't drum up enough emotion to care. All I felt was the ache of caring for my best friend and knowing that we couldn't go back to what we were before.

"Aysa?" Emre asked after a minute. "I should take you home."

My back stiffened, and I stepped back. "No. I'm not going home. If you love me at all, Emre, then you'll let me remain." *If these are my last days with you, then let me stay.* "You'll help me pick the right man."

Emre's jaw tensed. My heart shattered at the pain laying there as he slowly nodded. His face went hard, nothing in his expression telling me what he was feeling. He'd walled up and locked me out.

He turned toward the fire. "I should make us something to eat."

Not waiting for a reply, he stalked toward the supply tent. I lowered onto one of the mats, watching him. I cared for him, I admitted to myself, more than anyone in the world. It broke my heart to watch him as he stiffly roasted some meat over the fire without a word.

Swallowing the lump in my throat, I turned to look out over the golden sands, wishing I could travel back in time and change what I had just ruined.

CHAPTER TWENTY-FOUR

Emre

I handed Aysa the lamb that I had just finished roasting, cursing myself when I saw her hand tremble. I'd upset her, but I didn't want to get hurt again. Yet, there was no way this wouldn't end in us hurting. I didn't regret kissing her. It was the best thing I'd ever done. More intoxicating than any wine, and that was why I wouldn't do it again. Couldn't risk getting drunk on Aysa's lips only to have her ripped away from me when she married one of the eight.

"Emre, tell me something about you I don't know." Aysa was staring at her plate, the food untouched.

I swallowed. There was much about my life I hadn't told her. Aysa relished talking while I enjoyed listening. It was why we were friends. She knew I had wandered and why I had started. She knew I'd lived a spell with Tribe Hamid and Tribe Ender. But she didn't know what drove me from them, from the people and place that had been home.

"Once, there was a little boy whose otac sent him to Tribe Ender when he was eight years old. That tribe was known throughout the land as being the best to learn combat from—both hand-to-hand and the art of the sword."

Aysa nodded, already knowing this, and placed the still warm meat on a piece of pita as she listened.

"He worked hard to earn approval and praise, both from the tribal leader and the leader's sinovi. He honed his art, becoming fluid in hand-to-hand as well as the broadsword, which was a weapon only a few knew how to wield.

"One day, he defeated the tribal leader's sinovi in hand-to-hand combat. He was thrilled. The sinovi wasn't. Catching him by surprise that night, the sinovi beat the boy until he could barely move."

"Emre." She laid her hand on my leg, and I stared at it, trying to remain fixated on that rather than getting swept away in the memories.

"Once the boy was well enough to leave, he did. His otac had died of some strange illness and another man had taken the place of tribal leader. They wouldn't take the boy back. So, he wandered. A few weeks later, half-dead, he ended up in the Hamid tribe. They accepted him. Taught him to fish and work with his hands. He thought he had found a family. A good family. But all good things end.

"The leader of the tribe had a kćerka. Her name was Feray. She was beautiful, full of laughter, and she loved being out in the sunshine on her otac's fishing boat. She could talk the boy into anything, pull him out of all his moods. She was a lot like you, Aysa, and gave the boy a reason to stay."

My breath caught as I saw Feray in my mind's eye. A face I hadn't let myself dwell on for years. Aysa was so much like her—with a courage and fire that drew me in like a moth to a flame. Even though Aysa tried to hide it, I sensed it, wanted to treasure it, hold it close.

Clearing my throat, I continued, "But it didn't last. She got sick—quite sick. The healer said it was something inside her that was slowly killing her. The boy sat with her every day, read the sacred texts, and prayed for her and with her. She got weaker and weaker. Started to forget who people were. One day she asked the boy to kiss her goodbye, and when they finished, she let go of life.

"Her family didn't get the chance to tell her goodbye. She was gone that quickly. And the boy blamed himself. After a heated conversation with the girl's brother—who also blamed the boy—he left. He didn't say goodbye to her parents, to her brother, to anyone. Just packed his bag and took to wandering again."

"You're that boy, aren't you, Emre?"

"Yes. And Feray is—was Kerim's sister." My shoulders slump, remembering the kiss, her exhale that took her spirit with her. It had broken me, and when I'd told Kerim, he'd been enraged that I had dared to kiss his dying sister. "Kerim and I were friends, but I was closer with Feray. I've always felt as if he blames me for her death. He was always scared that her recklessness would get her hurt. Turns out, it was my kiss rather than one of our adventures that killed her."

"You didn't kill her, Emre. She was already sick and dying, and you said she asked you to kiss her."

I nodded. "I know. But I still blame myself. If I hadn't kissed her, maybe she would have held on longer. Perhaps..."

I trailed off as Aysa's thumb rubbed up and down on my knee, her voice soft as she asked, "Is what happened to Feray the reason why you're so protective of me, Emre?"

I never thought about it before, but perhaps that was the reason. "To be loved is wonderful. To belong, a special joy. But to lose those things?" I pushed to my feet, tearing off my turban and burying my fingers in my hair. "I can't lose someone else I've grown fond of."

"Only fond?" Aysa's voice was barely a whisper. If we had been anywhere but the silent, scorching desert, it would have been lost. I wanted to pull her close, speak the sacred vow and pledge myself to her in both word and deed.

But another vow, another promise, had me clenching my fists at my side, keeping my back to her as I said, "It can't be anything more, Aysa. I loved and lost one leader's kćerka. I won't lose another one. Not when it means never piecing my heart back together. If I have to love you from a distance, it's better than not being able to love you at all."

"And yet, you'll lose me regardless." A sob, the pattering of feet, and Aysa disappeared into the tent.

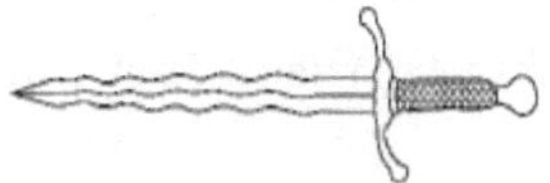

The Border of Taletha and Šeri—The day of the race

The sun sank in a burning red inferno behind the sandy hills of Šeri as Arqa of Taletha sat atop his great black stallion. The beast pawed the ground, shifting its weight with a snort of discomfort that mirrored the inner struggle of its rider.

Arqa grunted as his partner, Shaeen, halted his brown mare at Arqa's side.

"Has he arrived yet?" Shaeen's voice, a smooth as silk and as deadly as a viper, whispered over to Arqa.

The former military commander flinched, hating that he did, yet he was unable to fully trust the man at his side. Shaeen had, after all, attempted to murder Ameer Dhamar and pin it on the former malek. He'd threatened the amira, wanting her for himself when she was obviously in love with Dhamar. Arqa squeezed the reins in his fist. He questioned his sanity for sitting here with Shaeen now. Why hadn't he left when he'd had the chance?

"Well?" Shaeen hissed.

"Do you see the boy?" Arqa snapped.

Shaeen glared at him, his black beard trembling. "Don't talk to me that way. I'm the one with the plan, after all."

"This plan is reckless at best, certain death at worst." Arqa roughed a hand over his face. "Dhamar has already reduced us to middle class citizens. Why do we think this will regain us our positions?"

"It won't." Shaeen rolled his shoulders, his teeth gleaming in the faint light of the moon. "But won't revenge taste so, so sweet?"

War. Shaeen wanted war. Death. He was so much like the old malek in that respect. And now they were at the border, waiting for the key to reignite the enmity between Taletha and Šeri once again.

The sound of hoofbeats reached their ears as a young man pulled up beside the border marker, swinging off with an enviably grace. Arqa was several years removed from the boy, and jealousy filled his heart as the young man prowled forward with confidence.

"Are you—?" Shaeen began, but the man cut him off with a wave of his hand.

"You know who I am." He glared at them. "I have the...delivery."

"Good. Good." Shaeen's grin was wicked, and Arqa's stomach soured at the bundle squirming on the back of the young man's horse.

"Do you have my payment?" The man crossed his arms, and his light-colored eyes flashed. "And I expect that I will receive that other reward you promised."

Shaeen laughed, low and throaty. "Oh, you know that's up to you. Show your people your battle prowess. Besides" —Shaeen stalked to their ally's horse and pulled back the tarpaulin from the bundle. A woman's terrified face stared up at them, wild with fear. Shaeen's finger trailed over her cheek — "you did well with *her*. I trust that you can easily sway your people to your side."

The young man grunted. "Do you think you can topple the šefe?"

Shaeen waved his hand dismissively. "If I can't, nobody can."

"You failed to dethrone Taletha." The young man's smirk was challenging. Arqa cut a glance at Shaeen. His partner's back went ridged, his hand's fisted at his side—likely to keep himself from punching their one and only ally.

"We did." Arqa swallowed as both men looked up at him, still perched on his stallion. "But this plan will cause enough agitation in both nations. Unrest is the perfect time to strike."

The young man's grin turned almost as feral as Shaeen's, and he gestured toward the woman. "Well, I suppose I can assist in this plan. I'm not needed at the šefe's camp for a few days yet."

"I don't share well." Shaeen stroked the cheek of the woman, whose whimper was loud enough to be heard through the gag she wore. "But for our partner, I suppose I can."

"Where's your camp?" The young man swung back up onto his horse, turning away from Shaeen to face Arqa.

"This way." Heading toward camp, Arqa swallowed back his unease. There were a hundred ways this plan could end, and he had the unsettling notion that none of them would be particularly good.

CHAPTER TWENTY-FIVE

Aysa

I lay in Emre's tent, ignoring the sweat running in rivulets down my back and the pain in my shoulder. Tears made their way down my cheeks, but I didn't make a sound. The last thing I wanted was Emre knowing he'd made me cry.

What made him say it was better to let me go? Did he not see the way this contest was killing me? Did he not care that I had kissed him?

And why had I done *that*? It was a foolish, stupid decision that meant every kiss I had after that, I would compare to Emre's. None would ever be the same because whomever I kissed next wouldn't be him.

Majka's words after I'd gotten ill rattled in my mind, adding to the cacophony that I couldn't shut off. *If you see something in someone you think you can't live without, latch onto that. Don't let it go.*

Could I live without Emre? Before it had been easier to say *yes*. *Yes*, I could marry someone else. *Yes*, I would choose them over and over, fight the battle daily to love them. *Yes*, I could make myself forget what it felt like to be cherished as myself, rather than an ideal.

But was that what was best? Because while I *could* do all of that, I didn't *want* to. I wanted Emre to hold me when I was sick. I wanted Emre to cradle me as we slept and to wake to his soft breathing and gentle smile. I wanted him to be the one to tend my wounds, hold our babies, claim my lips, my attention, my heart.

I sat up, dizzy as the heat continued to press down. My shoulder pinched, and I stumbled out into the late afternoon and glanced around for Emre, fighting another wave of lightheadedness. My stomach growled, but I ignored it, taking another step forward. But the world tipped, my vision blurred, and I gasped as I blinked up at the cloudless blue sky.

"Aysa?" Gentle hands scooped my head into their lap and pressed a waterskin to my lips. The water was cold, and my fuzzy thoughts realized that Emre must have been at the oasis, fetching fresh water for us.

"Thank you." I pushed onto my elbows, Emre's hand settling against my upper back.

"What happened?"

"Dehydrated, I think." A sheepish smile bloomed on my lips. "And my head still hurts from yesterday. The heat of the tent didn't help that."

"I should have thought about opening the flaps for you."

"It's not your fault." I reached out and laid my arm on his bicep. My thoughts from earlier swirled in my mind as I met his gaze. "Emre, I—"

The pounding of hoofbeats interrupted my words as Kerim tore into camp. His horse had barely pulled up before he was leaping off the beast and racing up to Emre's side. I could feel the tension rolling off of Kerim—like the sand radiating the day's heat. "I warned both of you this would happen!"

"What are you talking about?" Emre stepped in front of me.

Kerim jabbed a finger in Emre's chest. "The pieces fell into place. It's started."

"What started?" I questioned the same time as Emre asked, "Why are you here?"

"I ran into my tribe. Apparently, the day after we left the šefe's camp, you," he jabbed a finger in my direction, "went missing." Kerim's brown eyes hardened. "Today, word reached the šefe's camp that the princezo has turned up dead."

"What?" The word whispered out on a puff of air, my legs feeling shaky once again. "But that's not me!"

"Clearly." Kerim met my gaze. "But who is it then?"

Emre's body went taunt. "Who told you this?"

"A messenger of the šefe, on his way to rally the eastern tribes. I was chosen to come tell you." Kerim cut a glance at me. "It might be a good idea for you to leave. Soon. The others are on their way here tonight, and tomorrow, they plan on returning to help fight the war."

"War with whom?" Emre asked. "Who is claiming to have killed the princezo?"

"Malek Dhamar is denying involvement, but..." Kerim's jaw was tight, a white-knuckled grip on his scimitar. "The woman's body was found at the border. Bloody and bruised beyond recognition."

"Then how are they claiming that it's the princezo?" Emre asked, his fingers tapping against his leg. "It could have been anyone."

"Perhaps. Except..." Kerim's gaze locked with mine. "An eye was delivered. An eye that matches Aysa's coloring perfectly. Whether or not it's Aysa's is irrelevant. The šefe won't take an insult from Taletha; not when his kćerka is missing. What will he say when he discovers you have her, Emre?"

"Is that a threat?" Emre all but growled. "I thought you said we could trust you."

"You can trust me." Kerim threw his hands into the air. "But can you say that about the other seven? What will they do when they find out Princezo Aysa has been here for two days?"

"Our reputation is not important," Emre snapped. "What matters is that the šefe is dragging us to war. Again."

War. The words rang in my ears, my aching head pounding out the beat of the war drums that followed us to the battlefield. My otac would go to war with Dhamar because, to him, I was dead.

"Emre." My chest tightened. "We have to go home."

He dragged a hand over his face with a groan. "But Kerim is right. It's not safe for us there, either. Someone has been targeting you, not because of this contest, but because they want to start the war again."

"It's my fault." I shook my head, my ears ringing. "The men will return, they'll discover I'm here, and I'll ruin you. I'm so sorry. I—"

"Aysa!" Emre grabbed my shoulders and I winced when he pressed on the wounded one. "You're not thinking clearly."

I yanked away from him. "No, you're wrong. You'll be destroyed. Otac will kill you, and it will be my fault."

"You'll do no one any good by panicking." Kerim stepped forward, hands raised as if he was calming a frightened colt. "You need to keep your head and listen to Emre and me."

"Why would you tell us what you discovered?" I shot back, panic continuing to claw at my throat. "You could have outed Emre to my otac and won my hand. Why didn't you?"

"Because I told both of you that you could trust me, and I meant it." Kerim shook his head. "I swear it on the sun, the moon, and all the stars, I am loyal to you."

As I watched Kerim fist his hand over his chest and drop to a knee before me, I wondered why he was doing any of this. Why would he swear his loyalty to me? He didn't know me, no one did. Emre was right, I didn't deserve loyalty when I'd never truly been myself.

A girl *died* because of me. Because someone was so upset by peace that they murdered her. *Murdered.*

I choked, barely able to breathe as I turned and ran.

Away from the shock.

Away from the reality.

Away from all the emotions and pain that were pounding against my chest.

I couldn't handle Kerim's loyalty. Emre's love. Though I craved both,

I didn't deserve them.

As I ran up a dune, the stars began to wink in the evening sky. The jangle of bridles and saddles sounded, signaling that Kerim's fellow tribesmen had reached the camp, but I didn't turn around. I dropped to my knees, curling my arms across my stomach, and burst into breath-stealing sobs.

CHAPTER TWENTY-SIX

Emre

At the very crest of the dune, Aysa stepped forward, crumpling to her knees and bursting into sobs. Her shoulders shook, her head bowing as she cried out all her frustration and fear.

I hesitated, wondering if she wanted me here. Aysa always pretended to be the picture of poise and grace. Yet that wasn't true, wasn't her. And right now, she wept into her hands, grieving for a woman she didn't know. Everything in me wanted to dash to her side and scoop her into my arms. I wanted to hold her until the ache stopped—an ache I knew all too well.

Slowly, I eased to her side, lowering myself onto the warm sand and letting my knee bump into hers.

Aysa sniffed, flicking a tear off her nose with the side of her finger as she hugged her legs to her chest. "Someone—someone died." She pillowed her forehead against her knees, undoubtedly pulling on her stitches. "Did you hear Kerim? The tribes think it's Taletha. That it's somehow Dhamar's fault. Otac will listen to the elders—who were against peace from the start— and go to war with Taletha. Everything I tried to stop, to avoid, will all crash down around us." She looked away from me, staring out at the stars winking in the black sky.

I sighed, wishing I had the words to comfort her, but coming up short.

She was right. War loomed on the horizon yet again. A war that neither Aysa nor Dhamar wanted. But someone had murdered an innocent woman, framed Taletha, and forced our hand. Someone was out for blood.

"Did I truly make such a poor choice that it will result in another war?" More tears slid down Aysa's cheeks, pulling me out of my morose thoughts. "I worked my hardest to end the last one. Why is it coming back?" Her voice cracked, and she leaned her head against my shoulder. More sobs shook her body, and I dared to curl my arms around her and hold her.

"It's not your fault, Aysa," I murmured. "It's cruel men enacting some type of revenge or plot against Taletha. Whoever they are, they're framing Dhamar, that much is clear."

"But that's been bothering me. How do they know I'm not in Otac's camp?" She sniffed and shivered as the cool desert night air brushed against our skin. "Either someone in our tribe knows and is against us, or—"

"Someone here in our camp." I leapt to my feet, knocking Aysa's head off of my arm in my haste to rise. Blood roared in my ears. "Someone else knows besides Kerim, and you're in danger. We have to leave right now."

Aysa paled, grasping my hands as I pulled her to standing. Her grip tightened as she stepped closer to me. "Where? Where will we be safe?"

"Taletha." I tugged her after me while staying in the shadows to avoid the few men still gathered around the fires, discussing the news from the border. Leaning close to Aysa's ear, I whispered, "Grab only the barest necessities."

She nodded, still trembling, and I pulled her into my arms as we stood in the shadow of our tent. "I vow to you Aysa, by the sun, the moon, and all the stars, I will keep you safe. Upon my life, I will."

"No." She shook her head, her arms wrapping around my waist so tightly it almost hurt. "No, I need you to stay alive, Emre. Please, stay alive for me." Tears dampened the front of my kurta, and her fists clutched the fabric at the back. "I can't do this alone."

Her admittance to that made my heart soar and fall all at once. She had dropped the façade for me, showed me the broken parts of her heart that she hid from the world. I was getting the real Aysa—the woman who was so scared to fall short that she hid her true self. The woman who was beautiful inside and out yet still doubted her value. The woman whom I loved more than anyone else in the world.

I pressed my lips against her forehead and murmured, "I will do my best. Now, hurry. Gather only what you need."

"All right." She paused only long enough to wipe her face with her fingertips and take a steadying breath before she slipped into the tent.

Trying to remain calm, I stalked to Esma and began to saddle her. Tension knotted my shoulders, my fingers trembling as I worked the straps and harnesses. I jumped when a hand landed on my arm, but I kept working as the urge to sweep Aysa away pounded at my temples.

"You're going?" Kerim's voice was low, his eyes watching me with barely veiled interest.

"Yes," I ground out between clenched teeth. "And I swear, if this is a trap—"

"It's not. I promise you that, Emre." He huffed a breath, the sound tinged with a million things that remained unsaid between us. He glanced at me, his eyes the same color that Feray's had been. "I meant what I said yesterday. I'm tired of the bitterness. You're my brother. Whether you run away again or not, that won't change. You loved my sister, and she loved you. That alone makes you family. But I—" He ran a hand through his hair with a sigh. "I've missed you, Emre. Why did you stay away so long?"

"I found a reason to stay." I looked over his shoulder, seeing Aysa darting from shadow to shadow toward us. "She brought the light back to my life...like Feray did."

"Have you told her that?" Kerim asked, his voice dropping lower still as Aysa continued to approach.

"In a way." I swallowed the lump in my throat, the memory of the kiss still fresh in my mind. I tightened another strap on the saddle. "But it doesn't matter. She has a duty to Šeri."

"If she's in love with you, you know I'd gladly step back from this challenge." Kerim smiled grimly. "I only came because my majka forced me to."

I laughed. "Your majka is a force to be reckoned with."

"Yes, imagine my absolute delight about being her successor." He chuckled, clasping my shoulder. "May Nicar go with you both, Emre. And come visit soon."

"I will." I felt a genuine smile tugging my lips up despite my fear as Aysa reached our side. Her eyes flicked to Kerim, and she graced him with a nod of respect.

I clasped her hand. "Ready?"

She eased closer to me as Kerim turned and walked back to the fire. "Do you trust him, now?"

"Yes. More than I thought I would." I took her hand, and Aysa dragged her gaze to meet mine. "He's a good man. He'll be a worthy leader of his tribe."

"All right." She nodded, a smile on her lips that didn't quite reach her eyes. "I trust you, too, Emre."

"Thank you, Aysa." My face flushed, and I turned toward my mount. She trusted me. It was a gift neither Aysa nor her otac handed out in excess. To be trusted by them was a high honor indeed.

I gripped Aysa's waist and helped her onto Esma's back. My thoughts unwillingly flitted to the week prior—cradling Aysa in my arms as we tore across the desert dunes. Now, it wouldn't be quite the same. She would still be with me in the saddle, far too close for rational thoughts. Her scent of oranges and earth would wrap around me like an embrace.

But instead of laughter and fun, we were in a race for our lives, trying to outpace and outwit a Šerian traitor.

Chapter Twenty-Seven

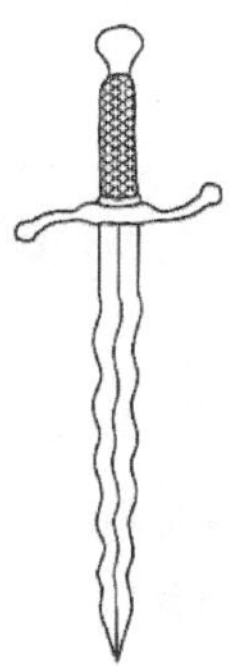

The Šefe's Tribe

I stared into the fire, my legs crossed with my elbows resting on them. We'd all returned from the race and were now gathered at the šefe's camp, awaiting our orders. The race had been exactly what I needed, though not to win Aya's hand. No, I had other pieces in play—ones far bigger than winning any stupid race that idiot guard and the šefe came up with.

Efe laughed at something someone said beside me, but I didn't hear. I was waiting for that boy, Cafer, to appear with Emre. I thought I knew who the boy was. Actually, I was nearly positive. No one had dove-gray eyes quite like Aysa. And Cafer's eyes? They mirrored hers exactly.

"You all right?" Kerim asked, sitting down beside me, and picking up a plate of pita and hummus.

"Why do you ask?" I shifted, trying to read Kerim's body language.

He raised a brow. "You've seemed a little on edge since we all arrived back at the šefe's camp. It doesn't take a scholar to see that."

"Well, if I'm on edge—which I'm not—there's nothing anyone can do about it."

Kerim raised his hands in surrender. "Fine! Have it your way."

I smiled at Kerim, though it felt a bit savage, and said, "I will. Thanks."

He shrugged and shoved a piece of pita in his mouth as he turned toward Efe's conversation.

Rage built in my chest. It had always been this way. Ever since I was a child, I had been expected to be a certain way. A certain smile, a certain docile personality. No one saw me as strong, confident, able to lead someday. I'd learned ages ago that being a leader meant hiding. Hiding the truth, the way things were accomplished, who you were.

These men—boys—weren't all that much to look at. Efe, Kerim, even Naz, they were just like me. So why did Otac see me as less than? Why did he love my sisters, yet treat me like I was refuse?

I stood, growling under my breath as I stalked to the horses. I felt Kerim's gaze on my back, but I didn't turn around. Didn't honor him with that bit of satisfaction. Besides, turning around would show him I was nervous. I couldn't allow that.

I focused on the corral of horses. They snorted as my mare trotted up to nuzzle my shoulder.

"At least you like me." The echo of a terrified scream rattled in my mind, and I pressed my forehead to the horse's neck. But the darkness let the memories play out.

Shaeen over the young woman with the eyes that matched Aysa's...at least close enough. Her hands bound as the sick man used her. Her skin had bruised, and she bled...

I shook my head, another growl slipping past my lips. *You chose this,* Shaeen's words whispered in my mind. *Live with the consequences.*

"It's not Aysa," I thought aloud, but even that didn't release any guilt. Because while I hadn't tried to harm the princezo, someone had.

Poison. Somebody had spiked her wine with poison. Someone, I dared to think, in the group behind me.

"If you're looking for Emre, he never returned from the desert."

I startled as Berk ambled forward, his bright blue eyes glowing in the moonlight.

"*Are* you looking for him?" The hulking man crossed his arms, all flattery gone without Aysa around.

"No, I just needed to clear my head." I straightened but still felt small compared to Berk. Compared to all of the men. Would I ever be good enough?

Berk leaned close. "Stay away from the princezo. Just because you have history, doesn't mean you deserve her."

"Did I say I did?" I snapped, shoving Berk away from me and spitting to the side. "Don't be an asp, Berk. Aysa is able to pick her own spouse."

He snorted. "Oh, of course. How foolish of me to think that the šefe will simply let his kćerka marry whichever of us she wishes." He rolled his eyes. "Surely, you're not that naïve. You know her otac and majka will have thoughts on the matter."

"Perhaps. But unlike some of our parents, they trust their kćerka to make the right choice with simply their advice." Unlike my otac, who barely trusted me at all. Although, with my recent actions, it didn't seem like he was wrong.

"Watch your step, runt." Berk all but snarled, his eyes cold as the North Sea. "I'd hate to see my knife stuck in that back of yours." And with that, he turned and strode toward his tent.

My stomach clenched as I stared at the horses.

Emre hadn't returned. Cafer was missing. Had I missed my chance to confront the guard and reveal Cafer for who he truly was? Was Aysa halfway across the Šerian desert? If that were true...Shaeen and Arqa were going to kill me.

Like you let them murder that girl? That innocent girl that Shaeen used and then threw away like spoiled food?

Shut up!

I swallowed bile as I rushed around the light of the fire to my tent. Throwing a spare set of clothes and a blanket into my bag, I strapped my knife and scimitar to my waist. The shadows were my friends as I hurried back to my mare, saddled her, and tore out of the šefe's camp as if the demons themselves were on my tail.

I had to warn Shaeen and Arqa. This plan was unraveling faster than an old tapestry, and I was not going to take the fall for it. I couldn't afford to lose yet again.

Aysa

The desert was eerily silent as we stopped for the night. The dunes rolled around us as Emre halted our flat-out race across the sands. My shoulder throbbed from the gallop across the dunes, and I rested a hand against it. A chill permeated my very bones as I inched closer to the tiny fire Emre had lit beside the oasis we'd stumbled across. It was small, the tiniest spring of water bubbling up from the ground. But the vegetation was determined to grow by the water, and it not only grew, but it flourished.

Have I ever felt like that? I wondered, wrapping my arms around my legs as I stared into the fire Emre had lit. The flames licked across the twigs and other underbrush that he'd gathered, and they curled in on each other. I understood that pain. That burning pressure that I succumbed to, day after day, until I was nothing but a pile of ash.

A sigh slipped past my lips, and Emre turned to study me. His gaze was all too aware —too knowing and probing. I didn't want that right now, didn't want to deal with any more life-altering news or decisions.

He opened his mouth, but I cut him off. "I'm not in the right frame of mind to talk, Emre. So please don't."

"All right." He smiled when I glanced at him with a furrowed brow. "I'm here for you whenever you are ready."

"For how long?" My voice quavered, and I swallowed against the pressure that was building behind my eyes.

Emre cocked his head to the side and waited for me to clarify.

"How long will you stand by me? Why am I so important to you?"

"You already know the answer to those questions, Aysa." He eased closer; the light of the fire reflected in his dark eyes. "I'll stand by you for as long as you'll let me, my princezo."

A pesky lump formed in my throat, and I looked away. Before, I would have said always—I wanted Emre to stand by my side forever and ever and never leave. But now, after him professing his love for me, I couldn't say that. Because to love Emre was a risk. It meant risking my status as princezo—because I knew the elders would hate it if I chose Emre. I would also be risking his welfare. How many times would he jump in front of whatever danger lurked in the shadows in order to protect me? And a small part of me worried that I was risking Šeri as a whole. Loving Emre meant I was thrusting my people into more turmoil simply because my heart wanted the man across the fire from me. But was that love worth the risk?

Logically, the answer should be no. No, a threat to Šeri wasn't a wise idea. Losing the one job I spent my whole life being prepared for was...ridiculous. A normal person wouldn't just give that up.

But as I looked over at my guard—my best friend—all logic failed me. He looked at me and saw me. The real me that was raw and wounded, uncertain and imperfect. He rushed into danger with and for me. He stood beside me for our nation because he saw what Šeri meant to me, what it could become someday. He cared for my sisters and loved my family. Looking at Emre, I saw my future, my life, my love. I saw something I couldn't live without.

But you have to. My heart shattered, and I looked out over the dark dunes, my mood falling like a star from the sky. Burning, dying, diminishing. I wiped away a tear, determined that Emre wouldn't see me cry twice in a single day.

"Let me check your shoulder." Emre brushed a strand of my hair over my shoulder.

"It's fine," I declared stubbornly.

"Aysa." His tone brokered no argument.

"I—I'll be fine until we make it to Taletha." The thought of him touching me again made my face flame and my stomach swirl.

"Why—"

"I can't do it. Can't handle you touching me. I'm afraid of what might happen if..." I swallowed the lump in my throat.

"Oh."

Oh? That was all he had to say? I bit my cheek and stretched out on the blanket by the fire. My heart broke. He wasn't even willing to fight for us? But Emre had always been that way. He stood by my decisions. And while normally I appreciated it, just this once I wanted him to fight me. To challenge me to pick us over Šeri.

Because I'm not brave enough to make the choice on my own.

Chapter Twenty-Eight

Emre

We rode fast, making the normal four-day ride from our place in the Šerian wilderness to Taletha's capital of Mordova in two. Aysa sagged against my back as we trotted through the city, people whispering and pointing with wide eyes. We stood out, dust-covered and with our dark tans. Plus, riding double wasn't common.

"How will we get into the palace?" Aysa whispered as we approached the sandstone walls and the gate set in the center. The red domes arched high in the air, the emblem of the Talethan royals atop the center one.

"We ask courteously?" I suggested with a nervous chuckle. Neither of us had thought this through, too anxious about getting out of camp and somewhere safe.

"I may have an idea." Aysa straightened, brushing as much dust off her kurta and salwar as she could before slipping off Esma and striding to the gate. "Please inform Malek Dhamar and Rania Inara that Princezo Aysa of Šeri seeks asylum along with her loyal guard, Emre, ogul of Tarkan!"

The mention of my otac's name rebirthed the ache that had been festering for over fifteen years. I rubbed my chest, remembering the day he sent me away to Tribe Ender, let me go without a backwards glance. He'd saved my life that day, though neither of us would know it for years.

A guard strode forward, his black salwar swishing with each step. I vaguely recognized him from when Aysa and I had captured Dhamar. His black hair was tied back at the nape of his neck, a few strands brushing his temples. He halted by the gate with crossed arms and eyed first Aysa—who stood with her hands on her hips—then me on top of Esma.

"Well, this is unexpected." His mouth quirked in a smile, breaking the stony veneer he'd been wearing. "Last I heard, Princezo, you were dead."

"A gross over-exaggeration, I assure you." She smirked up at me, then turned back to the guard. "Zahir, correct?"

"Yes." The guard inclined his head as he unlocked the gate. "If you'll wait by the steps, I'll inform the Malek and Rania that you are here."

"Thank you." Aysa smiled triumphantly at me as I dismounted. She stepped to my side. "I did it!"

"Apparently your bossiness is good for something," I teased, laughing as she jabbed me in the side. Pain lanced through my heart at the realization that Šeri didn't deserve her. I shoved down the rush of emotions that rolled through me as she eased closer, her head resting on my arm. Did she realize what she was doing? I brushed the back of my hand against hers, and she twined our fingers together as a bustle of people appeared at the top of the curved steps to the palace.

"Aysa?" Malek Dhamar of Taletha leaned his palms against the railing. His black curls were in disarray and his face looked drawn and pained. His eyes swept over Aysa, growing larger by the second as if not believing that it was his cousin in the courtyard.

"I'm alive!" She smiled, but the pinched look on her face told me it was forced. "Surprise!"

Dhamar flew down the steps, appearing rather undignified for a royal, and grasped Aysa by the shoulders. She winced, and his brows furrowed as his gaze flicked over her, looking for injuries. "Are you all right?"

She peeled his fingers off where her stitches were. "Besides being slightly mauled by a desert wolf, yes."

He quickly raised his hands. "Sorry!"

Aysa laughed and clasped Dhamar's hand as she grinned. "I'm fine."

Dhamar exhaled with clear relief. "I knew it couldn't be true, but General Beeran assured me it looked like you." Dhamar swallowed. "Apologies, I shouldn't bring this up to you."

"No, you should." Aysa's tone lowered, anger in each word. "I want to know it all. I want to seek vengeance for that innocent woman who was murdered, and I want truth to prevail. As you can see, I'm alive and well."

"I can see that." Dhamar's astute gaze landed on our hands as Aysa eased closer to me. "And what's this?"

Aysa blushed but wouldn't meet my gaze as she quickly untangled our fingers. "Emre helped me escape my suitors to arrive here. I didn't want them to know I'd been—well, spying on them, essentially."

She carefully avoided the part about sleeping in my tent. Probably for the best. I rested my hand on the pommel of my sword and straightened my stance. I couldn't let my emotions cloud my judgment here in Taletha. I had to protect Aysa—even if that was from my own feelings.

Aysa was reporting the events leading up to our mad dash across the wilderness to Dhamar when Rania Inara waddled to the railing. Her hands were settled on her rotund stomach, and I couldn't help but smile at the sight. In Šeri, it was common to see an expectant woman out doing chores before her abode, and it always brought me pleasure. Women were warriors, in their own right. Men fought for our land, for safety, for food. Women fought to bring new life into the world, faced the battles of raising little soldiers who would someday rise up and take their place in the war of life. And yet, women did it all with a grace no man could hope to obtain.

Inara squealed, clapping her hands before gesturing for Aysa to come up to see her. Dhamar followed, a soft smile on his face as his gaze settled on his wife. It swirled an emotion to life deep inside of me, one I'd rarely felt.

Jealousy.

I tightened my grip on my sword hilt, tapping a light beat to steady the rolling, ugly emotion rearing its head. Aysa was choosing to serve her country over her heart. And while it tore me up inside, I would let her do it. *She* would have to choose us. I wouldn't push it.

Inara enveloped Aysa in a hug. Tears coursed down the rania's face even as she laughed. "We'd heard you'd been brutally murdered, and we were so grief-stricken. I couldn't imagine anyone could have snatched you with Emre at your side, and no further information was shared beyond a declaration of war and—"

"What?" Aysa pulled back and turned to Dhamar. "War? Otac's declared war?"

"Yes." Dhamar sighed, scratching at his jaw which was tightly clenched. "I was waiting to pen my reply, hoping some more information might come to light." He smiled, gesturing to Aysa. "It turns out I was right."

Aysa chuckled, but I could see the weariness in her as she tugged the strap out of her hair and shook out the desert dust clinging to the dark tresses. "Who would want to set Taletha up for murder?"

Dhamar looked at Inara, a whole conversation passing between them. Then he turned to Aysa. "It's early, though I can tell the two of you are exhausted. I'll have a maid take you to the hot springs to bathe, Aysa. You too, Emre. We'll meet for a meal in our sitting room in a few hours, and then I'll explain it all."

Aysa nodded, easing closer to me again. "Thank you, Dhamar."

"Could a healer be sent with Aysa?" I dared to ask.

Dhamar's brows puckered.

"The wound she mentioned has stitches, and on our race here, there was no one to remove them."

Dhamar nodded. "I'll send for the palace healer. He's excellent."

"Thank you." I bowed, and Dhamar waved the formality aside.

"No need for that." His eyes flicked between Aysa and me. There was a perception there I didn't care for, and I stepped back to stand behind Aysa, as was befitting a guard. For that's what I was. Her guard. Not her friend, her lover, or her betrothed. I couldn't be. Wouldn't be. I needed to revert back to my position, no matter how much it hurt.

CHAPTER TWENTY-NINE

Aysa

A bath had never felt more welcome. After the healer had removed the stitches, I'd been stripped of my filthy disguise and sent to soak in pools of water warmed by the earth. The hot water, accompanied by a maid scrubbing the dirt from my scalp, had me feeling more human. She helped me into a clean, light blue kaftan and handed me a pale pink kerchief to bind back my wild curls.

"You look lovely, Princezo Aysa." The maid bowed, a smile stretching over her face as she took a final sweeping glance over my figure. "Would you like to rest before the noon meal?"

"May I?" The words were breathed out with a sigh of exhaustion, and the maid chuckled with a nod.

I followed behind the young woman—whose name was Hafza, Inara's personal lady's maid—as she glided down the hallway. Her yellow kaftan, though plain and unadorned, complemented her caramel-colored skin and her dancing dark brown eyes, which studied me as we moved toward my temporary lodgings.

"Are there any questions you have, Princezo?" Hafza asked at last, her hands folded before her. She moved with an understated grace, reminding me very much of Dilan. A pang of homesickness struck me, and I swallowed back the swirling emotions.

"No, I'd simply like to rest a bit." I forced a wobbly smile to my face.

Hafza nodded. "This is your room. Your guard's is across the hall. He should be back soon from his bathing."

I nodded, not trusting my voice.

Hafza reached out and squeezed my arm. "It's all right to feel overwhelmed. Inara's told me a bit about the trouble at the border. But you're safe here. Whatever happens, don't forget you have family and friends here in Taletha."

"Thank you." With a quick dip of my head—mostly to hide the traitorous tears sliding down my cheeks—I fled into my room.

Colored the orange that bathed the sands when the sun set, the bed was tucked into the wall on my left-hand side, gauzy curtains of yellow draping around it. A large, rug covered the off-white sandstone beneath my bare feet, and a square table settled on top of its swirling mosaic pattern. A heating pot and vanity were on the right. Ferns dotted the open spaces between two arching windows set with glass.

It was cozy, yet foreign. I closed my eyes as I leaned against the door, wanting to rest, but feeling out of place in the sprawling palace of Mordova. Dhamar was offering me sanctuary—attempting to protect me from whomever wanted to see me dead and set another war on our nations. But I had never felt more exposed.

A light rap on the door jerked me back to awareness.

"Who's there?" I asked, nearly afraid of the answer.

"Emre."

With an exhale of air, I eased the door open, leaning against its edge as if it were the only thing holding me up. It might have been.

Emre's gaze raked over me, uncomfortable in a pleasant way. One side of his mouth ticked up. "I see the maid helped you clean up."

"And the footman you." My eyes took in his still damp hair and his clean kurta and salwar in matching navy blue. The spicy scent of whatever soap he'd used filled the space between us.

I wanted to say more, to fill the silence, but pressure built in my chest and behind my eyes. I was fearful that if I spoke, I would cry.

"Are you all right?" Emre shifted, seeming as uncertain as myself.

No, I wasn't. I wanted to fall into his arms. Wanted to feel comfortable and secure in a world that was rapidly spinning out of my control. But instead, I shrugged, stepping back, and gesturing for him to enter.

"Aysa." He let the door swing shut with a click and braced against it. His chin was tucked to his chest, his shoulders taut with some emotion I couldn't identify.

Nicar above, I can't even name my own swirling feelings, and yet I'm trying to figure out his? I shook my head, unable to face my friend a moment longer. Striding across the room, I stood by the window, arms crossed. The clear glass distorted the images on the other side. Mordova's buildings and homes twisted and swirled with the imperfections in the pane. How like life that was—warped, unfair, unclear. How I wanted to smash my fist through all the expectations, through reality, and come back with my dreams in hand, triumphant.

"Aysa," Emre said again. His warm voice wrapped around me as his hands settled on my shoulders. "What's wrong?"

"I'm—" *In love. With you. I want you, but I can't have you.* The words lodged in my throat. Crossing my arms, I swayed toward him, my back brushing his chest. "I'm tired."

"Then lie down. I'll stand guard for you."

I wanted to curl up beside him, like we'd done in the tent mere days ago. But it was wrong to want, wrong to ask of him when I couldn't be his. With a sniff, I let his hand settle against my lower back as he guided me to the bed. He pulled the blanket over me, his gaze lingering on my face with a wrinkle of worry between his brows. It took all my strength to smile. "I'm fine, Emre."

He shook his head, sorrow of his own on his face as he whispered, "No, you're not. Stop lying to me, Aysa. I know you better than you think."

With a small smile, he sailed out of the door to do what he did best—guard me as I let my tears guide me into slumber.

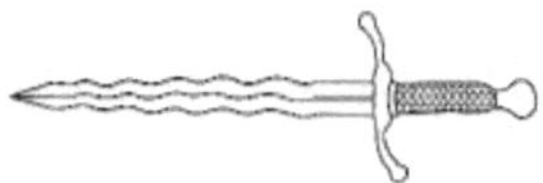

I woke far from refreshed. My cry had left a dull headache behind my eyes, and I rubbed at my temples now as Hafza guided Emre and myself to Dhamar and Inara's sitting room. Emre kept glancing at me, but I ignored him. I had to.

If you give in, you'll fall even farther. You want to marry him, but just think of what that will do to Dilan, to Otac and Majka, to Šeri. You can't be selfish.

But that logic only went so far when, with each beat of my heart, I felt it crack a little further.

We stopped at an open door between a deep red one and one painted sky blue. Two guards stood on either side, and I recognized them both.

"Good to see you again Zahir." I spun in a circle, managing a cheeky smile as the stoic guard raised a brow. "See? I'm still very much alive."

The other guard—Saif—let loose a guffaw that he attempted to cover with a cough. I winked at him and sailed through the door.

"Distracting my guards, I see." Dhamar smirked from his cushion at a round table. Steaming platters of shawarma, warm pita, and kofta sat before him, along with bowls of hummus, foul, and ice cold faloodeh.

My stomach growled, but the scent made me feel ill. What was wrong with me?

"Come, sit." Inara patted the cushion beside her with a smile, and my feet moved of their own accord. I sat beside her, Emre on my other side. He picked up my plate as Inara wrapped an arm around my shoulders in another sisterly embrace. "Are you doing all right?" she whispered against my hair, igniting another round of tears.

But these were tears of frustration. I was *fine,* and I was tired of being asked the same question over and over. I wanted to go out into the wilderness and scream. Holler at Nicar that it wasn't *fair*! My sisters could marry for love, fall for their shepherd boys, and raise families of tenderness and joy. My happiness was sitting beside me yet was completely out of my reach.

Pulling away from my cousin, I scowled down at the plate Emre sat in front of me, wanting to throw it across the room in my frustration.

Inara's gaze watched me, a concerned furrow to her brows, but she remained star-blessedly silent.

"So, who are your traitors?" Emre asked, popping a bite of kofta in his mouth as he eyed Dhamar.

My cousin wiped his fingers on a napkin and glared at the fabric. "Arqa and Shaeen. Formally on my council. They were more or less exiled from the palace and the upper city for their treachery against the malek and ameer."

"You let them go?" I scoffed a bitter laugh. "So that they could betray you further?"

Dhamar shrugged. "I wanted no more bloodshed to start my reign."

"Wise." Emre glanced at me before asking, "And what's your plan to stop them?"

"From my...sources, we know they're holed up in either a border town, or a tribe of Šeri who is loyal to them. They're getting help from somewhere, as the girl who was murdered was clearly Šerian."

"How so?" Emre asked, cupping his chin in his palm and drumming his fingers against it.

"She had a tattoo distinctive to your people's style." Dhamar gestured to his bicep. "A fox made of one unbroken swirling line."

My hand clutched my left bicep, where my seal was tattooed. My mark as a kćerka of the šefe. Dilan's was an eagle, Gulya's a wolf, Zlem's an owl. Each was unique to them, a blessing from Otac and Majka in our fifth year. The girl had one. No wonder Otac thought it was me.

I turned to Emre, my hands clutching the table's edge in my anger. I stared at his chest. If I met his gaze, I would dissolve into a weeping mess—something I wasn't used to. Vehemence lined my words as I whispered, "I want them to pay. In blood and pain, they should suffer for every form of abuse they inflicted on that innocent girl."

"And they shall." Dhamar leaned forward and pried my hand free from its strangled grip. "Trust Emre and me to see this through. This isn't a battle you have to face alone, Aysa. You helped me finish the last war, let me help you end this one."

Everything in me wanted to recoil, to stand up and face the traitors alone. I wasn't used relying on anyone—even Emre. But I nodded, trying to smile past the swirling anger inside.

Although, it wasn't just anger at the former lords of Mordova. It was anger at the eight leaders' sons that I had been paraded in front of, fury toward my otac and majka for making me do the stupid contest, even if it was just as out of their control as it was mine, and ire at myself for kissing the man at my side—a man I had no right to love and long for.

"Come, Aysa." Inara struggled to stand, and Dhamar leapt to his feet to help. She turned to me with a smile. "Walk with me in the garden."

Startled from my thoughts, I followed Inara out of the room without a murmur. She linked her arm with mine and guided me through the halls, the afternoon light warming the stones as we stepped through the doorway to the veranda. A screeching scream echoed over the stones, and

I jerked, my heartrate rising even as Inara laughed.

"It seems that the peacocks wish to welcome you."

"Peacocks?" I rested a hand over my thundering heart. "Sounded more like a wailing woman than a bird."

"I know." Inara laughed again. "They startled Dhamar so badly the first time they cried that he fairly fell out of bed. It took him, Zahir, and Saif most of the day to figure out what it was."

I chuckled, thankful for the distraction as I watched two of the male peacocks. They strutted forward, tails spread wide as an unsuspecting female pecked at some grain laid out in a low trough. They preened around her, trying to capture her notice and secure a mate. She appeared thoroughly unimpressed with either male, more concerned with her food than the attention.

"I feel like her." I nodded toward the birds as Inara lowered herself onto the fountain's edge.

"In what way?" Inara hugged her stomach and the child within.

"Men vying for my acknowledgement, my approval and praise. They want me but not the me I am." I bit the inside of my cheek with a sigh, gathering my thoughts. Inara remained silent. "I would be lying if I said I didn't enjoy it, somewhat. But the real side of me that I hide? She still feels worthless, despite all the flattery."

"That..." Inara hesitated.

"That what?" I probed.

"I understand that to a small degree. Men came to the Market, looked at me, some even praised my unusual features." She gestured to her blonde hair and light skin. "But just as many dismissed me and told me all my imperfections. It hurt."

"Men never point out my imperfections, Inara," I said.

"Do you let them see them?"

I flinched. No, I didn't. Emre accused me of that very thing. I hid deep inside anything that could be seen as weak or flaw. Because if people saw the real me, the person who was wild and bold and blunt, would they want me?

No, they wouldn't. The elders had made that point abundantly clear. I was headstrong and reckless. I didn't open my heart easily. I spoke my mind. None of that made me a perfect šefe for Šeri. So I hid myself away, under layers of surety and confidence, never allowing myself to be uncertain or confused. I had to make wise decisions and make them quickly. But even in that, I was called impulsive and rash. Not good enough.

Inara shook her head, bringing me back to the conversation. "Many of my defects are external. Blonde hair, pale skin, light colored eyes. To the men of Taletha, it was too glaring a fault to ignore yet Dhamar chose me. But then as husband and wife, he got to see the imperfections and wounds of my heart, the things easier to hide and wall up from those who wish to love us."

"The point?" I asked testily, some of the anger rising up once more.

Inara's eyebrows rose even as a smile twitched her lips. "The point is that no one is perfect. Not me, not you, not Dhamar, not Emre. Love is looking at the imperfections and seeing the beauty in them. An artist always sees the flaws in their work, and I think it's the same with people. The things we wish to change or remove from our lives are the very things that make us...well, us."

Inara fingered the hem of her gauze sash, her eyes distant. "I told Dhamar the ugliest parts of me—the things about myself I wanted gone. Doing that freed us to love one another wholly. We all have aspects of our character or history we wish we could change. We even try to smother it. But it made us who we are. To hide it is to hide a part of ourselves and not allow our husbands or family to love us completely."

"People don't like who I am," I whispered, shocked at how exhausting yet freeing it was to admit that truth to my cousin-in-law.

Silence reigned for a long moment before Inara asked, "Have you given them the chance to see you?"

I looked away, unable to withstand her probing gaze. My earlier thoughts of who I truly was assaulted me, along with memories that flashed like a lightning storm through my mind: Otac saying, "You're headstrong and wild, Aysa." Dilan's thoughtless words, "You keep your heart boxed up." Majka's comment of, "The council thinks you're too reckless, kćerka."

Wild and reckless and heartless. My chest tightened, and I buried my face in my hands, refusing to cry no matter how much the truth hurt. I had cried enough this week to last a lifetime. The real me I showed people pushed them away.

Everyone but Emre. He saw more of my reckless, headstrong ways than anyone and he still accepted me. Even called me out when I needed it. I loved it. I loved who I was when it was just Emre and me out on the dunes or at the oasis.

But it's not enough. It can't give me Otac's approval or Majka's praise. Can't give me sisters who love the wildness in me regardless of how it makes them look. What was it Inara had said? *Love is looking at the imperfections and seeing the beauty in them.*

Inara's hand landed lightly on my shoulder. "I'm sorry if my words were ill spoken. Are you all right?"

"No, but I will be." I sniffed, straightening from where I'd hunched over my legs and sighed. "Thank you, Inara."

"For what?" Surprise coated her words.

"For speaking truth." I pulled her into a hug, and she laughed before tightening her arms around me. "Thank you for being willing to do that."

Inara smiled as she leaned back, her hands clasping my shoulders. "Let me say one thing more—never be afraid to be yourself. You are fiery and brave. I love that about you, my sister."

Another tear slipped free, and I hissed, dashing it away as I lurched to my feet. "I want to see more of the garden."

Inara smiled as she linked her arm with mine once more. We slowly walked around the fountain.

"What else is bothering you?" Inara asked, not ready to let the matter drop. She leaned her head against my arm.

I growled, half-teasing, half-serious. "You mean besides the fact that the man I love is the one I can't have, and the nation I care about is about to go into another war? Nothing at all."

We stood before a small building in the corner. If one could call it a building. It had the frame of a house, but instead of walls, a sheer netting was stapled to the wooden frame. It created a small house structure with trees and flowers blooming within. Inara opened the door, and I followed after her.

Rather than answering my question, she said, "Dhamar showed me this during our wedding celebration. Here in Mordova, it lasts three days." Inara shivered, almost as if some part of those three days was infamously ingrained in her memory.

"What is it for?" I asked, glancing around. Then I noticed them. Dozens upon dozens of butterflies fluttered around the enclosure. Purples and blues, yellows and reds, every hue imaginable colored the tiny wings in a mosaic of moving shades. I spun in a slow circle, unable to close my mouth as I watched the butterflies dance around the space.

"They're so small, yet so bold." Inara's outstretched hand had a pretty little butterfly of black and blue perched on it. "I want to be more like them. They shed their skin and blossom into these little miracles."

"They're stunning."

Inara's blue-green gaze collided with mine, heated yet kind in its intensity. "And so are you. Shed the skin of expectation and step into the beauty and grace gifted to you by Nicar. You are brilliant Aysa. Live like it."

"I-I can't." I rubbed my arms, crossing them over my chest. "I have to marry one of the eight Otac chose. I can't—it's not—"

"That's an excuse. Something Saif told me years ago is that love is sacrifice. If you love Emre, you'll fight for it. It may mean letting something go. But I promise you, Aysa, if Nicar asks you to let go, something better will take its place."

I turned away. My heart stirred at her words.

What if… I swallowed, watching the tiny insects flutter about in near silence. They mirrored the swirls of anticipation in my stomach as I finally let the question that my family had tried to ask me for weeks break through the barrier I'd erected around my heart. *What if you chose heart over head? Desire over duty? Emre over Šeri?*

CHAPTER THIRTY

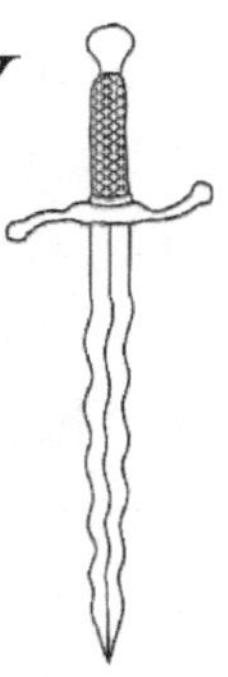

Emre

The door clicked shut as Inara and Aysa left. My index finger tapped the edge of my goblet as Dhamar turned toward me. "What was that about?"

I raised a brow.

"Aysa seemed..." Dhamar turned his hand in the air, trying to choose the right word. "She seemed withdrawn. Angry."

"That's likely because she is." Trying to not feel the same frustration at our situation, I sighed and took a sip of my drink. "She's been ordered by her otac to marry."

Dhamar's brows shot up below his hair. "He picked the man? I didn't take Dayi Aydin to be so...authoritarian."

"He's not. He chose eight sons from the tribal leaders of Šeri. Aysa gets to choose the one she wishes to wed."

Dhamar nodded slowly, watching me like a lion stalking its prey. He said nothing for a long moment, his dark brown eyes far too perceptive. I was not prone to squirming, but the sudden urge to fidget overtook me.

With a smirk to rival Aysa's, Dhamar said, "You care for her, don't you?"

"She's my charge to guard," I choked out. "Of course, I care."

"No, that would be the look that Saif and Zahir give to my wife." Dhamar crossed his arms and leaned them on the table. "You *love* Aysa.

You have a look that I see in Saif's eyes when he looks at his wife, or the one I undoubtedly give Inara daily."

Panic clawed at my throat, and I could only shake my head in denial of the truth. I closed my eyes, willing away Dhamar, the room, the stomach curdling scent of spices and meats.

"I can't love her," I whispered, anger infused in the words. "I am her guard. She's the future šefe of Šeri! To love her means one of us will lose."

"Lose?" Dhamar shook his head again. "I'm afraid I don't under-stand."

I glared at him. "No, you don't. Aysa wants to be the ambassador to Taletha. The council sees her as unfit and unprotected here unless she's wed. She either has to marry one of the eight leaders' sons or give up her dream of being the ambassador."

Dhamar snorts. "That's ludicrous."

"Ludicrous or not, it's what she has to do. I can't fit into those dreams, and I won't ask her to give it up. Not for me."

"Do you love her, Emre?" Dhamar asked.

"Yes." I met Dhamar's gaze. "And that often means letting go. I learned that lesson long ago."

Dhamar's looked over my shoulder, and I turned to see Inara standing there.

"The baby?" Dhamar leapt to his wife's side, his hand landing over her rounded stomach.

She smiled up at him, complete adoration pouring from her gaze. "The baby is fine. But, Emre, Aysa would like to speak to you in the garden. Saif will show you the way."

I nodded, pushing to my feet to bow toward the malek and rania before following the guard to a small portico. The sky was perfectly blue, not a cloud to be seen as the light reflected off the white stone wall around the sprawling courtyard. The air was tinged with the scent of eucalyptus and jasmine, the bubbling fountain joining the song of the breeze through the sycamore trees that lined the wall.

Aysa sat on the fountain's edge, worrying the inside of her cheek as she rubbed her chest—the place her golden coin necklace had hung. In her blue kaftan and pink headscarf, she glowed in the afternoon light, more lovely than the desert roses and blood lilies that bloomed around her. I could have stared at her for hours, but she turned and met my gaze with a hesitant smile.

"Hello," she said, gesturing me forward.

Trepidation settled in my stomach. What did she want to talk about? She'd been upset during the meal. Was that anger going to be directed at me now?

I sat beside her, trying to hold my twitching fingers still. Aysa smiled. I attempted to return it but was certain it looked more like a grimace.

"Don't look so concerned." Aysa bumped her shoulder into mine, filling my senses with her earthy, orangey scent. "I just wanted to talk to you."

"About?"

Aysa leaned back, dropping her gaze to her lap. "Inara and I talked."

I waited, letting her order her thoughts, find the words. Unable to hold still, my fingers tapped against my thigh, a manic staccato that matched the thundering of my heart.

Her voice dropped to a whisper. "I love you, Emre. And I—I want to marry you."

The thundering of my heart stopped, and I'm fairly certain I forgot how to breathe. Aysa looked up, tears gathering on the edges of her eyes. She reached out and hesitantly clasped my hand in her own. "Majka told me that, if I saw something I couldn't live without, I should latch onto it and not let it go. Well, this is me, latching on. Will you...will you have me?"

Aysa loved me. *Me*. She wanted to marry me. But—

"Your dreams," I rasped out, my heart screaming at me to accept this offering. "I can't ask you to—"

"You're not." Aysa stood, turning to stand in front of me. With me seated on the fountain's edge, she stood a few inches taller. Her hands settled on my shoulders and my eyes flicked to her lips of their own accord. "Emre, you never pushed. Never asked for me to choose you. This is my choice. Majka, Dilan, Gulya. They all wanted me to pick you."

"Zlem wanted me to tell you." I dared to reach up and run a lock of Aysa's hair through my fingers. "But I couldn't."

"You're too good for me, Emre." Her chin trembled, and a tear fell free. I could count on one hand the number of times I'd witnessed Aysa cry, and in the last five days I'd seen it twice.

"Don't cry, my princezo." I cupped her chin, wiping at her cheek with the pad of my thumb.

"I—" She stepped back, still clasping my hand and tugged me to standing. Shaking her head, she slipped her arms around my waist. Aysa had hugged me before, but never with the admittance of love on her lips. She trembled as I wrapped my arms around her. "Marry me, Emre."

"Aysa, you want to be the ambassador. And what if the tribal leaders don't let you be the šefe because you chose to marry me? I won't let you give that up."

"Love is sacrifice," she whispered, tightening her hold on me. "And while I love Šeri, I've been...struggling with the thought of giving up what I truly love for the sake of leading. It will be hard to let go, but this?" She eased back enough to look me in my face. "I can't live without you, Emre." Then, with barely a warning, she pulled my face down to hers, pressing her lips to mine.

My hands moved to her waist, drawing her closer. She began to pull back, but I cupped her cheek, leaning in and returning her kiss with the desperation of a man who was drowning. For I was. I was sinking in my love for Aysa, and her kiss was the air I needed to breathe. All the while, my mind screamed that I shouldn't. I shouldn't let her sacrifice her dreams for me—a wandering soldier of Šeri who couldn't offer her a family or a home.

I broke the kiss, chest heaving as I leaned my forehead against hers. "You want to marry me."

She smiled at my bewildered statement. "Yes. If you want me."

"Nicar above, yes." I chuckled. "But are you certain? Do you want to pledge the sacred vow to a man with no home, no family, no tribe? I can't offer you anything while you're giving me everything. That's not fair."

"You're giving me the very best thing, Emre." She threaded her arms around my neck, her nose brushing mine when she whispered, "You're giving me you."

Restraint gone, I kissed her, getting lost in the woman I'd loved for years, yet hadn't let myself long for. Her arms tightened, pulling our bodies closer to each other as she deepened our kiss.

A cheer had us breaking away and turning to the portico. Inara and Dhamar leaned against the railing, grins on their faces that were brighter than the sun reflecting against the sand. Inara clapped again, laughing as she said, "I think we have a wedding to prepare for!"

Aysa's fingers threaded with mine, and she leaned up against me. "Would it be too rushed to do it tonight?"

"Tonight?" I asked, looking down at her.

"I don't want anyone or anything to tear us apart." Her grip tightened, and she leaned her head against my shoulder. "And now that you're mine, I don't want to be away from you."

I glanced over at Dhamar, who was looking at Inara, who was beaming at Aysa.

"Yes!" The rania nodded, bouncing as much as her expectant state allowed. "Oh, Aysa, I get to help you prepare for your wedding!"

Aysa laughed, the sound real and crisp and clear. She hadn't laughed like that since the contest started.

I glanced at Dhamar and said, "Although this may start the very war we're trying to avoid."

"If this becomes the catalyst, then there was no hope of maintaining the peace to begin with." Dhamar chuckled, his arm wrapped around Inara's waist.

The raina jabbed her husband in the ribs. "Now, none of that talk! Aysa's family will be happy she found love."

I hoped Inara was right. My chest tightened at the thought of disappointing the šefe. Of losing his respect. But a glance at Aysa's glowing eyes and blushing cheeks and I knew—I knew I'd choose her over and over again because she was worth it all.

Inara beamed down at us again. "It's time to get the bride ready!"

Aysa threw her arms around my neck again with a sigh. "I'll see you in a few hours, my love," she whispered before she pressed a small kiss against my jaw. A shiver raced down my spine.

"I love you," I whispered, pulling her back into a hug before she could escape. "Thank you for choosing us."

"Always. From this day on until forever." She giggled, appearing happier than she had in months. With a smile, she practically danced up to the portico and linked arms with Inara. In a flurry of laughter and silk, they moved back into the hall.

Dhamar leaned his elbows against the railing and smirked. "Apparently, you do fit into her dreams."

I tried to glare, but a smile slipped free as Dhamar laughed.

"Come!" He gestured for me to follow him. "It's time to prepare for a wedding!"

CHAPTER THIRTY-ONE

Aysa

Inara was huffing by the time we reached the hall for the bathing pools. Hafza kept glancing at her with a worried expression pinching her mouth into a frown.

"Are you certain you should be walking this far, my rania?" Hafza asked.

"I'm certain. Quit fretting, Hafza." Inara smiled over her shoulder, her hands pressed against her bulging stomach. "Honestly, the amount of hovering over me is positively stifling."

I chuckled. "You are with child, Inara."

"And the healers and midwives all say I'm in perfect health." Inara's hand slid down to cradle the lower part of her stomach as she walked beside me. "Now, tell me. What made you finally decide to choose Emre?"

"I..." Heat flooded my cheeks. There was a plethora of reasons, but some sounded so selfish and childish. I thought of how Emre had stood by me through the entire contest. He'd protected my virtue and honor, strove to find me the very best man he could that *wasn't* him. He truly was selfless, and that selflessness showed me more than all the gallant words and deeds in the world that he loved me.

I turned to Inara and bit the inside of my cheek. "I love him very much. It's just hard to put it into words. He's been...so good to me through this whole ordeal. He's fought for me, for the right to find a man worthy of my love, and all the while, he loved me. He cared, and he put aside his desires to help me get what I wanted. He's protected me, body and soul."

"What made him change his mind?" Hafza asked as we stepped to the steaming bathing chamber.

"I chose him." I shrugged, warmth pooling in my chest at that thought.

Inara lowered herself beside the middle pool. She trailed her fingers through the warm water as she watched me with the slightest tilt to her head.

"And what made you do that?" Hafza asked

I fiddled with a button on my kaftan. "Inara did."

Inara's brow rose. "Me?"

"Yes. You challenged me to be myself, and it made me realize that Emre is much the same. He doesn't expect perfection."

"No one should expect that, Aysa." Inara's face held all the tender softness of someone who knew the pressure of perfectionism. She'd been for sale at the Wife Market here in Taletha for years before being bought and wed to Dhamar. She understood far better than most. "And if Emre is the one that sees all the imperfections and struggles, the sorrows and pain, and he stays? He is worthy of you, my sister." Inara struggled to her feet and wrapped me in her arms.

A tear—one lone, hot drop—scalded its way down my cheek. Inara's hug tightened, feeling so comforting but in a different way than Emre or even Majka. Inara's hug was one of understanding, seasoned with a strength earned from trial that she was willing to share with others. A sob caught in my throat, and I choked it back.

Leaning away from Inara, I brushed the tear away and forced a smile. "I think it's time for me to get ready for a wedding."

Inara smiled. "Yes, and I have just the kaftan for you."

"We'll have you looking like an amira," Hafza vowed.

I shook my head. "No, not an amira. A bride." *One worthy of the man who's stood by my side through it all.*

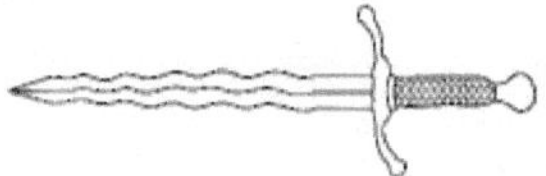

I blinked at my reflection, not believing the sight.

Inara helped to button the millions of tiny white pearl buttons along the back of the golden-colored kaftan while Hafza began to brush luminescent power to my cheeks and eyes. She highlighted my eyes with a kohl stick, brushed a pink balm to my lips, and deftly braided the sides of my short, curly hair before attaching a sparkling diamond maang teeka into the tresses.

"Do you have...?" I bit my cheek and shook my head. They wouldn't have a pair of nimets, surely. It was an old Šerian custom that wouldn't be practiced here in Taletha.

"Do we have what?" Inara asked, pushing against the small of her back before waddling over to sit on the edge of her bed. The clean white of her bedclothes and the whitewashed walls were dazzling but comfortable. Though, they were vastly different from the tents and sands of Šeri. Another pang of homesickness hit me. I longed for my desert, the wide expanses and endless sky. I wished for my majka and sisters to be here, helping me get ready for my marriage. For Otac to place my hand in Emre's with his blessing. But if I couldn't have them, I was thankful for

Inara at my side—my sister in all but blood.

A knock sounded on the door before I could reply, and my Teyze Lenna glided in. She looked happier than the last time I'd seen her. She'd visited Šeri for a few months, but when Inara had announced her pregnancy, my teyze had hurried home to be with her.

Now, Teyze Lenna clutched a small ebony box in her hand, glancing first at Inara before smiling down at me. "How is everyone?"

"Nervous," I admitted, surprising myself. "And excited."

"All normal feelings, I assure you." Lenna smiled and held the box out to me. "I found this in the vault. Dhamar said I could give it to you as a wedding present."

I lifted the lid and pressed my fingers to my lips as I gasped. Nestled inside the box on a bed of red velvet was a pair of large, jewel-encrusted earrings. A bride in Šeri wore no jewelry on her wedding day beyond the maang teeka and nimet earrings. The earrings were special as they were picked by the bride's parents specifically for her in the days after her engagement. Each day leading up to the wedding, her parents would pray blessings over the adornments—for her marriage, her husband, herself. For love and happiness and peace to fill her home and her heart. I knew it was a strictly Šerian custom, so the fact that my teyze not only remembered but had thought to gift me a pair brought tears to my eyes.

"Thank you." I traced the tear-drop shaped diamonds that fanned out into what almost looked like a peacock tail. "These will look stunning with my kaftan."

"May I?" Teyze Lenna took the box and slid the earrings into my ears. One had an intricate, swirling cuff with a chain that curled around the top of my ear. "I pray that Nicar would bless and keep Emre and you. May the sun rise each day on new love between you and your koca. May joy ever be among you. I pray you are blessed with many children. Children who will grow due to your cherishing and love. May your tribe be one of peace and prosperity. Through all the trials and tribulations that will come, I pray that you will choose each other over and over again. May a long and sweet union thrive between you and Emre. I pray this all and more as I gift you the nimet."

"Amen." I whisper, smiling even as tears misted my vision. Turning, I looked into the mirror once more. I was ready. I was a bride.

My hands trembled as I stood, smoothing out my skirt. I turned toward my teyze and squeezed her hands. "Will you walk with me?"

"Of course." My teyze cupped my cheek with her hand. "You are a beautiful bride, my Aysa. Your father will be so proud of you."

My stomach knotted. No, he wouldn't be proud. He was likely going to be furious. I was breaking his trust, not following the orders of the tribal leaders for the first time in my life. I pressed a hand to my stomach. The fabric of the kaftan pulled tight against my hips and chest, making it hard to breathe.

Teyze Lenna gripped my shoulders. "Stop it right now! He will be proud of you, dearest, because you are going after the one you love. He loves your majka very much. I know he wants you to find love as well."

"But at the cost of Šeri? Of my peoples' welfare?"

"And what about your welfare? Your happiness?" Inara asked as she stood and walked over to us. Her hand clasped around my bicep, her eyes insistent as she whispered, "You are worth more to your otac than anything. Do you remember when Dhamar and I went before your father? When Šeri was at war with Taletha?"

"It would be a little hard to forget that." I chuckled weakly, still feeling nauseous and dizzy.

"We were all terrified," Inara continued. "And you asked me how much you trust a father's love. Well, you can trust it completely. You swore on the sun, moon, and all the stars to protect Dhamar and me. Your otac didn't kill us. That wasn't because of our flowery words, Aysa. He did it to keep you safe."

Tears pressed in the corners of my eyes. I hated them. Hated the weakness they made me feel. I brushed away the moisture with my knuckle, trying to not ruin the makeup that Hafza had done. "But—"

"No!" Inara shook her head. "No *buts*. You told Emre you loved him. That you were choosing him over Šeri. Is he the one your heart longs for?"

I smiled through the moisture in my eyes. "He is."

"Then embrace it." Inara squeezed my arm. "Love him. Build a family with him."

A knock sounded on the door before Dhamar poked his head in. "Emre is waiting." He blinked at me, his eyes sweeping over my kaftan and hair before he smiled. "You're going to take his breath away. I can see how you stole his heart."

A blush climbed into my cheeks, and I chuckled. "Thank you, Cousin."

Dhamar inclined his head and held out his hand for his wife. "We'll be waiting!"

The door clicked closed behind them, and I sucked in a sharp breath.

"Are you ready, my dear?" Lenna held out her arm and I wrapped my hand around it.

"I think I am."

The walk from the room to the small temple within the palace walls felt like an eternity. Teyze Lenna kept a steady pace, and I glided at her side, my palms sweaty as we moved toward my future, my love. My heart thundered, my ears buzzed, and I prayed to Nicar that this was the right choice.

I lowered my head when we reached the temple doors. The scalloped edge was painted a golden orange, the sunset brightening its hue. They groaned as they opened, but I couldn't move, couldn't breathe.

Love is sacrifice.

Lenna began to walk forward, and I followed, chin to my chest as we walked toward the front. Toward Dhamar and Inara, Hafza, Zahir and

Saif. Toward Emre.

A sudden anxiousness settled in my gut. I loved Emre, but was he the best choice? What if my love was clouding my logic? I pictured all eight of the men I had been told to choose. Efe, Derin, Ömer. Naz, Berk, Kerim. Kagan and Ulvi. Each had strengths and weaknesses. Each would bring assets to Šeri that we desperately needed. But none of them strengthened *me*. Supported me and loved me. Perhaps I had been looking at love the wrong way. Did it truly matter how they would help my country if they didn't build me up?

Love made a person stronger. Braver. Bolder. Love bonded together. Love rose up. Love was selfless, yes, and strove for the good of the one loved. And when I thought of all those attributes, they all pointed me to one man.

I raised my gaze and met Emre's. Worry furrowed his forehead, but when I smiled, his face relaxed. Energy coursed through me and the desire to sprint to his side had me quickening my step.

Teyze Lenna chuckled. "I suppose you've stopped trying to logic yourself out of this then, hm?"

"Yes," I breathed out on a sigh as we neared the spot in the private temple that was tiled with a blazing sun. Cushions rested all around it, and our witnesses all sat upon them.

Lenna stepped up to Emre and placed my hand in his before wrapping hers around them. She looked first at me then my betrothed before saying, "Treasure each other. Seek the good in every challenge. Love each other no matter the faults that lay between you." Her throat bobbed. "In all things, work together. You are stronger as a pair than on your own. Never try to be perfect but embrace the beauty of flaws and failure."

Patting our clasped hands, Lenna pressed a kiss to my cheek. Then she turned and sat beside her son. My lower lip trembled as I looked up at Emre. He was staring at me with a mixture of love and fear in his eyes—brown eyes that contained flecks of gold I had never noticed. I swayed closer, and he tightened his hold on my hands as the priest waved incense around.

He guided us through the traditional Talethan vows. We pricked our fingers, and the priest directed us on how to do the markings. It was strange, as Šeri didn't have such customs.

I knew we wouldn't be able to do our one sacred custom. Neither of us were prepared for a wedding. I prayed to Nicar that Dhamar hadn't tried to foist one of his jewels onto Emre. That would have defeated the tradition. It was supposed to be crafted by the groom's hands or passed down to him from his family. Emre had no family. I was all right with that. I had the love of my life, and that was all that mattered.

"Now, Emre, ogul of Tarkan, has something he'd like to say." The priest's monotone voice broke through my thoughts.

I blinked as Emre drew something out of his pocket and held it before him in his palm. He stared at it, his throat bobbing before he said, "I have held onto this for years. My otac gave it to me before I left for Tribe Ender to train as a warrior. I wore it on a chain around my neck, told no one, and treasured it because it reminded me of the one woman who ever loved me enough to tell me. My mother."

He dragged his eyes up to mine, the sheen of them betraying the depth of his emotions. "Aysa, kćerka of Aydin, *you* are my new treasure." He held up a sparkling ring. A dark orange sapphire sat in the center, surrounded by a circle of tiny emeralds. "With this ring, I vow that you will always have my heart, my love, my protection. By the sun and stars, my love for you will burn for all eternity. I love you."

A reverent silence hung around us, and for once I ignored the tears trailing down my cheeks as Emre slid the ring onto my fingers and pulled me closer.

The priest smiled and said, "In the sight of these witnesses, they are bound by the vows they have spoken. By the word of our law, they are one. Tonight, they shall be bound by flesh. What is joined this day, let no man break. Emre, you may now seal this vow."

Emre grinned, a lightness in his countenance that hadn't been there before as he leaned in and kissed me. His arms twined around my waist and pulled me to him as our few friends and family clapped and cheered. Breaking our kiss, I laughed and hugged him tightly.

As in the garden, being in his arms felt so right, like coming home after a long journey. Or sitting by a warm fire in the chill of winter. I loved his kisses, and I knew there would be more tonight. I was his wife, after all. But for that moment, all I needed was his arms, his embrace. It was more than enough for me.

The feasting wasn't a large party. In fact, it was the same friends and family that had been witnesses at our ceremony. Saif's wife, Ranya, had been invited by Inara. She was a sweet woman with a rambunctious one-year-old who kept slipping barazek from the table when no one was looking. I was fairly certain Emre might have been helping him in his escapades, though I couldn't prove it.

Inara hugged me tightly, her smile genuine as she said, "Enjoy tonight. You've picked a good man who will treat you like the jewel you are."

I smiled, pulling her in for yet another embrace. "I will, Inara. You enjoy your koca, too."

"Perhaps in a few more weeks when this" —she patted her belly with a grin— "is a wailing infant."

I tipped my head back and laughed. Inara was much more comfortable than she had been in Šeri months ago. Her whole bearing was more regal, more poised, more confident in who she was. I looked over at my cousin, who was talking with Emre and Zahir, and smiled. His love was the reason for the change, subtle though it may be.

Would Emre change me? Most likely. My prayer to Nicar was that the changes would grow us to be better—better leaders, better spouses, better people. I pressed a hand to my chest, overwhelmed and a touch dizzy from the tight dress.

"Let's be off." Inara nudged me toward the men, linking her arm with mine as we glided across their common room toward Dhamar and Emre's sides. She exchanged my arm for Dhamar's as she leaned her head against his shoulder. "I'm getting rather tired, my love."

Dhamar wrapped his arm around Inara's shoulders and pressed a kiss to her temple. "Is that the signal for me to remove everyone from our rooms?"

Inara giggled, her cheeks growing pink. "Perhaps."

Dhamar turned to me. "Congratulations, cousin. I pray your marriage will be a happy one."

"Thank you, Dhamar." Feeling impulsive, I hugged him. I was surprised when he returned it. "And thank you for all you've done for us."

"Yes, thank you." Emre bowed. "For everything."

Dhamar nodded, something unspoken passing between them.

My husband curled his arm around my waist. "Time for us to make our exit."

I grinned, giddiness making me fidget with the beads on my kaftan as we walked out the door and toward our rooms.

My teeth gnawed on my cheek, the poor skin raw from all my nerves today. My eyes flicked up to Emre as he guided me into his room and shut the door. The colors were different from mine. The bed stood between two round windows. A light blue and yellow patterned blanket and matching tapestry pillows lay across it. Gauzy curtains were draped around the bed to ward off insects. A small table sat in the corner beside the door, a heating pot to the left. Along the right wall stood a wardrobe and vanity. It was cozy and comfortable, but it did nothing to calm my stomach that was riddled with anxious excitement.

"How are you?" Emre asked, stepping closer. His hands settled on my waist as I reached up and pulled the maang teeka off my forehead. The air of the room brushed against the hot skin underneath, cooling it as I swayed closer to my husband.

"I'm tired," I admitted, smiling up at him. "But not too tired to be with you."

"Good." He smiled.

Nicar above, did I ever want to kiss him. I leaned my forehead against his shoulder, breathing him in. He smelled good, like cinnamon and sunshine. Longing welled up in me to be closer to him, to kiss him senselessly, to get lost in his love. But a thought had been bothering me all through our meal, and I eased back.

"You didn't swear by the moon," I stated.

"Hm?" He dragged his eyes away from my lips.

"During your vow, you didn't swear by the moon."

"No, I didn't." He reached up and began to unweave the braids holding my hair back from my face. His fingers buried into the locks, massaging my scalp, and sending shivers down my spine. "The sun shines during the day, yes?" When I nodded, he continued, "It's bright, beautiful, and warm. I want our love for each other to be that way, too."

I smiled as he reached around me to pick up a comb that sat on the vanity, his chest brushing against mine as he invaded my space. The spicy scent of cinnamon filled my nose again, and I barely refrained from pressing my face against his chest once more.

"And the stars?" I asked. I gasped as he turned and nuzzled his nose against my neck. He'd never held me like this. Barely touched me at all until now. But with our vows to cherish and love one another, we were bound until death claimed us. He was mine, and I was his. I smiled at that thought as I wrapped my arms around his neck.

"The stars," he breathed as the comb he hadn't used *thunked* back onto the vanity. "They are vast and many. So many that it would take an eternity to count them all. *That's* how long my love for you will last. Forever unto eternity."

I leaned back, forcing him to straighten. My fingers trailed down the front of his kurta, pausing to fiddle with a button near the middle. "And why not the moon, Emre?"

"It waxes and wanes. It's a cold light, too." Emre's brows puckered as he stared down at me. "Never do I want to fade from you. I want us to blaze and burn and multiply. I want people to look at us—and someday our family—and know that we are forever."

"Forever," I repeated, shivering as he ducked his head and let his nose brush my forehead. Tipping my head up, I pressed my lips to his as my hands slid back up his chest, around his neck, and buried into his hair.

Emre deepened the kiss, his lips almost desperate as they moved over mine. Fire blazed in my chest, stronger than any I'd ever felt. I wanted Emre. His highs, his lows, and everything in between. He was my best friend, and now I longed for him to be my partner, my lover, my husband in every form of the word.

My kisses moved from his mouth to his cheek and down his neck. A groan rumbled in his throat as his hands moved up and down my sides. My fingers found the top buttons on his kurta and undid them.

"Wait." His voice sounded strangled, and he took a step back.

"What?" My voice was husky, and I felt a bit disoriented, riding the high that was kissing Emre.

"If we're doing this..." he hesitated. "If we're going to be koca and kari,

I don't want either of us to regret it. You chose me, Aysa, but do you *want* me?"

"Of course!" I cupped his cheek when he dropped his gaze. "I married you, Emre."

"You did." His throat bobbed, but he still wouldn't meet my gaze.

Biting the inside of my cheek, I stepped fully out of his embrace. "Are you doubting me? My love?"

"No." He still didn't raise his head. "But I don't want you to regret this. You chose me over Šeri. Over our nation that you love fiercely."

Did that bother him? Right now, I didn't regret choosing Emre. Yet his posture said he worried I would. I clasped his hand in mine. "I could still be the šefe. We don't know what the tribal leaders will decide, Emre. Will that be a burden for you? Being married to the šefe of Šeri?"

His head snapped up, his eyes burning with desire as he growled, "Never. I want you." He eased closer, tightening his hold on my hand. "Whether you're šefe or slave, I love you for who you are inside. That daring woman who charges into danger, who faces challenges coolly and calmly. I told you during the contest that you're fierce and brave, wild and free. That's what I love. Your courage and strength are beautiful, not revolting. And I'll keep reminding you of that, no matter how long it takes for you to believe it."

Tears pricked my eyes, and I looked away. Emre had seen me cry far too much in the last week. I still didn't want to admit my weakness—my own imperfections.

When no words spilled forth in the gathering silence, Emre asked, "What are you thinking?"

I glanced at him, at his dark brown eyes and black-brown hair gleaming in the lantern light. His brows were furrowed, his lips plump from our kiss. He was a stunningly handsome man. But I saw more than that when I looked at Emre. I saw his willingness to fling himself in front of a desert wolf and assassin, his care that had him riding out into the wilderness with eight infuriating men, his tenderness as I cried on his shoulder. I heard his encouraging words, his advice, and yes, even his reprimands. The man before me was one I didn't deserve, and yet the one Nicar—in her infinite wisdom—knew I needed.

"Aysa? What are you thinking?"

"I'm trying to think of a way to prove to you that I do want you, Emre."

He blinked twice before pulling me to his chest. "By action, by word, by love."

"But how—?"

He pressed his finger to my lips, making them tingle before Emre's calloused fingers traced over to my cheek. Then, he kissed my forehead, exhaling wearily through his nose.

"Stop thinking, Aysa. Feel. What do you feel?"

My logic. It was muddying all of my choices. I'd thought I'd known my feelings when I'd spoken with him that morning. But it didn't work. You couldn't reason yourself out of love; and you also couldn't logically fall in love with someone either—both of which I'd attempted. Love didn't always make sense. Perhaps that was what made it so wonderful. It wasn't perfect, it wasn't without fault or failure, and yet it was one of the most beautiful things in all of creation.

I tipped my head back and met Emre's gaze. Pushing away all my worries, all my need for perfection, for that one solitary moment, I let myself *feel* what I had long denied myself.

"I feel as if I'm falling, Emre," I stated. "I'm falling into a world I don't know what to do with. I'm being tossed to and fro by winds, and I'm terrified because I don't know what to do. But" —a lone tear rolled out of my eye —"I have you. And I know that this fall will end well if you're there to catch me. You anchor me in the storms of life." My lip quivered, and I let it. "I love you and want you to kiss me."

Emre's eyes flicked between mine. "Truly?"

I laughed, a few more tears slipping free. "You asked me to feel and *that* is what I—"

His lips crushed mine as his arms pulled me to his chest. The kiss was frantic at first, but after a few minutes it slowed, searching and full of desire and hope. As he kissed me, Emre guided me toward the bed, sitting and pulling me to stand between his legs. His fingers on one hand played with the buttons on the back of my kaftan while his other hand cradled my hip. Still, he kissed me. And all the while, I let myself feel. Ignoring the logic, refusing to think about anything except Emre and my love for him. Because this was beautiful. This was our moment. And as we stumbled through our wedding night, I knew. With Emre by my side, life would never be the same.

Chapter Thirty-Two

Emre

I woke slowly, warm contentment settling over me as I blinked my beautiful wife into focus. Her hair was curled in wild disarray around her face, her breathing slow and measured as she continued sleeping. Her arm was curled about my waist, her head against my shoulder. I tugged her closer, breathing in the scent of oranges and earth that was my Aysa.

Nicar above, I don't deserve you. I pressed a kiss to her forehead with a sigh. *But thank the goddess that I have you.*

My eyes closed, and I let myself slip back into that blissful almost slumber.

What felt like mere seconds later, Aysa jerked awake, rubbing her eyes as she sat up. She looked around the room. Then her gaze landed on me. Her brows furrowed a moment before a saucy smile bloomed on her face. "Good morning, my koca."

I chuckled, pulling her back down beside me in bed. "Good morning, kari."

"You're the best thing to wake up to," she declared, pressing a kiss to my lips.

"I know." I laughed as she smacked my shoulder. Wrapping her in my arms, I kissed her again, killing any fight she had.

She deepened the kiss, burying her fingers into my hair with a sigh, right as a knock sounded on the door.

Aysa groaned as I rolled over and quickly threw on my salwar from yesterday. Crossing her arm and pouting, she muttered, "Let's pretend we're still asleep."

Before I could respond, the knocking came again, and I raised a brow at her. She huffed and flopped back onto the pillows, tugging the blanket up to her chin.

I opened the door enough to stick my head out. Saif stood there, rubbing the back of his neck with an embarrassed expression on his face. "Malek Dhamar wishes to speak to both of you over breakfast in his room. He said he wouldn't disturb you if it wasn't completely necessary."

My hand not clutching the door handle tapped nervously against the trim. "Is something wrong?"

Saif opened and closed his mouth twice before he sighed. "It's best for you to speak to the malek and rania. It's not my place to say anything."

"Of course." I nodded once and then shut the door.

Aysa sat up, her brows furrowed again. The sheet was still clutched under her chin, and I could tell she was worrying the inside of her cheek with her teeth. "It has something to do with Šeri, I know it."

"No matter what it's about, we will face it together." I settled back into bed and pulled her into my arms. Aysa sighed and slumped against my shoulder. Inadequacy slammed into me like a charging rhinoceros. What if I wasn't enough for her to lean on, not strong enough to support this brilliant woman beside me? Would someone else have been better for her? I vowed to love and cherish, but what if that wasn't all Aysa needed? Not allowing myself time to filter the words, I asked, "Will that be enough for you, my princezo?"

"Facing it together?" She sat up, her eyes filled with hurt. "Of course, Emre. You're my koca. Whatever the challenge, we're stronger together, and we will overcome it as a team."

"You don't feel as if..." I swore under my breath and tore my fingers through my hair. Clutching a fistful, I tugged slightly, focusing on that pinpoint of pain rather than the upset expression on my wife's face. "I feel as if I'm unworthy of you. You had sons of leaders to pick from, yet you got burdened with me."

"Burdened with—?" She scoffed, cutting off the end of her question. She cupped my cheek and forced my gaze to meet hers as she whispered, "I want you, Emre. I chose you to love for the rest of my life. None of those other men came close to the magnificence that is *my koca.*"

I smiled, feeling weary to my very bones. But as Aysa leaned in and claimed my lips yet again, I found that I was grateful for her love, for her laughter, for her support. Perhaps I wasn't good enough for her, but I was going to spend the rest of my life showing her how very much I loved and admired her. For better or for worse.

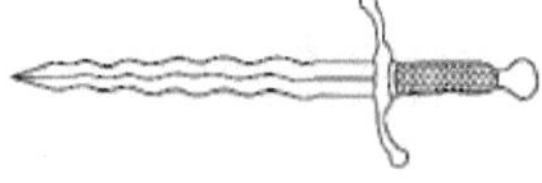

My fingers drummed against Aysa's hand on my arm as I guided her toward Dhamar and Inara's common room. She kept glancing at me out of the corner of her eye, a humorous smile twitching her lips.

"Please relax." She halted me a few feet from the malek and rania's door, tugging me closer as she wrapped her arms around my waist. "I swear you're more fidgety than Ranya and Saif's little one was last night."

"I'm...concerned." I cleared my throat, unable to meet her probing gaze.

"Logically, it's likely about the war brewing at the border. Our marriage can't be known yet." Aysa's gaze dropped to my chest.

"I'm not certain I'm wise enough to deal with such a threat. The traitors killed a woman to enact revenge on Dhamar. What will they do once they realize you're alive? That doesn't include the rage of the tribal leaders. Nicar alone knows what they'll do once they realize that your otac did not sanction our marriage." My throat hurt as I swallowed, my hands trembling against Aysa's back.

"I choose you." There was such vehemence in her words that I stepped back, out of her embrace. I wasn't certain what to do with such devotion. I tried to turn away, but Aysa clutched a fist full of my kurta and drew me closer, her gray eyes blazing. "Flames take what they think. I love you, Emre. I love our marriage, new as it is. I love knowing that, no matter what, you're with me, supporting and protecting through it all. No other man comes close to you."

"Do you believe that?" I asked in a whisper. Her body's heat rippled over me. It felt like coming home—something I had long been denied. Standing so near her, even without touching her, was an embrace, a kiss, the interlocking of fingers in a hand hold. She was absolutely everything I needed.

I waited, watching as she gazed up at me and tightened her grasp on my kurta. Her lips twitched in a soft smile as she replied, "I do."

"It's true about you, too." Kissing her was what I wanted, but I needed her to know—without a doubt—what she meant to me. "Because you are perfect to me, princezo. All I want, all I need. You're a rock, strong and sure, even when you're not." Her brows lowered, and I chuckled. "Perfection does not equal worthiness."

"I know." She swallowed hard, glancing down toward Dhamar's door. "We need to go. They're waiting."

She wasn't ready to talk about her perfectionism. That was all right.

When she was, I would be there to help her gather the broken pieces she was trying to force back together by sheer will alone. While that was a gallant act, it wouldn't last. I'd seen the shattered pieces of Aysa days ago on the dune when she'd let me in close enough to understand that side of her. To me, it was as beautiful as the fierce warrior I knew so well.

We glided into Dhamar's room without further words. Inara reclined on a mound of pillows, her hands once again cradling her belly. She smiled and waved as Dhamar all but lurched to his feet. He appeared pale, and he furiously scratched at his jaw with his index finger as I helped Aysa settle onto a cushion of her own around the low table.

"How was it?" Inara whispered loudly, causing Aysa to turn red despite her tanned skin.

I smirked. "It was lovely."

Aysa swatted at me, her blush deepening before she hid her face in her hands. "Dhamar, save me!"

Her cousin chuckled. "You expect me to stop my wife? That's like trying to stop a charging rhinoceros."

"I rather look like a rhinoceros these days, don't I?" Inara huffed and rolled her eyes dramatically before smiling at Dhamar.

Aysa snorted, a bemused expression on her face. "You look wonderful. You have that beaming glow of a soon-to-be majka."

"*Majka.*" Inara tried the word, rolling it over her tongue as one would a new food or drink. "I like that."

I turned to Dhamar. "I don't think you summoned us to breakfast solely to embarrass my kari, did you?"

"No, I didn't." The malek of Taletha seemed to wilt, staring at the table of food none of us had touched. His eyes flicked to Inara, another wordless conversation passing between them as they gazed at each other.

Aysa's fingers wove through mine as she gripped my hand beneath the table. Slowly, her shoulders rolled back, that steady mask of bravery and serenity slipping into place. "What's going on, Dhamar?"

"There is a gathering of Šerians at the border," Inara stated when Dhamar hesitated yet again. "It appears to be the war camp from eight months ago. We think it has something to do with the body that was found."

"Which wasn't you," Dhamar interjected. "But your father doesn't know that. Neither do his...what do you call his council?"

"The tribal leaders." Aysa's grip tightened painfully. "We could send word. Proof of life. We didn't fight for this peace only to lose it now."

"We think..." Dhamar leaned his elbows on the table, folded his hands and pressed them to his lips. With a great sigh, he said, "We had guards trailing Arqa and Shaeen. But communication with the guard simply stopped and just this morning we found the bodies of both guards at the palace gate."

Inara eased forward and set a hand on Dhamar's leg. "It isn't your fault. Their deaths aren't on your conscience."

"It's corrupt men doing evil things," Aysa whispered, setting a hand against Dhamar's arm. "We will fix this, Dhamar. By the sun, moon, and all the stars, I swear it."

"A noble sentiment, Aysa, but one you can hardly fulfill." Dhamar waved at the food with a grunt, dismissing the topic for the moment. "Let's eat."

Conversation was stilted as we all nibbled on the food. The savory spices did nothing to slow the churning of my stomach, and Dhamar's dour expression only fueled the unease.

Throwing down his pita bread, Dhamar stood and began to pace. "I don't know what to do. War will return to our nations if we can't figure out a way to calm the animosity between our peoples, Aysa."

"My otac is not an unreasonable man. Surely if we explained—"

"I tried." Dhamar's voice cracked, fear written in every line of his face. It wasn't an expression I'd ever seen on the man before, and it thoroughly startled me. "I sent a letter explaining the details of the death and the manner in which we found the corpse."

"Which was?" I cleared my throat glancing at the Aysa. "I'm afraid that's something we're unaware of. Our information was given second hand."

Dhamar paused his pacing and turned a touch green. "I—It was found propped up against a border stone. She was—naked. It was clear what they had done to her. Chunks of her hair had been shorn and possibly pulled by the wildlife. Bruises and cuts littered her body, but it was her eyes..." Dhamar shook his head and turned away from me. "Even after Beeran verified it was Aysa, I went out to make sure. But I couldn't. The eyes had been gouged out, bloody sockets where her gray eyes had been and—it was awful. I don't know who the young woman was, but I pray to Nicar that they killed her quickly."

Bile coated my tongue, my hand clamping around where my sword hilt should have been.

Aysa, rather than looking ill, leaned forward with venom in her gaze. "If they're as twisted as that, they'll be at the border to see the reward of their handiwork. We ride there, along with your guard, and we hunt them like the beasts they are."

"No." I gripped her shoulder, forcing her to look at me. "They want you out of their way. They'll murder you if they see you anywhere near the border."

"They deserve to die!" Aysa's voice trembled. "Emre, they killed that woman because of me."

"No, not because of you." Inara clasped Aysa's hand. "You are no more responsible for Arqa and Shaeen's actions than Dhamar is."

Dhamar scratched his jaw as he began to pace one more, his strides short and erratic in his agitation. "I want no more blood on my hands. It was mercy that stayed my hand toward them the first time, though Nicar knows they didn't deserve it. Now, they've broken one of the sacred laws. I cannot ignore that. Yet the thought of killing them—"

"Turn them over to Šeri," I stated. His gaze snapped to mine, and I shrugged. "You want peace; they want vengeance. It's the solution. Besides, I know my marriage to Aysa will cause an uproar. Giving them the ones who murdered a Šerian kćerka will also help with that."

Aysa nodded, but her jaw was set in that stubborn way of hers. "Then their deaths will no longer be your problem."

Dhamar met Aysa's gaze. "I know you want to be there, but Emre is right. It's not safe. Especially with them wanting you dead."

"And I'm very near my time." Inara's hand settled against the curve of her stomach. "I want family here when I bring my babe into the world."

Aysa looked at me, her expression torn. I clasped her hand, squeezing it as I flicked my eyes toward Inara. Aysa's brows lowered but she nodded once. "I'll stay, if only for Inara and Emre's peace of mind."

Dhamar nodded. "Then let's ready to leave within the hour."

"I'll be ready." I stood, pulling Aysa up with me. Dhamar was embracing his wife when the door clicked closed behind us.

"I don't like this," Aysa declared as I threaded my fingers with hers.

"I know." I truly didn't like it either, so I could only imagine my headstrong wife's distaste for staying behind. "But I'd rather have a reason to come home."

Home. No longer a tribe or a nation, but a person. Dove-gray eyes that captured my attention and wrapped around me with love. An embrace that told me I wasn't alone, and never would be again. Her kiss that sent my heart soaring yet grounded it in a reality far sweeter than any fantasy.

Aysa leaned her head against my shoulder. "I didn't plan on you running away from me so soon after our wedding."

"I'm not running *away* from you." I turned her to face me when we reached our room. "I'm running *toward* you. Toward our future. To have any hope of being together, we need to face this threat. Face it and destroy it."

She nodded, stepping willingly into my embrace. I leaned my cheek against the top of her head, committing the feeling of her arms around me to memory for the coming days.

"I need to pack." I pressed a kiss to her temple and eased out of her hold. As much as I wanted to remain here, there was a war to stop, an evil to end, and a future to reach. Together.

Chapter Thirty-Three

Aysa

I sat on the bed, watching Emre hurriedly throw fresh salwar and kurtas into his pack. His lips were pressed into thin lines, his brows furrowed. Every so often he'd pause, his fingers drumming against his thigh.

"Emre." He turned from fastening the straps of his satchel. He'd packed in under five minutes, not much to collect for his trip back to Šeri—a trip I wished I was going on with him. "Come here."

One side of his mouth curled up as he climbed onto the bed and pulled me into his lap. "What does my princezo command?"

"Nothing. Just sit with me a moment." I slid my arms around his back, letting my head settle against his chest. His heart beat a steady rhythm against my ear, a reminder that this was real. He was mine, I was his, and nothing and no one could change that now.

After a moment I mumbled, "Are you certain I can't go with you?"

"You know the risk that would be. As much as I want you with us, it's safer to have you here, with Inara."

"But I don't want you to leave!"

"Aysa, I'm coming back." His arm around my back tightened. "No one and nothing could keep me away."

Squeezing my eyes closed, I muttered, "Death could."

"Do you doubt my skills as much as all that?" There was a teasing lilt to his voice, but I could hear the note of hurt as well.

"No, of course not." I sat up, cupping his face with my hands. "It is selfishness, pure and simple."

His hands rested against my hips, his thumbs rubbing slow circles. "Is it now?"

I hummed my affirmation, leaning in to brush my lips mischievously against his own. "Because I'd much rather have you here."

His brows wiggled. "In bed?"

Heat bloomed in my cheeks, and I moved to climb off his lap, but Emre's strong arms pinned me, pulling me back against his chest. His fingers tickled my sides, eliciting a squeal of protest. He chuckled, the sound rumbling against my ear as he pressed a kiss between my neck and shoulder.

Sliding me onto the mattress, Emre propped his head in his hand, his other arm wrapped around my waist. Adoration and longing rested in his gaze as he stared down at me, warming me through.

"Emre." I grabbed hold of his kurta, pulling him close. "Don't let Otac and the leaders bully you. Come back to me in one piece. Keep us safe." Then I pressed a quick, desperate kiss against his lips.

Emre returned the kiss before whispering, "Always, my princezo. Always."

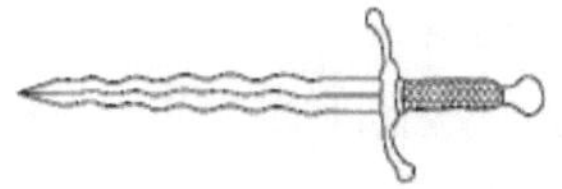

The front yard was a flurry of activity as the afternoon sun beat against the stones. Emre was tightening his sword belt, his steady gaze watching the chaos with that unwavering composure I adored. Finishing with his belt, he threaded his fingers with mine, his lips pressing flat.

"It will be fine." I willed my words to be true. Nicar above, if anything happened to my koca, I'd never forgive myself. He was fighting for me, for our life together. Nothing was assured, and my innate desire to control the outcome balked at that knowledge.

Emre turned to look down at me, a small smile ticking up the corner of his mouth. Feeling impulsive, I tugged him down to kiss me. We'd been married less than a day, and already he was off into danger and death. I eased back, cupping his cheek as I whispered, "You be careful."

Emre's brow quirked up. "I really don't think you should be the one to tell *me* to be careful, Aysa."

"Perhaps not." That earned me a small laugh. My throat tightened, and I wrapped my arm around him as Dhamar and Inara glided to the top step.

Curved scimitars were strapped to Dhamar's back, daggers along his belt. Dressed in a black turban, kurta, and salwar, he struck an imposing figure. A medallion with his coat of arms—the soaring swallow that marked the royals of Taletha—sat against his chest. Inara had her arm wrapped tightly around his waist, and her face was grim as she watched the bustle of the army preparing to leave.

"Try to avoid bloodshed," I ordered Dhamar.

"That's the plan." He pressed a kiss to Inara's forehead as his hand cradled his unborn babe. "And I'll do my best to be here for the baby's birth."

Inara smiled, but her chin shook as Dhamar pressed a kiss to her lips. "Hurry home," she whispered.

With a nod, Dhamar turned to Emre. A hard look shuttered whatever he was feeling as he clasped my husband on the shoulder and then strode down the stairs.

"I'll be home soon." Emre pecked my temple before following my cousin.

Inara stepped to my side, threading her arm with mine and resting her head on my shoulder. "I tell myself it will get easier, watching him leave. He's been on many trips around Taletha without me, but somehow this one is much harder."

"It's war." I swallowed the lump of fear. "It could bring more death to all our lives."

"Then I'll pray to the goddess that it can be resolved quickly and with as little blood spilled as possible."

I exhaled with a sigh. "May it be."

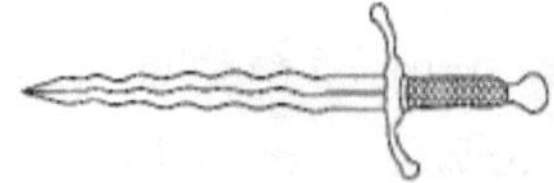

Five days later, we were sitting in Inara's room. Hafza was embroidering one of Inara's kaftan as the rania sat sipping some tea. I fingered a piece of baklava, my normally talkative self rather pensive as I stared toward the window. Toward the south and my husband. No word had reached us from the border about what was happening. We were left to wait and wonder, and the anxiety was threatening to drive me mad.

"Aysa?" Inara's soft voice drew me back to the room, to the women around the table.

"Yes?"

"Tell me a Šerian story." Inara leaned up against the wall, her hand rubbing the swell of her stomach. I'd kept it to myself, but it appeared lower than it had before, and I wondered how near her time Inara was.

"What type?"

"An adventure." Hafza smiled. "I know your people love a good adventure."

I laughed with a nod. "Have you heard the tale of the eagle and the wolf?"

When they shook their heads, I set down my tea and pastry and began.

"Once, there was a mighty wolf named Cetin who roamed the great plains of our desert. He was the largest of all, strong, fast, and cunning. He led the largest of the wolf packs but remained aloof and arrogant to those beneath him.

"One day, Cetin was met by the mighty eagle, Asuman, who told him his great pride would be his undoing. For arrogance, left unchecked, breeds devastation to the bearer. But the great wolf simply laughed and told the eagle he knew nothing."

"Rather unwise," Hafza muttered.

"Indeed." I smiled. "And that is why Asuman challenged the great wolf to a race. The pair would hasten to the nearest oasis. Once there, they had to collect a pomegranate and return to the very spot where they currently stood. The winner would choose the fate of the loser."

"Seems simple enough." Hafza shrugged.

"Ah, but the eagle knew something Cetin did not. The pomegranate grove was greatly overgrown, and it would take the wolf hours to reach the center. For Asuman, he could fly over the tangle and dive down to grasp the ripest, plumpest pomegranate in the entire oasis.

"Back on the dune, the eagle waited for Cetin. When the wolf at last arrived—scratched, mangled, and quite enraged—Asuman ordered Cetin to forever wander alone. For boastfulness makes one less. And thus was born the lone wolf, not exiled by his pack, but by his great and awful pride."

"What a wonderful story, Aysa!" Hafza laughed and clapped her hands.

"Yes, it was—" Inara gasped, grabbing the sides of her rounded stomach and squeezing her eyes shut.

"My rania?" Hafza lurched to her feet, halting when Inara's frightened gaze landed on her. "What's wrong?"

"I think—my water broke," Inara said, tears filling her eyes.

Hafza helped Inara stand, wrapping a supportive arm around her waist. "It will be all right. We're ready for this beautiful babe, yes?"

Inara nodded, her eyes shutting as another labor pain squeezed her middle. "I thought they were the false labor pains, as I've been having them off and on all week. But all through the story, they grew worse." Her frightened blue eyes met mine. "Aysa..."

"I'm here." Stepping to her side, I clasped her hand while Hafza ran to the door to alert Saif.

"I'm so scared." Inara leaned against me, her words whispered. "The baby's coming, and my husband is off trying to end yet another war. I don't know if I can do this."

CHAPTER THIRTY-FOUR

Emre

Two days prior...

Esma's hooves churned up the sandy soil as Dhamar and I galloped toward the border. My fists gripped the reins of both the horse and my simmering temper. This was wrong; I was heading to the border mere days after I'd wed the woman I loved. But we didn't have a choice. My love for Aysa was why I was here, facing down a man I'd worked ten years to please. Ten years of loving his kćerka silently and painfully, only to lose the home I'd fought so hard for. Was it always going to be this way? Gaining what I desired most only to have it ripped away days, weeks, months, years later? Was loving worth the risk of heartbreak?

Aysa's smile filled my mind, and I relaxed in the saddle. Perhaps so. Despite the pain, it had been worth loving her from a distance. It was worth loving her now, no matter how difficult the confrontation I faced. And regardless of what lay ahead, it would be all right if I had Aysa by my side.

Even if I lose her, I'll be fine. Nicar knows what I need. I had to believe that. I closed my eyes and willed it to be true, because if it wasn't, I couldn't face Šefe Aydin.

Dhamar dismounted, eyes scanning the dunes ahead of us. "Where are they?"

"He'll arrive when he wants to. The man—while not as ridiculously pompous as your otac was—has his own flair for the dramatics."

Chuckling, Dhamar looked up at me. "Something his daughter seems to have inherited as well."

I nodded. Aysa had a style all her own, that was for certain.

Tension coiled in my stomach, threatening to make me ill. This was worse than watching the men fawn over Aysa, more difficult than seeing Feray's body wither away. It sent my heart thundering faster than when I'd braced for the beating from Ulvi years ago. This was on par to receiving the news that my otac had succumbed to an illness days after I'd run from Tribe Ender. This was me waiting not only for my šefe, but for Aysa's otac. She could deny it all she wanted, but she wanted his approval. Nicar help me, *I* wanted his approval.

They say she's too headstrong, too wild. Will her otac ever see her as more than that? I swallowed another wave of righteous indignation. *Perfection over self.* It seemed as though they would keep trying to beat her into a mold she didn't fit. They wanted demure grace, a šefe who was methodical in all her decisions and ways. But what was wrong with passion and fire? Nothing. Nothing was wrong with Aysa, yet she felt the need to be what they wanted. They'd made her an overthinker, a logic user. She had so much heart and spirit, but the approval of others was slowly draining the life from her.

"You look ready to charge their ranks alone, Emre." Dhamar's chuckle sounded. "What has you so livid?"

"Aysa."

Dhamar's brows rose. "You're fighting already?"

"No, nothing like that." I chuckled and rubbed the back of my neck. "I simply have a problem with people forcing their expectations on her." *And watching her let them.*

Dhamar said nothing, looking out over the dunes once more. A flash of metal caught my attention as a churning cloud of dust moved toward us. The šefe and his armies had arrived at last.

I swung down beside the Malek of Taletha as we strode to the border stone. Zahir fell into step behind Dhamar, his gait measured as his dark eyes studied the horizon.

"What should we expect?" the guard asked, his voice low and steady. I envied his composure. My stomach was threatening to empty itself onto the sand.

"Šefe Aydin will be controlled, but he will be angry." I tapped my fingers against the hilt of my sword. "I'm not certain what he will have heard. We must be prepared for anything."

Dhamar nodded. "I think we should lead with your marriage to his daughter."

"That may only enrage him more." Though, perhaps hearing that his kćerka was alive would be enough to win the šefe to our side.

Dhamar turned to Zahir. "Send some men to scout the town. We need to catch Arqa and Shaeen before this turns into a disaster."

"You mean it's not already?" Zahir chuckled dangerously and bowed, his dark eyes narrowing to slits as he rose. "Yes, my malek."

With a snap of his fingers, five guards followed after Zahir. My eyes watched the steadily approaching column of desert mounts. "There's something both Aysa and I failed to mention."

"Oh?" Dhamar didn't move from my side.

"There was someone in the tribe who was trying to kill her."

"What?" Dhamar's gaze snapped to me.

"One of her suitors, I think..." Bold words rested on the tip of my tongue. Treason to Šeri, the šefe, and the princezo was no small thing. But it was the only logical solution. The only way they could have known the exact style of Aysa's tattoo that hid under her bicep. The only way they could have captured a kćerka of Šeri. I moistened my cracked lips with the tip of my tongue. "I think someone is working with your traitors to plunge our nations into war."

"To what end?" Dhamar asked. "And why try to kill Aysa?"

"I don't know." I rubbed my neck with a sigh. "But I know it's the only way they could have known what they did."

"So twofold treason—both nations attacked from the inside out." Dhamar growled as the šefe—his dayi—pulled up to the border stone. "Time to end this, once and for all."

My stomach took to churning once more as Dhamar stalked forward. The šefe stood with an entourage that was comprised of Aysa's eight suitors, the tribal leaders, and a score of guards.

But I only saw Aydin. His gaze was hard as Dhamar bowed and said, "Peace to you, Dayi Aydin."

"Peace?" Aydin fairly spat the word. "You dare to say *peace* after torturing and slaying my kćerka?" His voice cracked, and I took a moment to study the šefe. He seemed to have aged a decade in less than a week. Dark circles marred the underside of his eyes, and his hand shook as he gripped the hilt of his scimitar. "I demand justice for the death of my kćerka! Death by your hand means the death of *your* rania!"

Dhamar paled, his words missing as he opened and closed his mouth in shock.

"Šefe Aydin." I bowed as his gaze swiveled to me. "Your kćerka—"

"You've joined them?" Aydin fairly roared, his usual restraint vanishing in the wake of his grief. "You're a traitor to Šeri, Emre! A traitor to—"

"I am no traitor!" I shouted, leveling a glare at his outburst. My hands shook, and I bowed my head. "I saved Aysa's life. Even now, she's back in Mordova with Dhamar's kari, waiting for my return."

"*Your* return?" a voice asked, riding to Aydin's side. Kagan's shoulders were slightly hunched as he leaned against the pommel of his saddle. "Why you, Emre?"

Before I could respond, Dhamar found his voice, his posture straightening as his bearing returned. "Last evening Emre and Aysa exchanged the sacred wedding vows. They are one in the sight of Nicar."

I had never seen the šefe's face turn so pale. He looked at me, a mixture of horror and—was that pride in his gaze? His lips parted, but Kagan interrupted. "You will just let this—this *nobody* take your kćerka to his bed? He broke the oath he made to you to protect her! He used her!"

"He is her koca!" Aydin turned his steely gaze to Kagan. "There is no longer a contest, not now that Aysa has picked her consort."

Naz snorted. "Likely he soiled her so she had no choice."

Fire burned in my veins, my sword drawn and pointed toward Naz in the span of a heartbeat. "That is a challenge not only to Aysa's honor but my own. By the sun, I would never harm Aysa; by the moon, I never tried to persuade her to choose me; and the stars as my witness, I will slay anyone who dares attempt to sully her good name!"

Silence reigned for several tense moments before Aydin cleared his throat. He turned to Dhamar. "Who was the girl then?"

"We're trying to find out. The men who harmed her were former councilmen of mine." Dhamar's face darkened. "They're here somewhere, and my men are hunting them even as we speak."

"Good." Aydin's brows furrowed, his gaze dropping to his hands.

Dhamar cleared his throat. "We fear that some among your people were helping them, Dayi."

Aydin's gaze snapped to me. "Who?"

While Dhamar had been talking to Aydin, I'd been watching the eight young men. Naz was glowering at me, while Efe, Ömer, Derin, and Kerim were studying me with curious—yet somewhat disgruntled—expressions. There were two, however, who were scanning the horizon. Watching. Waiting. My gaze narrowed.

"Dhamar, Šefe Aydin." I pointed at the men. "Arrest Kagan of Alïm and Berk of Zafer. They are the two helping our enemies."

Before I finished speaking, Berk dug his heels into his mount and bolted. No sooner had he taken off than three mounted men of Dhamar's, along with Derin and Ömer, took off on his heels, Derin drawing his bow from his back as he did so.

Kagan was trapped between the šefe and Kerim, both who glared at the surprisingly defiant looking young man.

"What is the meaning of this, Kagan?" Aydin's voice pitched low.

"You're listening to the grievance of a common guard over me?" Kagan scoffed. "Of course, you are. You're the same as everyone else. Same as the elders, my otac, and all the tribesmen who sees Kagan of Alïm as a pathetic waste. No one wants me to rule—too headstrong, too brash, too angry. Oh, and I am angry! Angry at being treated like cattle dung!"

"Who treated you as such?" Aydin scoffed. "Your otac loves you, Kagan."

The young man sneered, his words biting. "My otac didn't stand up to his elders, didn't give me a chance to rule before I was tossed aside for my eldest sister. So, I had to take what I wanted. I went after it, and Dhamar's disgruntled councilmen promised it to me. Aysa, as my bride. You, dead so we could rule. But she had to go and marry *him*." He spat at me, his hazel eyes hardening with pure hatred. "I wish Berk would have succeeded in poisoning Aysa now. Dilan was much more likely to marry me."

Aydin growled a low order, and Kagan was ripped from his horse. The šefe then turned to me. "I fear the council will say we should remove Aysa as princezo. She failed to listen and follow orders."

"We were expecting that, as well." I inclined my head then met his gray eyes without flinching. "And she understands. Aysa weighed her options and is willing to face the consequences. You must do what you think is best, my šefe."

"You love her, don't you, Emre?" Aydin's gaze softened marginally.

My throat tightened, and I nodded. "More than anything or anyone else in the world, my šefe."

Aydin smiled now, some of the tension leaving his shoulders. "Then Aysa made the right choice."

Relief had my body relaxing. "Thank you, my—"

A shout sounded to our left and we all turned, weapons drawn, as Zahir hustled a man forward. His hands were bounded behind him, his dark gray eyes wide with fright. He met Dhamar's gaze and paled even further than his already ghostly complexion. "Beg mercy, your majesty! I beg mercy!"

Dhamar seemed to loom over the man as Zahir shoved him to his knees before his malek. "I extended the hand of mercy, Arqa, yet you and Shaeen spat on it."

"I was pulled into this, my malek. I swear by blood and blade!"

"Your vows do nothing to sway me." Dhamar shrugged, a hard look shuttering away how much I knew this choice was destroying him inside. "You are the šefe of Šeri's problem. It was his subject you tortured and murdered. It is to him you will answer for those crimes."

"Shaeen used her! He ordered the young Šerian to capture her, and it was both of them who performed the acts!" the former lord babbled, his eyes wide and panicked.

My blood boiled as I turned to Kagan, his hands bound much like Arqa. The defiant look was still on his face, but I could read his eyes better than most. And he was terrified.

Good, I thought as I stalked forward. Aydin watched as I slammed my knee into Kagan's groin, causing the man to double over. I gripped the front of his kurta, keeping him from crumpling to the ground. "Any man who treats a woman as an object is no man at all. He is the scum of the earth. Thank Nicar above that she protected Aysa from the likes of *you.* I pray that the šefe enacts every penalty imaginable upon your head, Kagan."

I shoved him away, letting him fall to the sand without a backwards glance. My vision blurred as I stalked to Esma, swinging up into the saddle with barely suppressed rage.

The men who had chased after Berk returned. Bile coated my tongue as my gaze focused on his mount. Berk's body was thrown over the saddle, an arrow protruding from his back.

Dhamar settled atop his charger, his gaze flicking to the dead man before landing on his dayi. "We will continue to hunt for Shaeen. Once we have him—"

"Cut him down." Aydin was glaring down at Kagan, disappointment and anger burning in his gaze. "As Emre said, no one who harms a woman in such a way should be allowed to live."

With a nod, Dhamar said, "It shall be done. Does the peace stand?"

"Yes. It stands." Aydin looked up, studying his nephew. His mouth softened, and I could see that expression of pride in the depths of his eyes; the one that was so fleeting, but as heady as fine wine. "And as proof, you shall decide what happens to this traitor." He gestured, and Dhamar's guards took control of Kagan.

I glanced at Dhamar; his dark brown eyes were hard. He hadn't wanted the job of deciding the traitors' fates, but it appeared as if he was going to have to do it.

Dhamar gathered up his reins, wheeling around toward Mordova. I moved to follow, but Aydin's voice stopped me. "Emre, tell Aysa I'm proud of her. That I love her and that no matter what the council decides..." he hesitated, waiting until I met his gaze. "No matter what, she will always be my kćerka."

"It shall be done, my šefe."

Pointing Esma north, we urged our mounts back toward Taletha and our wives.

CHAPTER THIRTY-FIVE

Aysa

My heart raced faster than a runaway stallion as I gripped Inara's arm. Her body seemed to seize as another labor pain took her, leaving her trembling with tears in her eyes.

"It will be all right, Amira." Hafza somehow remained calm as she turned to me. "Help Inara into bed, get her comfortable, then light the heating pot. I'm going to fetch the midwives."

"And Ranya?" Inara asked between clenched teeth as another labor pain grasped her.

"Yes, Saif's already sent someone to fetch her." Hafza strode out the door with determined steps.

My arm around Inara's waist, I guided her to her bed.

"My labor kaftan is in the wardrobe." She braced a hand against the bed's edge and cradled her stomach with the other. When I stepped to her side with the kaftan, she whimpered, "It hurts, Aysa."

"I know, Inara. But it will be worth it, I promise." I unbuttoned her kameez and helped her step out of the soiled salwar before tugging the labor kaftan over her head. All the while my heart thundered, and my hands shook. I wasn't qualified to do this. I'd been with Majka when she'd delivered Zlem, but that had been ten years ago. All I remembered was Majka's screams of pain and the blood that made ten-year-old me dizzy.

Inara needs you. That's why you're here. She's terrified, and you're strong and steady. You can do this. With a sharp inhale to keep myself calm, I drew back the linens on the bed and helped Inara in as the midwives bustled through the door along with Hafza and three other servants.

"I would like you to sit beside the rania and hold her hand," the head midwife ordered me. Her black hair was pulled into a severe bun and a kerchief was tied tightly around it. "She will want to squeeze something when the pains become hard."

Inara's frightened blue eyes met mine. "I wish Dhamar was here."

It was my fault he wasn't. I bit the inside of my cheek and smoothed my hand against Inara's brow. "He'll be home soon to find himself with a happy and healthy kari and a new child. I'll get to hold his baby first and tease my cousin endlessly about it. Perhaps I'll even be able to convince Emre that we should try for a babe of our own."

Inara's face turned red, and I didn't think it had anything to do with her labor pains or the heating pot warming the room to an uncomfortable temperature.

I smirked, clasping her hand in mine. "You'll complete this task as you've done so many others, Inara—with beauty and grace."

Instead of replying, Inara tightened her grip on my hand and gasped, curling up slightly and bearing down. Tears trailed down her cheeks.

"You must breathe, your highness!" the midwife ordered as she propped Inara's legs up. "It will do no one any good if you pass out."

I turned away from them all and focused on my cousin's face. "Do you hear that, Inara? Breathe." Listening to the midwife's measured breaths, I mimicked it for Inara, who seemed to focus on it in between the pushes.

Time blurred. Inara screamed, pushed, relaxed. On and on, the labor went, each minute coiling the tension in my stomach. I wanted the baby here as much as Inara. In so many ways, Taletha needed this little life. Šeri needed it, too. He or she would be the first born to total peace between the nations—Nicar willing.

Be with us.

Inara flopped back against the pillows, panting. A servant pressed a cup of water to her lips, and she sipped some before turning toward me. "We settled on names the other night." Dark circles marred the underside of her eyes, but she managed to smile. "Would you like to hear them?"

"Yes. Very much." My heart quivered at the joy in Inara's eyes. Was that what loving a life looked like? Loving a babe that grew for months inside of you, that you slaved to bring into the world, seemed like another level of adoration. And yet my heart jumped at the thought, longing to feel little hands and feet brushing against my stomach and to watch Emre cradle a child of our own in his arms. We'd been married less than a week, been together as husband and wife one night. But I knew I wanted him to be the otac of whatever children I was blessed to receive. And I knew he would be a good one.

"I picked the name for a girl, Dhamar for a boy." Another labor pain, this one lasting longer than the others. It passed, and Inara sighed in momentary relief. "Imran if it's a boy. It means *prosperity*. And if it's a girl, we want to name her Razaanah, which means *peaceful*."

"Beautiful, either way." I squeezed her hand gently.

"Now, if my child would just get here." She laughed but stopped short. A strange look came over her face, a wild determination she'd been missing. "It's time. The baby is coming now!"

CHAPTER THIRTY-SIX

Emre

We were a day's ride from Mordova. I wanted nothing more than to ride through the night, pushing our bodies and mounts to make it home to our wives. But Dhamar had more sense.

"Better to camp one last night under the stars than break your neck," he teased as we swung off our horses, the moon rising big and red in the sky.

"I'd rather push on," I grumbled as good-naturedly as I could.

The malek laughed. "Undoubtedly. I had to berate Inara when she came to rescue me from Šeri last year. She made the three-day journey in a day and a half." He shook his head. "Crazy woman."

"Love makes you do reckless things." I glanced at the men setting up our camp. "It doesn't often make sense."

"Indeed." Dhamar moved forward, his gaze locked on the fire that a soldier was making.

A commotion sounded to my left, and I turned, hand on the hilt of my sword as a shadowy figure broke into a run toward Dhamar. Something glinted in the moonlight, and I shouted, "Dhamar! Duck!"

The malek listened, dropping to his stomach as a dagger flew, end over end, and landed in the sand inches from Dhamar.

A savage growl echoed through the clearing as the figure pounced onto the malek, his hand closing around his throat. I ran forward, drawing my sword. "Release him! Now!"

"Ah, ah, ah!" The man turned, hauling a thrashing Dhamar to his feet. He seemed to have superhuman strength, his gaze a little deranged as he pressed another blade to the soft flesh of Dhamar's neck. The malek stilled. "Take another step, and I'll relieve Dhamar of his head."

I froze. Not from the man's words but rather from the looming shadow that was inching around the fire and toward the man holding his malek.

Zahir.

"Might I assume you're Shaeen?" I asked, letting my gaze settle on the man.

"A pleasure, Emre," his voice rasped, his black hair pulled into a low tail and his eyes gleaming like onyx in the firelight. "You made it quite difficult to get that problematic princezo out of the picture."

"The pleasure is all mine," I scoffed. "What can you hope to get out of this? Murdering the Malek of Taletha won't make you a lord again."

"No," he pressed his cheek against Dhamar's temple, his voice lowering to a hiss. "But with Dhamar out of the way, his wife will be available, won't she?"

I could see Dhamar's anger, feel it through the warm air as he struggled not to react to Shaeen's words.

"Too bad she has the heir of Taletha in her womb," I said.

"Ah, but only if it's a lad." Shaeen turned to me. "Talethans don't let women ascend to the throne."

"A pity," my gaze cut to Zahir. He was close, a dagger of his own in his hand. "For your women are a special type."

"Are they?" Shaeen's grip loosened ever so slightly, and Dhamar's gaze snapped to the arm pinning him in place.

I struggled to think of an argument strong enough to keep Shaeen preoccupied. "They're gentle, yet strong. Graceful and fierce. Surely you must see their beauty?"

"Indeed." Shaeen's wild look didn't leave his face, and I prayed that Zahir stabbing him wouldn't kill Dhamar in the process. "They're—"

His words were cut short. Zahir plunged his knife into the former lord's throat, ending whatever he was about to say. Dhamar, gasping, caught hold of Shaeen's knife wielding hand, pulling it away and ducking under it with fluid grace. Leaping back, he pressed a hand to his throat, trying not to gag.

"That was too close." I braced my hands against my knees as Zahir stood over the gasping and gurgling Shaeen. "Don't ever do that again."

"Care about me a bit there, Emre?" Dhamar chuckled, swaying as the rush of almost dying began to fade.

I clasped his shoulder. "No, I just don't want to face the wrath of your kari if you were to die."

Dhamar tipped his head back and laughed. It echoed around the small valley we were camped in, bouncing off the rolling hills, and warming the place more than any fire could ever hope to.

Quickly, the guards cleaned up the mess of Shaeen's dead body. Dhamar sent it back toward the border, to be presented to Šefe Aydin as the proof that all the traitors were disposed of. The fire was moved away from the spilled blood, and we settled in for one last night of camping.

Kagan was tied to a scrub tree out of the ring of firelight. His chin was pressed against his chest, his shoulders drooped in defeat as I approached him with a chunk of travel bread and dried lamb.

"Here." I held up the bread to his mouth, but the stubborn man glared at me.

"Are you trying to humiliate me?" he asked.

I raised a brow. "I'm trying to keep you alive."

He scoffed, looking toward the fire. What was he thinking? That Dhamar was likely to kill him anyway, despite whatever sins he'd actually committed? That perhaps the pain of starvation would be better than whatever tortures that Talethan malek would serve him? Little did Kagan know how different from the last malek Dhamar truly was. He wasn't perfect, but over the last five days, I'd seen his quiet strength and the way his men respected him for it. He was good and just.

"Why are you still here?" Kagan returned his glare to me. "Haven't you disgraced me enough? You took the only woman who's ever been kind to me. You took her and bedded her and now—"

I slammed my arm against his neck, choking him as I let the food fall to the ground. "Be *very* careful about your next words, *traitor*. First, Aysa is my kari. You will respect her if only for that and not shame our union—which we did the proper way in the sight of Nicar's laws.

"Secondly, the only reason I am trying to be kind to you is for Aysa's sake. You are her childhood friend, and regardless of what you did, you are a human and worthy of human decency. You may have tortured and murdered an innocent, but I won't stoop to your level."

I shoved off him, letting his lungs fill with air as I glared down my nose at him. "But since you're too proud to accept my help, I'll return to the fire and let you think about how pathetically low you've fallen."

Blood roared in my ears as I lowered myself onto a cushion by the fire. Dhamar's brows quirked up as he bit into a pita filled with meat, but I didn't have the will nor the strength to answer his silent question. Kagan was so proud, so arrogant, and look where it had landed him; tied to a tree, destined to die a traitor's death.

Weariness pressed against my shoulders as I sat staring into the flames. I wanted Aysa. Wanted her arms and scent to envelop me and tell me everything was going to be all right. We might not have a tribe, we might not have a family, but we would be all right. Because no matter what, we would always have each other.

My body ached as I swung off Esma and onto the stone-laden courtyard before the palace of Mordova. Zahir was shoving Kagan toward the prison when Dhamar strode toward me. "Ready to—"

Whatever he'd been about to ask was interrupted by Saif fairly vaulting down the palace steps. "Malek Dhamar! Come quickly!"

"Inara?"

"Is in labor!" Saif gasped.

Dhamar looked at me before taking off at a dead sprint for the palace stairs. I raced down the hall on Dhamar's heels, my own pulse frantic with the speed at which we raced. We'd only been gone five days, but apparently that was more than enough time for a baby to decide to join the world. Not bothering to knock on his wife's door, Dhamar flung it open and strode into Inara's chamber.

Hurrying to her side, he brushed a strand of her blonde hair out of her eyes. "Are you all right? And the baby? Is it a boy or a girl?"

Inara laughed. "I'm fine, my love. Meet your son, Imran."

"Son." Dhamar sat beside Inara, careful not to jostle the bed as he gingerly accepted the swaddled bundle of life from Inara. Awe and reverence lined his face. "Hello, my son."

I felt like an intruder, standing in the doorway as Inara's maid bustled around the room. The midwives were gone, and I wondered how long it had been since the baby had been delivered.

"Oh, and Dhamar?" Inara smiled, gesturing to someone sitting on a cushion in the corner. Aysa stood and glided forward, a bundle of her own in her arms. "Meet your daughter, Razaanah."

"Two? Twins?" Dhamar's mouth curved into an *O* of surprise, and he met my gaze as a large grin split his face. "I have a son and a daughter."

Aysa smirked. "And I got to hold them both before you."

"Aysa, darling. Now isn't the time." I stepped up to her, tucking her against my side as I stared down at the baby girl in her arms. Razaanah had a perfect little button nose, her eyes were screwed shut, and a thatch of dark brown hair covered the top of her head. She squirmed when a little baby grunt escaped. She was perfect, a tiny human cradled in my wife's arms.

"Would you like to hold her, Emre?" Inara asked, gesturing for Aysa to hand me the baby.

"Oh, no I don't think—" I gasped as Razaanah's weight settled in my arms. Her eyes squinted open as she puckered her lips and wiggled a bit more. She looked up at me, the blue eyes matching Inara's before they closed, and she sighed.

Aysa wrapped her arm around my waist, gazing up at me with suspiciously bright eyes. "Life is a wondrous miracle."

I nodded mutely. My throat ached as I stared down at the babe. She was perfect, warm, and tiny. Desire welled up in me to be an otac. Perhaps not in the near future, but someday. Someday I wanted a little family to call my own. Someday I wanted Aysa to curl next to me like Inara was nestled against Dhamar, despite the sweat and dust coating him. I wanted to smile down at a sinovi or kćerka of my own like Dhamar smiled down at his.

I wrapped my arm around Aysa's shoulders, pressing a kiss against the top of her head. My memories of my otac were few and far between, but I knew I had longed for him to be a part of my life. I'd wanted a family to call my own and had wandered most of my life looking for one. Kerim's family had been mine for a short while, then I ran from it. Šefe Aydin had been like an otac. Still was, in a way, which was something I would have to talk to Aysa about before we retired for the night. But despite of all of those failures and rejections, I had the love of the woman at my side. She picked me, and together we would build a love that would last. From the ashes of nothing, we would forage a family unlike any other.

A new tribe, a new family, and a new life. I pressed another kiss to Aysa's head, feeling her sag against me.

"Time for bed?" she asked, her words somewhat slurred.

"Yes." I gingerly handed Razaanah off to Inara. "Congratulations, Inara. Dhamar."

"Thank you." Inara smiled, cradling her kćerka closer. "We've truly been blessed."

Dhamar nodded, still staring fixedly at Imran.

"Good night to the new majka and otac." Aysa winked as Dhamar finally looked up with a smile.

"Thank you for being here for Inara, Aysa." Dhamar's smile faltered. "I wish it could have been me."

"Next time, love." Inara leaned her head against Dhamar's shoulder. "Anyway, you wouldn't have done a thing besides drive Zahir insane with your worry."

Dhamar began to mock argue with his wife as I guided Aysa into the hall and toward our rooms. "What was her labor like?"

"I think Imran was born after about five hours of labor." Aysa yawned. "Razaanah was a few minutes after him."

"A first-born son." I smiled down at her. "What do you hope our first one is? A boy or a girl?"

"You're thinking about this already?" Aysa grinned at me, her eyes dancing with hope. "You want a family?"

"Of course." I paused, dragging her to a stop. "Don't you?"

"Yes! And—" She looked away, worrying the inside of her cheek. "I'd like to start soon."

I nearly laughed, shaking my head at the good fortune of Nicar. "I would, too."

Aysa chuckled at that as we continued to move down the hall. It took a dozen more steps before I worked up my courage and said, "There were some...developments at the border. Your otac fears that the council won't be happy with us, Aysa."

She winced. "But is he?"

"I think so. He said to tell you that you will always be his kćerka. But he fears the council will want you removed as princezo."

Which was the same as disowning her. My heart ached as Aysa's gray eyes went distant, frozen in some memory. She stopped walking, her eyes closed, and she crumpled against me. "I knew that was likely."

"Did you?" I asked, wrapping my arms around her back.

"Yes." Aysa didn't say more, and she didn't cry as I thought she might. Rather, she clutched the back of my kurta and held on as if I was the only thing grounding her to reality and the present moment. "What are we going to do?"

"Start our own tribe in the wilderness of Šeri. A home for outcasts and wanderers. Šefe Aydin will acknowledge it, as he said you will still be his kćerka in his eyes. You won't be šefe of all Šeri, but you can be on the council. Besides," I tipped her chin up, forcing her to look at me. "I'll gladly follow you as you lead our new tribe. Our new family."

"No." Aysa shook her head. "*You* will lead our family. You have always guided me, Emre. Always been my anchor. Now, I ask you to direct what we're building. Set the foundation and give me the rules to follow."

"Or how about this?" I stepped back, raising her hands to my lips as I stared into her gray eyes. "I will guide our family and marriage, of course. But I need you to lead *with* me. Help me stay on course by offering me your suggestions and ideas. Argue with me and challenge me to think bigger and wider. And when you get stuck in that logical mind of yours, I'll talk you out of it. Let's learn how to lead a new tribe together."

"I like that." She smiled.

I tugged her to my chest, cradling her hips in my hands. Her arms wrapped around my neck, holding on as I pressed my forehead against hers with a small sigh. "I want to build this new life. To create a love and a family that is passionate and bold and brilliant. But I can't do it without you. You're my partner, my lover, my friend. I love you, Aysa." With those words, I ducked my head and claimed her lips.

She kissed me with the same passion she did everything. Not bothering to end the kiss, I stumbled into our door and fumbled with the handle before managing to open it. Once inside, I pressed my wife against the wall, finishing our kiss with tiny ones along her nose.

"You know what we need?" she whispered, her voice husky.

"What?" I asked, not bothering to move back as Aysa's arms tightened around my neck.

"There are some bathing pools around here." My wife wiggled her brows. "And we're both in desperate need of a bath."

"That sounds like a brilliant idea." With a growl that had her laughing, I kissed her again, more thankful than ever to be home in her arms.

CHAPTER THIRTY-SEVEN

Aysa

There was nothing better than waking enfolded in Emre's strong, safe embrace. I took the quiet moment to study him—my husband. His chest rose and fell against my hand, his heart a steady rhythm against my cheek. A lock of his hair fell over his closed eyes, and his hard lines seemed to soften as he slept, gentling his expression to one that was almost youthful.

There was still a sorrow that seemed to cling to him, even in sleep. There was so much heartbreak in my best friend. Some of it I hadn't even been aware of. I knew his history, the childhood he'd been denied. His otac had sent him to Tribe Ender to learn sword-fighting after his majka had died. Emre told me how hard that was, yet he'd excelled. He'd heard little from his otac during that time, but he wanted to make him proud. When Emre left, he'd discovered that his otac had died of illness. A tear trailed down my cheek as I stared at him now. What must it have been like for young Emre as he wandered, eventually finding Tribe Hamid? And how heartbroken must he have been when he'd left that tribe and found mine?

I reached up and smoothed the hair off his brow, tracing my fingers lightly against his jawline. My husband, best friend, supporter, guard, comforter, love. How had I denied it for so long, I didn't know, but now that I had Emre's love, and loved him in return, there was no doubt in my heart. He was the man I needed, wanted, treasured.

He stirred at my touch, his black lashes fluttering as his eyes open. They were the deepest brown they could be without being black; equally soft and hard in their depths. I loved his eyes, his smile, his embrace, his physical strength. They added to the charm of the man that I'd known for ten years; the one that leapt into danger, listened to me share all my fears and frustrations, comforted not only me but my sisters as well. The man whose heart was full of mercy and grace, who had been willing to let me go because he knew it was what I needed.

"Good morning," he said, his voice husky with sleep. His arms, still around me, tugged me closer so that he could kiss my forehead. "How is my beautiful kari this morning?"

"Happy to wake with you by my side." I sighed, letting my eyes slide closed as he rubbed small circles against my back.

After a long moment, Emre said, "We discovered who the Šerian traitors were."

"*Traitors*?" I popped my eyes open to look at him. "More than one?"

He sighed as he nodded slowly, rolled to his back, and stared up at the canopy top. "I wondered about both of them but wanted to give them the benefit of the doubt, especially because..." He sighed again and roughed a hand over his face.

"Because?"

"One is your friend." He waited, watching for my reaction.

But I had none. Numbness filled me, tainted with sadness. *Kagan*. My old childhood friend, the boy I'd run with through the tent paths with and around the flocks and herds when his tribe had come to visit. He'd been there when I'd broken my arm at eight, right before he'd been adopted by the tribal leader of Alïm. And yet he had betrayed Šeri. Betrayed *me*.

With a sigh, I curled into Emre's side, relishing his presence as I struggled to understand.

"He felt the need to be perfect," Emre whispered against my hair as he pressed a kiss to the crown of my head. "He said he had to prove himself to his otac and to the tribe."

"Promise me something," I whimpered, the first fissures of sorrow welling up in my heart.

"Anything, my love."

"Promise me that, when we have children, we won't expect perfection." I dashed away a stubborn tear with a sniff. "That we'll have expectations we make clear but won't make them feel like they're foolish for failing or messing up once in a while."

"Oh, Aysa." He rolled to his side, propping his head in his hand as he stared down at me. "Do you feel that?"

"Every day," I whispered.

Emre tipped my chin up, brushing the dampness of the tear away with his thumb. "You know you never have to be perfect with me. I don't expect it. It's impossible to be perfect. Everyone makes mistakes. It's what you do after you make a mistake that matters to me."

"And what are those expectations?" I asked, a bit of my façade crumbling right there. It often came down around Emre, but there was something about this moment that had it falling even further.

My need for perfection had driven me for years; I had to be the perfect šefe, the perfect kćerka, the perfect sister. The only time I'd felt comfortable failing was with Emre—mostly because I could make the same mistakes over and over, and all he would do was quietly correct me. For that reason, he'd taught me how to race Kismet over the dunes, how to wield a dagger, and, most importantly, how to love without reservation.

"My only expectation is this: when you fail or make a mistake, I want you to come and admit it to me." He leaned closer and whispered, "Because I'll do the same. Just like we're learning to lead, let's learn to fail together, my princezo."

For a moment, my heart stopped beating. The thought of admitting a failing choked the air from my lungs and made it hard to see straight. But then I met Emre's gaze, remembering all the times I'd failed before him. He'd never laughed, never gotten angry or put out. No, he just guided me back to the right path and then held my hand as I navigated the twists and turns of life.

"I'll do it, but only if you're willing to forgive me when I do."

"Always, Aysa." The tension in my chest eased as Emre smiled and pulled me closer. He kissed me, slow and deep and without reservation. I savored it, knowing I had a lifetime of them ahead of me but not wanting to miss out on the exquisiteness that was this moment with my husband.

We may have been without a tribe. We didn't know what the future would hold or how we would survive. But for that moment—everything was all right. It would always be all right because I had someone to love, someone who loved me, and even if the sun and stars fell from the sky that very night, we would make it to tomorrow because we weren't alone. We would fight and live as we had for the last ten years...together.

Epilogue

One year later

Emre

I held the tiny bundle that was my one-month-old son, Zeki, in the crook of my arm as I clasped Aysa's hand in the other. Bouncing on the balls of her feet, she watched the horizon as the dust cloud that signaled a caravan drew closer.

"Will you settle down?" I chuckled, tugging her closer to wrap my arm around her waist and pressing a kiss to the top of her yellow kerchief.

"Do you think he'll like what we've built?" she asked as she fingered the charm of her necklace. The tiny gold butterfly glinted in the sunlight. Aysa wore the gift from Inara every day, a reminder to be herself.

I looked over my shoulder and out at our tribe. Tribe Luta was a collection of outcasts, wanderers, and even displaced Talethans looking for a fresh start. Our people loved Aysa nearly as much as I did. They looked up to her, followed her without a murmur. With pride, I watched her fiery nature thrive under the rough and oftentimes stubborn people that we called our tribe. She fought with both blade and words to earn her place as leader, and she did so with grace and passion.

Still her guard and guide, I stood by her side as a sign of support, leading when she asked me, but also knowing that this was the woman I'd married—one who strove for perfection in everything she did. She was growing, becoming better at admitting when she couldn't do a task or when she'd failed. Always I encouraged and loved her.

Zeki squirmed, his tiny lips smacking together before his face screwed up, and he let loose a wail of anger.

"He is his majka's sinovi," I stated, carefully lifting him up to my shoulder to pat his back as he continued to scream into my ear.

Aysa smirked. "Yes, because he loves his otac so very much."

I chuckled, bouncing my legs to quiet my wailing son. The sound of Zeki suckling his fist sounded in my ear, and I wrinkled my nose in displeasure.

Aysa laughed, wrapping her arm around my waist as she turned her attention back to the horizon. The caravan was taking shape, distinct forms of figures atop desert mounts. One broke from the rest, eating up the distance at a breakneck speed. Aysa swayed forward, as if she planned to run and meet the figure on the horse.

"Wait," I warned, my hands too busy holding Zeki to keep a hand on Aysa.

She didn't move any further. Rather, her arm tightened against my waist. Her head leaned against my arm as we watched her otac approach. Aysa trembled as she leaned out a bit more but still kept her feet planted in the sand. We hadn't seen Šefe Aydin since I'd left him at the border, Arqa his prisoner while Kagan was ours. Dhamar had chosen mercy for Kagan, with some input from Aysa and me. He'd been reduced to a servant, helping to clean the very prisons he now lived in. Dhamar had promised my wife that he would keep an eye on the young man, and perhaps Kagan could redeem himself. Though, he hadn't seemed all that repentant at his trial.

The desert mount halted in front of us, and before a word could be spoken, Šefe Aydin was before us, pulling Aysa into his embrace with a

soft cry of relief. Aysa returned the hug, tears in her eyes as she clung to her otac.

"Oh, my beautiful kćerka," Aydin choked on the words, a sob following the endearment. "How I've missed you so."

"I missed you, too, Otac."

I eased Zeki back into the crook of my arm, feeling the invader to such a tender moment.

"Ah, and there is my sinovi."

Thinking Aydin meant my child, I stepped forward. "Yes, this is Zeki."

"I didn't mean your babe, Emre." My gaze met Aydin's as he said, "I meant you."

I swallowed, a host of emotions crashing over me. My otac, sending me away to train. My otac, giving me birthday gifts when Majka had been alive. My otac's hugs, praise, and affection that were few and far between. He'd been a good man, but when Majka had passed, he hadn't known how to raise a child.

To hear Aydin call me his sinovi, it healed a tender spot in my heart I hadn't known was bruised to begin with. The šefe smiled. "You are my sinovi, as much as Dilan's koca is. No matter the council's choices, I acknowledge you as one of our tribes, as my sinovi and kćerka by the sun, the moon, and all the stars."

Aysa and I both smiled.

"Thank you, Otac," I said, my voice cracking a bit on the final word.

"Now, let me see my unuk!" He chortled as Aysa took Zeki from me and settled him in her otac's embrace. "Oh, it does my heart good to hold your child, Aysa." He pulled my wife into his other arm and pressed a kiss to her forehead. "Your sister has yet to have a child, even though she married not long after you."

"How is Dilan?" Aysa looked up at her otac, pain on her face for her sister. "Is she adjusting to the role of princezo?"

"Yes. Her koca has been incredibly supportive." He smiled, though it

was somewhat pained and wistful. "Had you married him, Aysa, I think he would have been a fine consort."

"I'm quite happy with my koca." Aysa bristled for one moment before stepping from her otac and into my arms. "Emre is a wonderful koca and a fantastic otac."

"I didn't mean that disparagingly. Merely as an observation." Aydin grinned. "Now, I wish to see all your tribe has become."

With the caravan setting up behind us, I tucked Aysa under my arm as we led her otac into our tribe. Tribe Luta bowed to the šefe, the man that held the power to acknowledge us as a tribe of Šeri or as merely another blight on the land.

"Otac!" I turned, barely in time to catch the little spitfire that launched herself into my arms.

"Ah, there's my Silaah!" I tossed her into the air, relishing her giggles as I caught her and pressed a kiss to her nose. "Where were you? You missed greeting your deda!"

"Deda?" She peered over my shoulder as she wrapped her arms around my neck, suddenly shy.

Aydin raised a brow. "Now this you failed to mention in your letters."

Aysa chuckled. "We wanted to make sure no one came and claimed her. Otac, this is Silaah. We discovered her a few months ago, wandering along the border of Taletha and Šeri." Aysa met my gaze, and I nodded. We'd fill in Aydin later on regarding the state the young child had been in—half-starved, bruises covering her little body, and scars along her back. Aysa turned back to Aydin. "We think she's about two or three."

Handing Zeki to Aysa, Aydin hunkered down to Silaah's level. I peeled her arms from around my neck and knelt down with her on my knee.

Aydin smiled, his tan skin wrinkling around his eyes and mouth. "Hello there, my unuka."

"Hello, Deda." Silaah tried to bury her nose in my neck, but I leaned back.

"There's no need to be afraid, Silaah." Aysa's words were gentle as her hand settled against the little girl's back. "He's nice. He's my otac, like Emre is yours."

"Otac?" Aydin met my gaze with a cocked brow.

"We adopted her," I murmured as Silaah turned and hugged Aysa. "She was...terrified of me for a very long time."

It angered me, the way men treated children and women. If I had to spend the rest of my life protecting them, I would. With every breath, I would fight for the safety of all the innocents of both Taletha and Šeri. It was the least I could do.

I scooped Silaah onto my shoulders, knowing she would become accustomed to Aydin as she had everyone else in Tribe Luta. It simply took time.

"There is much for me to learn about your tribe, isn't there, kćerka?" Aydin smiled again, joy pouring out of him as he stood.

Aysa laughed at her otac's observation, cradling Zeki close to her chest as she slipped her hand into my free one. "Yes, Otac. And the first is that this"—she grinned up at me before her gaze moved to Silaah and then down to Zeki—"this, right here, is exactly where I belong."

The End

ACKNOWLEDGEMENTS

There are so many people to thank. It takes a village to write a book, and *By the Sun and Stars* is no different.

To my wonderful publisher, Quill & Flame Publishing House, and the woman behind it, AJ Skelly. Thank you for taking a chance on Taletha and for bringing my books to life through edits, covers, and printing. None of these books would exist without you.

Thank you to my wonderful cover designer, Emilie Haney. I am still blown away every time I look at my covers for Taletha and I can't believe how blessed I am that you designed them. Thank you for allowing me to feel confident in marketing these books. I love being able to dare people to judge a book by its cover.

To my dear Q&F friends—Amber, Vanessa, and Crystal. I'm so blessed to have you four to banter with and bounce questions off of. You're always there when I need you. This little community we've built is beautiful. I'm so proud of you ladies and where we're all headed in this world of publishing!

To Nate and Anna. Thank you for always believing in my writing and for cheering me on from the beginning (and that awful contemporary story that shall not be named). You're the reason I'm where I am, and I'm forever thankful.

Thank you to all of the readers who've returned to Taletha and the world of Wife Markets, canvas tents, kaftans, and manakeesh. I'm so glad you loved Dhamar and Inara. I pray that Aysa's story resonates with you

too. Thank you for making this writer an author!

Thank you, Mom, Dad, Andrew, Clara, Abby, Alex, Allison, and Azariah. Thank you for always encouraging me to pursue my dreams, for tolerating my incessant need to create, for reading my books and celebrating my accomplishments—even when you don't understand. Most of all, thank you for being a family worth mirroring in the books I write and for always being there. I love you all!

Lastly and most importantly, thank you Jesus. Thank You for the gift of storytelling. You created the very best Story ever told—the Story of Salvation and Redemption—and all I can pray is that these stories are a dim reflection of its beauty. Thank you for using these words in ways I cannot begin or hope to understand. Thank you for never leaving me and never demanding perfection in order to earn your love. Thank you for daily molding me more and more into your likeness, for adopting me into your family as your kćerka, and for being the otac that will never disown me, despite my flaws. You are a good, good Otac. And I'm beyond blessed to be loved by You.